PRAISE FOR

THE NINTH METAL

"[In *The Ninth Metal*], debris from a comet drops a fabulously valuable new metal on Northfall, Minnesota, turning it into a bloody, brawling boomtown. Great characters, fine writing, totally engrossing."
— STEPHEN KING

"Wildly entertaining and highly original mélange of northern Minnesota lore and slam-bang near-future SF action . . . Percy's dead-on local color, strong central characters, and well-integrated flashbacks into the making of a modern samurai will delight and entertain both comics fans and serious science fiction readers. This is an impressive series starter."
— *PUBLISHERS WEEKLY*, STARRED REVIEW

"Take one part dystopia, one part sci-fi, two parts apocalypse, then ride them roughshod through a bleak and bloody western, and it still wouldn't get close to what Ben Percy does here, which is blow open the core of humanity's dark heart."
— MARLON JAMES, BOOKER PRIZE–WINNING
AUTHOR OF *BLACK LEOPARD, RED WOLF*

"Whether you choose to think of him as the Elmore Leonard of rural Minnesota or the Stephen King of science fiction, Ben Percy — with his extraordinary and unrelenting eye — dishes up humanity like some kind of otherworldly blue-plate special, at once deeply familiar and wildly new."
— MARGARET STOHL, *NEW YORK TIMES*
BEST-SELLING AUTHOR

"When Benjamin Percy publishes a novel, I have got to read that novel. *The Ninth Metal* continues his streak of thrilling, incisive genre-bending goodness. It's a sci-fi novel, a crime novel, and a superhero novel too. Audacious and intelligent and exactly what I was dying to read."
— VICTOR LAVALLE, AUTHOR OF *THE CHANGELING*

"Percy takes the darkest conspiracy theories you can imagine and makes them the stuff of nightmares . . . humankind is held responsible for its irresponsibility, paying the price for all the convenience we take for granted, for our obsession with the digital world . . . the message is effective and scary . . . there's something undeniably creepy about the thought that your smartphone can possess you. A gory cautionary tale."
— *KIRKUS REVIEWS*

"*The Dark Net* kicked my ass with its deft mash-up of both blackhat hacker culture and black magic. Percy reveals an upgraded, rebooted battle between good versus evil — a fast, fantastic, throat-punch of a read."
— CHUCK WENDIG, *NEW YORK TIMES* BEST-SELLING AUTHOR OF *BLACKBIRDS* AND *ZEROES*

"*The Dark Net* channels the spirit of your favorite sprawling and epic 1980s horror/thriller novels into a tightly paced, nasty, unrelenting twenty-first century nightmare. An addictive and frightening read."
— PAUL TREMBLAY, AUTHOR OF *A HEAD FULL OF GHOSTS* AND *DISAPPEARANCE AT DEVIL'S ROCK*

"Beautifully written, as extravagant as the night sky but way more cool . . . Benjamin Percy's soft-footed yet industrial-strength imagination, storytelling mastery, deep curious infatuated humanity, and his total willingness to throw himself off one narrative cliff after another. This is horror literature's bebop, bold, smart, confident in its capacity to redefine its genre from the ground up. Read this book, but take a firm grip on your hat before you start."
— PETER STRAUB, *NEW YORK TIMES* BEST-SELLING AUTHOR

THE UNFAMILIAR GARDEN

BOOKS BY BENJAMIN PERCY

The Language of Elk

Refresh, Refresh

The Wilding

Red Moon

The Dead Lands

Thrill Me: Essays on Fiction

The Dark Net

Suicide Woods: Stories

GRAPHIC NOVELS

Devil's Highway

Year Zero

James Bond: Black Box

THE COMET CYCLE

The Ninth Metal

The Unfamiliar Garden

THE
UNFAMILIAR
GARDEN

BENJAMIN PERCY

MARINER BOOKS
An Imprint of HarperCollins*Publishers*
Boston   New York

Copyright © 2022 by Benjamin Percy

marinerbooks.com

Library of Congress Cataloging-in-Publication Data has been applied for.
ISBN 978-1-328-54488-9 (trade paper)
ISBN 978-0-358-33271-8 (hardcover)
ISBN 978-1-328-54420-9 (ebook)
ISBN: 978-0-358-57845-1 (audio)

Book design by Chrissy Kurpeski

Printed in the United States of America
1 2021
4500842886

For Lisa

PROLOGUE

t begins with a comet.

Decades ago, an infrared telescope captured the thermal emission streaking through the solar system. Eventually it was determined to be 300.2 kilometers wide and orbiting the sun in an elongated ellipse that would bring it within five hundred thousand miles of Earth.

The moon, by comparison, is 238,900 miles away. This would be, scientists said, a beautiful light show that everyone should enjoy all the more, knowing that we'd narrowly escaped planetary annihilation.

The official name of the comet was P/2011 C9, but most people called it Cain, the surname of the astronomer who'd discovered it. Twenty years later, it burned into view and made its close pass by Earth.

People took off work. They gathered at soccer fields and in parking lots, on rooftops and along sidewalks, setting up lawn chairs and picnic blankets and grills and coolers as though readying for a fireworks display. Everyone suddenly owned a telescope. Vendors sold comet T-shirts and hats and key chains and plush stuffed toys. Surfers stacked up on beaches waiting for the big waves they believed would come from the gravitational flux. At least two cults killed themselves off, announcing this was the end of the world and the comet a gateway to the vault of heaven.

Professors and scientists and religious leaders became regular guests on cable news shows, where they talked about how comets had long been associated with meteorological and human disasters — tsunamis, earthquakes, and droughts. In 44 BC, when Caesar was assassinated, his soul was said to depart the Earth and join the comet flaming overhead. In AD 79, a comet's arrival aligned with the eruption of Vesuvius. In AD 684, when Halley's comet passed by, the Black Death broke out, and in 1066, when it made another appearance, William the Conqueror won the Battle of Hastings. Celestial judgment and providence. Or an instrument of the devil, as Pope Callixtus III called it.

"Heaven knows what awaits us," one professor said. "It is a reminder of our irrelevant smallness and accidental existence in the universe, a glimpse of something violently outside the bounds of human existence, as close as you can come to seeing God."

Local news reporters interviewed people on the streets. "I don't know — it's just kind of cool," one man said. "Special. Once-in-a-lifetime sort of deal. You want to be able to say, *I was there*. It's almost like we were living this two-dimensional life, and now there's this sense of it being three-dimensional, if you know what I mean."

Cain looked like a roughly drawn eye, some said. Or a glowing animal track. Or a slash mark in the fabric of space. A wandering star.

For a few days, the comet made night uncertain, hued with a swampy green light. And by day, the sky appeared twinned with suns. And then — gradually — the comet trailed farther and farther away, and people forgot all about it.

Until one year passed. The planet finished its orbit of the sun and spun into the debris field left behind by the comet. The residue of Cain's passage.

This June, the sky would fall. That's what the newscasters said.

The meteor shower was not as long-lasting as August's Perseids, but for several nights the sky flared and streaked and wheeled, the constellations seeming to rearrange themselves with ever-shifting tracks of light. At first hundreds and then thousands and then hundreds of thousands and finally an uncountable storm of meteors.

The ground shook. Windows shattered. Grids of electricity went dark. Satellites shredded. Radio signals scrambled. Dogs howled and people screamed their prayers. Many of the meteors dissolved in the atmosphere, but many struck the earth, sizzling into the ocean, splintering roofs, searing through ice, punching craters into fields and forests and mountainsides, like the seeds of the night.

It was then that everything changed.

THE UNFAMILIAR GARDEN

1

Five Years Ago
The Night of the Meteor Shower

Jack was known as the fun dad. His wife said it like an accusation. He never dealt with the discipline or the tears. He never remembered that screen time had to be earned with chores or that baths were limited by a half-hour timer. Maybe Nora had a point when she said he only trafficked in laughs and cuddles. But maybe, he argued, that's what made them a good team? They each brought a different skill set to the parenting game. She was the organizer, he was the improviser. His wife supervised hair- and teeth-brushing, while he told elaborate bedtime stories and checked under the box spring for monsters before kissing Mia on the forehead and saying good night. His wife made the grocery lists and cooked precisely from recipes, and he cleaned up the mess in the kitchen while blasting music and teaching their daughter about 1980s hair metal bands. "What's extra annoying," Nora once said, "is that you like to point out your successes. When you make her put the graham crackers back in the cupboard or change out the toilet-paper roll, you proudly mention it to me. Like you deserve some kind of trophy."

Maybe he deserved a small trophy — or at least a high five and a "Good job" — for today. Because there were no water parks or movie theaters in store for them. This was a full-on dadventure. It was four a.m., and in the predawn gloom, he and his daughter were about to tromp around in the woods hunting for mushrooms.

Jack didn't have a choice. His research required it. And his wife, a detective, had been gone all night working a case. He could either hire a babysitter — and what babysitter would even answer a call at this hour? — or drag Mia along with him. But he wasn't complaining. And neither was his daughter. They were happy for the challenge.

Mostly happy, anyway. He hadn't gotten enough sleep and felt fuzz-brained and mildly crabby. Mia didn't want to get out of bed; nobody wants to get out of bed at four a.m., but especially not an eight-year-old. She'd pulled the sheets over her head, crying out as if in physical pain when he flipped on the lights. But after a few minutes of back rubs and soft words, he finally convinced her to get up and pee and change out of her jammies, and her voice soon brightened, asking about where they were going and what they were doing exactly.

She never got to ride in the front seat with her mother — one of Nora's many rules Jack actively defied — and Mia delighted in climbing into the cab of the pickup and snapping her belt into place and pushing on the radio and opening and closing the glove compartment. He had made her an egg and cheese sandwich and wrapped it in a paper towel. She took little nibbles of it and clicked the flashlight on and off and talked in her chirpy voice as they drove.

Last night they had watched the meteor shower together. He'd made popcorn and they munched it while lying on a blanket on the driveway. The light show had been beyond anything seen on the Fourth of July. Flaring streaks and booming flashes that never seemed to pause.

This early morning, the meteors continued to flash with a strobe-like intensity, and Jack's eyes jogged between the road and the sky. "There's one!" he said, and "Hey, there's another one!" They reminded him of snowflakes fleeing across a window at night.

"That one was a pretty one," Mia said.

"Pop quiz: What are the meteors made of?"

"I can't remember."

"Try to. We talked about it last night?"

"I can't remember, though. That was too long ago."

"Pieces of rock. Space debris."

"What's debris?"

"Like the leftovers from the comet."

"I remember the comet. We had a picnic party then."

"Right."

"That was when you and Mommy weren't arguing all the time."

"I — yes — we don't argue *all* the time ... but anyway, as the comet travels through space, it leaves behind a mess. So the debris is the mess, the junk, the dandruff, the litter. After you eat a bowl of Cheerios or a bag of Doritos, I have to clean up the *debris* you leave on the table."

"Mom says I'm not supposed to eat Doritos. She says they taste like cancer."

"Then I guess cancer tastes good."

"What?" she said.

"Never mind."

"But." She tapped at the window with her fingernail. "Why do the meteors blink on and off?"

"They're burning up in the atmosphere. Pop quiz: What's the atmosphere?"

"I know this one," she said, clapping her hands as if to conjure this answer, "but I don't know this one."

"The invisible shield that protects us from space."

"Now I remember. But it sounds kind of weird and made up?"

"But it's true. Pop quiz."

"Not another one!"

"Just one more. What's the difference between a meteor and a meteorite?"

"One of them doesn't burn up in the sky? One of them you can find in the ground and is worth lots of money?"

"That's right! Which one is the one that survives? Which is the one that strikes the Earth?"

"Meteor . . ." — she dragged out the *r* and looked at him with a scrunched-up face — ". . . ite?"

"Meteorite. Yes."

"Will any survive? Will there be any that come down and survive?"

"Given how busy the sky is, I'd say definitely."

"Oh," Mia said and fogged the window with her breath as she peered outside. "The sky is falling, the sky is falling," she said in a singsong voice. "But the meteorites that survive can't hurt us. Right, Daddy?"

"No, sweetie. You're safe. Totally safe."

"Okay. That's good."

Once they drove out of Seattle, once the buildings and streetlamps slid away, once they pulled off the interstate and then the highway and the firs and hemlocks walled them in, Mia grew quiet. Mist ghosted the air. The truck moaned and clanked as they traveled the rutted logging road. "This is creepy," Mia said.

"Just imagine it in the sun," Jack said. "That's not creepy, right? A dark space is *exactly* the same as a sunlit space, only without photons and infrared rays and electromagnetic radiation."

In response, Mia clicked on her flashlight and shone it out the window as if that might brighten the world. "Still creepy."

Mia was born with a lot of hair, a dark mess of curls that didn't respond well to a brush. She had gray eyes and bony shoulders and big feet that she was constantly tripping over. She always seemed to have lost another tooth, so her smile was never the same, changing with the gaps. She rarely stopped moving. Even when sitting, she shifted her weight, twitched her face, picked at her scabs.

This was a good age. Maybe the best age. Eight. Between seven and twelve, Jack's friends told him, kids weren't tantrum-prone whiners who couldn't tie their own shoes and they also weren't asshole teenagers who slammed doors and demanded unlimited data plans. Eight-year-olds worshipped you but didn't cling to you. Mia could go on a five-mile hike, fish a river, watch *Raiders of the Lost*

Ark, read *The Hobbit,* and talk to Jack, really talk, asking hard questions and testing out opinions and shaping her tastes.

But Jack could also say, *You know what, Mia? I'm busy as hell with work.* Or *I've got a killer headache. Could you go play Legos? Give Daddy some space for a bit?* And she would. She would take off without complaint for two hours or more, doing her own thing. It felt miraculous compared to the black hole of infancy and toddlerhood. It was great. Mia was a great kid.

Jack felt spoiled by this age, happily accustomed to it, and maybe that's why he got so irritated when he parked the truck along the edge of the road, slapping the grille through a cluster of ferns, and she said in a trembling whine, "I don't want to get out."

Jack killed the engine. The truck wheezed and ticked and then the silence of the forest set in. "What do you mean, you don't want to get out? You have to get out. I have to work. This is my job."

No response except a wiggle.

He continued, trying to keep his voice calm. "We talked about this, Mia. You seemed excited then. To help."

"Yeah, but." Mia clicked the flashlight off, then on. "I didn't think it would be like this."

"Like what?"

She was almost crying. "Like—I don't know—a freaky fairy-tale forest!"

The Olympic National Forest did look like an illustration from an antique leather-bound book. The old-growth evergreens reached dizzying heights, their trunks as wide as Jack's truck was long. And everything—the rotting stumps and knuckly boulders—was carpeted with moss. In this, the wettest rain forest in the country, it wasn't difficult to imagine a gingerbread house tucked into a clearing with a witch peering cruelly out its frosting-rimmed window.

"Why do we have to go in the middle of the night? Why can't we just come back in the daytime? When there's—whatever you call it—electric-magnet radiation."

"Electromagnetic. And we have to look now, because there was a good rain yesterday. Rain is fungi fuel. That's going to bring out a lot of new growth. And also because this area will be crawling with mushroom hunters by dawn. Those guys are the worst and they're going to ruin my work. And *also* because my UV torch picks up mushrooms better than the naked eye, and in the daylight, it won't—"

"I don't even know what any of that means!" Mia said, shrieking now.

Usually Jack kept his cool; he rarely lost his temper, but he could feel himself getting close. The early morning and long drive had thinned his nerves. One more whimper from Mia and he would probably start yelling and then she would start crying and then it would take fifteen minutes to calm her down.

"Chill, daddy-o," he said, and she said, "What?"

Instead of answering, he took a deep, calming breath. He unscrewed his thermos and drank his coffee and tried to focus on the warm, tingly feeling that spread from the center of his chest. A minute passed, and his headlights automatically clicked off. The blue of the starlit night—pulsing with meteors—set in and the forest somehow seemed less threatening.

"I was thinking . . . as soon as we're done here . . . we go to the bookstore?" Jack said this in his cheeriest voice. "Pick up a few graphic novels? Maybe even some of that weird candy they sell by the register? Those jelly-bean things that taste like boogers." He didn't think of it as bribery as much as payment. His daughter was doing him a solid, after all. "And—how about this? You can choose *any* restaurant for dinner."

At this she perked up. "Even TGI Fridays?"

"Even there."

"Even though you hate that place?"

"Even though it's totally gross, I'll go. For you."

"I can get dessert, right?" Mia turned the flashlight on Jack now, making him squint. "One of those big brownie-cake sundaes?"

"Fine."

"And a Coke?"

"Sure." He put his hand over the flashlight and it glowed through his fingers. "Quit with the light. You're ruining my already crummy night vision."

At that Mia unclicked her seat belt and pushed open the door. "Let's go!"

Jack was an assistant professor in the biology department at the University of Washington. He taught two classes every semester, but most of his energy went into research, publishing, and grant-writing. He was a mycologist. Surely the least sexy profession in the world, his wife, Nora, used to say, right after garbageman, sewer-pipe cleaner, and roadkill collector. People called him the mushroom man, which sounded like a lousy superhero name.

For the past few years, he had been working on a project titled "Diversity, Production, and Dynamics of Fungal Organisms in the Hoh Rain Forest." Hectare by hectare, season by season, he was mapping out the fungal landscape of the wettest environment in the country.

The trouble was, his surveys were constantly interrupted and his data compromised by pickers. As Seattle's economy continued to boom — encouraged by the tech industry — so had the locavore food movement. Restaurants paid as much as fifteen dollars a pound for the chanterelles, lobsters, shaggy manes, morels, matsutake, cyans, ringers, cauliflowers, pig's ears, hedgehogs, angel wings, and boletes that grew here. Fourteen hundred species altogether.

And then there was the hallucinogenic crowd — the dealers and druggies — who were after the *Psilocybe azurescens*. Also called blue runners and blue angels and — Jack's favorite — flying saucers.

By dawn, the woods would be busy with people, some carrying permits, all of them carrying knives so that they could snip the stems of new growth. A few wore pistols holstered to their belts, and Jack had read in the newspaper about shoot-outs and robberies in the Mount Rainier wilderness over prized patches.

Today, Jack would be surveying two hectares of woods and meadow. He looped a camera around his neck and shrugged on a backpack that rattled with specimen jars. The meteors continued to flash constantly in the sky, but he kept his eyes on the ground, and the canopy of evergreens shielded most of the light show anyway. A milky mist seeped through the woods, streams of it curling around trees. He took slow steps and swept his UV flashlight —what he called his torch—like a pendulum before him. The mushrooms popped in the light, standing out against the heavy, sodden greens and browns that defined the rain forest, blindingly white and wrinkled. Like the ears and snouts and genitalia of the underworld.

An owl hooted. A fir cone fell. A twig snapped. A spotted green banana slug oozed along a log, leaving behind a glistening trail of mucus. A deer startled from its bed of flattened ferns, and Mia cried out and hugged Jack's leg hard, and Jack said, "It's okay. It's just a doe. We woke her up." The mist swirled in the deer's wake and they listened to her crash off into the darkness for a minute or more.

Jack tried to talk to Mia, keep her distracted, telling her a few terrible fungus jokes, like "What kind of room has no windows or doors?" He pointed out the different varieties of mushrooms, which ones were safe to eat—like the honey mushroom—and which ones were poisonous even to touch, like the fly agaric with its sinister red cap.

"What's so interesting about dumb old mushrooms anyway?" Mia said.

"What's so interesting about mushrooms? What's so interesting about mushrooms!" Jack gave her a joking nudge and a tickle. "Seriously? How about the fly agaric I just pointed out to you? You know how it got its name? People used to mix it with milk and leave it out in a bowl to kill flies. Isn't that interesting?"

"I guess."

"How about that they've been evolutionarily static for ninety-nine million years?"

"I don't know what that means. You're always saying things that don't make sense to kids."

"Okay," Jack said, scanning the underside of a half-buried log.

"How about this — if it weren't for mushrooms, there would be no life on this planet. You know why? Because they eat and recycle debris."

"Debris!" Mia said, remembering the word. "Wait. Mushrooms eat space junk?"

"No, I mean the debris of our world. Plants. Carcasses. Fungi eat them and turn them into nutrient-rich soil. And if they didn't do that, the surface of the Earth would be buried beneath several feet of horrible dead stuff."

"Oh. Gross."

Jack set down the torch in the moss, photo-stamped a matsutake with the GPS coordinates, bladed the stem, and capped it in a specimen jar. "And a mushroom's spores are made from chitin. That's the hardest naturally made substance on earth. Harder even than steel."

"Really? But they're squishy."

"It depends on the nanostructure and density. It *can* be harder than steel, I should say."

"Okay."

"And a lot of scientists believe fungi originally came from space."

Mia pretended her flashlight into a lightsaber and swung it around. "Do you believe that?"

"Maybe. Oh, and get this. A certain kind of mushroom contains a compound that can give you crazy dreams — and you don't even need to go to sleep to experience them."

"You dream with your eyes open? Can I do that?"

"Well . . . no. It can be dangerous. And illegal." Jack hurried his words. "But! That same compound — psilocybin — might be a great way to fight depression. There are some clinical trials happening right now."

"You mean like what Mom gets? The blues?"

"Yeah."

"Mushrooms can make her better? Can I pick some for her, then? Like a bouquet?"

"It doesn't work like that, I'm afraid," Jack said, the energy falling out of his voice. "But that's a nice thought, sweetie."

They tromped in silence for a few minutes, then Mia said, "I found something! I've got one!"

Not one, but many. Dozens and dozens that made up a circle of mushrooms, twenty meters in circumference. They pushed aside ferns and peeked behind logs to find them all and trace the perimeter. It was a fairy ring, Jack explained. "Some people think it means good luck and some people think it means bad luck."

"What do you think?"

"Good luck. Definitely."

He explained how you could see the sporocarps above, but there was mycelium below that bound them all. "In other words, all of these mushrooms are separate but together. They're the same fungus."

"Separate but together," she said. "Like you, me, and Mom."

"Yeah. Sure. A family."

Jack got down on his knees, muddying his jeans, and crept along, lifting branches, brushing aside fir needles, peering under logs and into stump cavities, straining his eyes to take in every inch of the forest floor. Maybe fifteen minutes passed without him really registering anything other than the next fungus sample.

Then he noticed a voice calling to him with impatience. "Daddy? I said, Daddy!"

"Yeah?" He sat up and rubbed the bridge of his nose.

"I've called for you like a hundred times."

"Sorry." He swung his flashlight toward the sound of her voice. She stood twenty yards away, her back to him. "I'm just concentrating."

"I think I found something."

"A mushroom?"

"No. A hole."

"I don't have time for holes right now—okay, sweetie? The sooner I get this survey done, the sooner we can get back home."

"It's a big hole. A really, really, really big hole."

"Show me later, okay?"

"But what if it's from a meteorite?"

"It's not from a meteorite. We're here for fungi, remember? Let's look for fungi."

He soon forgot about the hole. An hour later, he made an effort to stand up straight, but his spine didn't really want to comply. He pressed his knuckles into the small of his back, massaging the muscles and urging out a few pops and cracks. Above him, in patches glimpsed through the canopy, meteors continued to sketch chalk lines across the blackboard of the sky, but they were fainter now as the horizon brightened with the promise of dawn.

Mia wasn't scared anymore, but she was tired, slumping her shoulders and dragging her feet and slurring her words and weighting her voice when she said, "Can we go? This is *so* boring. This is taking forever and ever and ever and ever."

Jack unzipped his pack and pulled out a Snickers bar and a water bottle. "Here you go, sweetie." He handed them over and then hoisted the girl onto a stump that marked the edge of the meadow. "Sit on your throne and watch the sun rise. I've got another fifteen minutes and then we'll bolt. Okay?"

Mia tore open the candy, took a bite, and said, around a mouthful of chocolate, "Promise?"

"Fifteen minutes. I promise. I'm going to keep moving," Jack said. "But you'll be able to see me and talk to me the whole time. I'll be right here." He swept his hand in the direction of the meadow. Channels of mist moved through it like white-water streams.

Mia said, "Can I play a game on your phone?" She held out her hand and made grabby fingers, because she already knew the answer.

Jack dug out his cell and plopped it in her hand and said, "Fifteen minutes."

It turned out to be thirty. The air was so fecund, so humid, that breathing felt like drinking, and he could barely take a step without another pod of mushrooms popping into view. He snapped photos. He took measurements and plucked samples. He jotted down notes.

He looked back only once. The sky was pinkening, but the forest remained dark. His daughter was seated against the great wall of trees, kicking her feet, her face lowered to the aquatic glow of the screen.

And that was the last time he saw her. He told the story over and over, but no matter how many questions he faced—from Nora, the rangers, the police, his colleagues and neighbors—he could not recall anything more. No, he hadn't seen any cars on the drive up the logging road. No, he hadn't fought with his daughter. No, he'd never struck her in anger, never, not even so much as a spanking. No, he hadn't thought it was a bad idea to bring her up there—in the dark —and leave her unsupervised. Maybe it wasn't the best idea, but it wasn't a bad idea, was it? No, there was no cry for help. No snapping branches. No sign of a cougar or a bear or anything. Nothing. There was nothing, nothing, *nothing* but the hush of the wind and the buzz of his UV torch and then his own voice calling out, "Finished!"

But there was no response. Because there was no Mia. Only the candy wrapper snagged in a fern, the water bottle balanced neatly on the stump, and the phone caught between the roots of a nearby tree.

2

◎

Five Years Later
After the Drought

For Nora, it has already been a long day. Twenty calls to follow up on from the sarge, from the coroner, the family of a victim, reporting officers, and on and on. Case files to close and open. Reports to write. Five witness interviews. A visit to an attorney's office. A court appearance delayed by a fire alarm. And then there was the mandatory demonstration down at the station.

This took place in the basement firing range, a dim concrete-walled space that smelled like mildew and sulfur. Sarge stood before the dozen detectives selected for this beta program. Nosler — the bullet manufacturer based out of Oregon — had developed an omnimetal cartridge that required no gunpowder. The strike of the hammer transferred enough kinetic energy to send the bullet out of the barrel at 2,500 feet per second.

Sarge was an old white guy with hair sparely salted onto an otherwise bald head. He could never button his shirts around his beefy neck, and his face turned red when he spoke at a yell, his voice clapping back and forth through the corridors of the range. He held up the seamless bullet, the size of a pinkie finger, that seemed to give off its own silvery light. He loaded it into his pistol. He aimed at the paper silhouette at the end of the range. "Shouldn't you pop in some earplugs, Sarge?" one of the detectives said, and he said, "No need."

There was no shout of gunfire. Just a snap, like a spent fuse, and a hole punched through the target's chest. "See that?" he said. "Easy-peasy. No noise. No lead." And the bullets could be reused if collected. "It's not pure omnimetal," he said. "It's just a thin shell. What it's cored with, I don't know. Chewing gum and dog shit. Doesn't matter. Just telling you in case you think you can take this down to the pawnshop to feed your coke habit."

A few laughs.

"This stuff is powerful. Maybe too powerful. Punches through concrete. Punches through steel. Probably capable of traveling all the way around the world and zapping you in the ass if you shoot straight and stand still long enough. So be careful. Got that?"

Nods. Shuffled feet.

"Because you're all a bunch of responsible assholes, you each get a seventeen-round magazine. Hopefully you'll stay holstered, but if you do by chance fire your weapon, in addition to the usual rigma-role of pain-in-the-ass paperwork, we've got to fill out some data sheets for Nosler. Okay? Okay. Now get the hell out of here."

Now she was finally done for the day. And bed was calling. Her job was chaos, so as an antidote, her time at home was ritualized. At 9:45 every evening, she takes a hot shower and scrubs herself until her skin prickles. By 10:00, she has rubbed her body with lotion and taken her 30 milligrams of Abilify and 40 milligrams of Paxil with a full glass of water, and by 10:15 she has softened her hair with co-conut oil and slipped on a bonnet and her pajamas and tucked herself under the covers. In bed, propped up by two pillows, she reads a mystery novel for forty-five minutes until her preferred bedtime of 11:00 p.m. Before shutting off the light, she studies the photo of her daughter that she keeps on the bedside table, the last thing she looks at every night and the first thing she looks at every morning. In the photo, Mia is sitting in the grass, squinting in the sun. She is wearing a white Easter dress with a lavender pattern, and a golden crown of woven dandelions perches on top of her curly fluff of hair. A smear of chocolate edges her smile.

But tonight, just as Nora cranked off the water and the shower-head dribbled and she reached for the towel, her cell rang.

It is currently 10:17. Instead of pajamas, she is wearing a black pantsuit. Instead of reading in bed, she is hurrying into the mud-room and collecting her badge and pulling on her shoulder harness and scooping up her car keys.

In her back pocket, her phone chimes, and she checks it to find a message from Detective Augustino Chives. He has pinged her the GPS coordinates so she knows where to find him inside of Schmitz Preserve Park, thirty acres of forest in West Seattle. As long as traffic is clear on the 5, she should be there in twenty. She taps out a quick message saying as much, but before she leaves, she has to fit on her mask.

Nora buys masks in bulk. She stores a package by the front door, tucked away in a decorative cabinet, so she can slip one on just in case a deliveryman rings the bell. She stows another package here in the mudroom, next to the dish where she keeps her badge and car keys. She doesn't leave the house without a mask looped around her ears and fitted over her nose and mouth. She prefers them in black to the standard white because the color matches her hair and makes the mask look more like an accessory and less like a bandage. They are carbon-filtered and anti-dust, antiviral, anti-spore, antibacterial. The only time she doesn't wear one is inside her townhome, but she is so accustomed to their shielding comfort that she feels a little raw and naked without one.

Yes, she carries hand sanitizer with her, and yes, she opens doors with her sleeve, and yes, she avoids shaking hands — but her disgust with germs and contamination is more focused on breathing. Because when you breathe, you're allowing something inside of you. An intimacy equivalent to sex. The average adult inhales and exhales eight liters of air every minute. That's around eleven thousand liters of air a day. Only 20 percent of this is oxygen. The rest is made up of gases, smoke, pollen, fungal spores, and microbial organisms recklessly ingested. Can you imagine chugging four big soda bottles full of toilet water every minute? It's the same thing to her. You can't soap out your lungs. But you can armor them with a mask.

She didn't used to be like this. Or she didn't used to be this bad, anyway. Part of it could be traced back to COVID, sure. Part of it could also be linked to her lost daughter and failed marriage, of course. Her obsession with control and safeguarding. She wasn't in denial or unaware that many considered her behavior freakish. She just didn't see what the problem was. She was surviving, wasn't she? She was great at her job, wasn't she? She had no tolerance for her mother constantly calling to say she was worried about her. Or a colleague at work offering to introduce her to a therapist or sign her up for a dating app. Nora will admit she is sometimes so obsessed with detail that she tunes out the noise of the world and fails to care what other people think. But who gives a damn if she's alone? That's what people always seemed to target—her aloneness. They seemed to think she needed to date, needed to join a hiking club, needed to drink chardonnay with pals after work at happy hour at Applebee's. Or whatever. Alone didn't mean she was unhappy. Alone meant she didn't need to compromise herself. Chasing somebody else's version of happiness was the last thing she wanted, and vulnerable was the last thing anyone could call her. Nobody had ever worried about diagnosing Sherlock Holmes, so they should leave her the hell alone too.

In the garage, her Prius awaits her. She would own a Tesla if she could afford it, but the low emissions of this omnimetal hybrid will have to do. The car is black, like her hair, like her mask, like her pantsuit, like her. She prefers tidy simplicity. That's why she styles her hair short and reads mystery novels exclusively and eats the same seven meals for dinner throughout the week. Fashion especially annoys her. Worrying over what to wear is such a waste of time and mental energy. Her partner, Chives, once said that there was something funereal about her taste in clothes, and she supposes that's fitting, given the job.

The night is overcast, and the lights of Seattle reflect off the furrowed bellies of the clouds when she drives to West Seattle. The radio remains silent. She finds the news depressing and music distracting. A few scattered raindrops splat on the windshield. Once, this wouldn't have seemed notable in Seattle, but they've been experiencing a severe drought.

Five years ago, the violent meteor strikes wounded the planet, upsetting weather patterns, creating climatological uncertainty. That's what the newspapers — and her ex-husband — said. The energy expelled was the equivalent of several nuclear bombs or volcanoes exploding at once. Only now is Washington beginning to recover, to settle into a new normal. Over the past week, the rains have returned to the Pacific Northwest, and with them, the defining green-and-gray color palette of the region. Trees are shrugging off their dead needles. Moss is thickening, flowers are exploding, and mushrooms are popping.

In the visitors' lot — a damp patch of asphalt walled in by evergreens — she finds several squad cars, Chives's Jeep Cherokee, the forensics van, and the medical examiner's van. They are parked messily, with no attention paid to the white lines, and she clucks her tongue as if they were children who have carelessly left their toys lying about.

She can't smell the air, but she can feel it — the cold clamminess like the breath of earthworms on her skin — when she steps out of her car. She collects her Maglite from the glove compartment and heads toward the woods. Some crime tape garlands the trailhead, and she ducks under it. A flashlight bobs in the near distance. A beat cop named Matt Bowers is walking up the trail as she walks down it. "Detective Abernathy," he says.

"What's the sitrep?" she asks.

He explains what he knows so far. Some high-school kids were coming out here to party. Up ahead — about a hundred yards or so — there's a faint path that branches off the main trail. Follow it another fifty yards and you hit a stony clearing with a hot spring bubbling at its center. It's a common site for illegal camping and bonfire bashes. The teenagers were so scared at what they found there, they left behind a twenty-four-pack of Rainier and some edibles. "Hope you packed your barf bag," Bowers tells her. "It ain't pretty."

Nora doesn't thank him but continues on—and a few minutes later, she stands at the rim of the rocky clearing. It is bowl-shaped and patched with moss. Along the perimeter, several Nomads have been arranged, and the portable spotlights busy the air with intersecting cones of light and conflicting shadows. When she enters a house, a restaurant, a grocery store, a crime scene, she always pauses, assessing her surroundings.

Down below, there is a body, and all around it, a slow, familiar dance is under way; cameras flash and notes are jotted and evidence bags are filled. She fights a tightness in her chest. Because she sees her daughter.

This happens a few times a month. There are an average of thirty homicides a year in Seattle, but she investigates many more bodies than that. In a warehouse, an alley, a canal, a living room. Waterlogged beneath the docks or locked in a trunk or tied up in a storage container. Mia was never found, so every death could be hers. This body—sprawled out on the rocks, one leg immersed in the hot spring—is hers.

Nora pinches shut her eyes so tightly her vision goes red. When she opens them again, the vic comes into focus. Not her daughter. Not a girl. Not even a young woman. It's a man. He is naked and lies sprawled in the shape of an X, one of his legs floating in the hot spring. A spotlight brightens the water, and she can't tell if it's colored a silty red because of blood, algae, or iron. Steam rises, rippling the air, making this rocky depression in the woods look like the dregs of a witch's cauldron. She will inspect the vic more closely in a moment, but even from a distance she can tell that the murder was not a hurried act of passion but prolonged, even ritualistic.

She takes in the rest of the scene. There are two mountain bikes, one of which is hitched to a rolling trailer with several bins bungee-corded to it. Set upon a folding table is a propane cookstove and a washbasin and several milk jugs full of water. There is a mold-spotted orange tent with the mouth flapped open. A taut blue tarp, dirty with fir needles, hangs at an angle between four trees. Beneath it sit two folding chairs arranged around a firepit.

She knows that she is poor at socializing, but she believes that she is excellent at categorizing people. She narrows in on isolated details — the lustrous hair and thick fingernails of a pregnant woman, the pinched wrinkled mouth of a cigarette addict, the five-hundred-dollar watch favored by bankers, the loping gait of roofers, the brittle, pocked skin of a meth addict — and develops an instant profile.

Seattle has a homeless crisis, but there are so many subcategories to the population: The single moms living in shelters and transitional housing. The mentally lost men who wear ten layers of clothes while dragging three shopping carts full of junk down the street. The druggies and runaways squatting in abandoned buildings. The anarchists and romantics camping in the woods. She guesses this man was one of the latter, given his gear and the organization of the camp. She spots a Misfits and E.L.F. sticker on a Nalgene water bottle that lies on its side. In the tent he will likely have soiled, broken-spined paperbacks by Kerouac and Abbey. She guesses his body will be marked by a tattoo of the tree of life, an ankh, or a yin-yang symbol. He will have a social media account with #eco or #green in the bio.

She picks her way down the trail and finds Augustino Chives on his cell — talking to someone from the Park Service, it sounds like. He waves to her and motions with one finger to indicate he'll be free in a minute. His eyes are turned down at the corners, giving him a permanent look of sadness. He has a graying crew cut and the body of a former wrestler — broad shoulders, short legs, a paunch. He wears his standard uniform of fleece and khakis. His voice should sound like gravel, but there's something whispery and gentle about it.

She pokes her head into the tent first. Two sleeping bags have been zipped together, and they're deeply bloodied, almost jellied. There is a flashlight lantern near the pillow. A mesh pocket is sewn into the wall, and a copy of *The Dharma Bums* and the *Audubon Society's Field Guide to Mushrooms* are tucked into it. At the foot of the tent is a duffel stuffed with clothes. She spots a sports bra amid the tangle of flannels and thermal long sleeves. Nothing so far surprises her except the hiking boots. Two sets of them—a man's size twelve and woman's nine—sit just outside the tent, within arm's reach of the flap.

The medical examiners unfold and unzip a body bag that looks like a loose, black pupa. But before they can hoist the body out of the water and into it, she says, "Stop."

They look at her and slump their shoulders, clearly unhappy to deal with her, ready to call it a night. "Shit," one says. "It's *her*." They mean something else. Names she has been called before. *Control freak. Wack-job. Psycho. Bitch.*

She has encountered these two before—Tom and Lance—but can't remember which man belongs to which name. Two balding white hipsters in their late twenties with oiled beards and sleeve tats. She considers them incompetent and lazy and said as much when it took four months for them to sign off on a death certificate on one case and three months for them to deliver blood results on another. Their labs are constantly backlogged. She knows the two of them always share a vape, leaning their weight against the bumper of their van and puffing purple and green smoke, before driving a body off to the King County office, and she imagines their lungs are shellacked with a grape-flavored chemical sheen.

"I believe it takes seven minutes to smoke a cigarette," Nora says. "I don't know what the equivalent is for a vape pen. How about you go find out?"

They mutter and snap off their gloves and tromp away to the edge of the clearing.

Somewhere in the night an owl calls. The spring burbles, heat coming off it. A rain shower quits before it can really get started. She pulls on a set of latex gloves, clicks on her Maglite, and crouches close to the vic. He appears to have died from a single deep stab to the heart. She quickly checks his hands for signs of struggle and finds the palms dirty and callused but uncut.

One of his eyes has been gouged out, and saw-like gashes edge the socket. He has been roughly shaved. His scalp and cheeks and chest and groin are scraped down to bare skin. She spots nearby the remains of what must have been a long head of hair and a bushy, brown beard. Tossed aside, it looks now like a damp bird's nest.

It is difficult to tell beneath all the blood, but she can see a curious series of lacerations, a kind of cross-hatching on his body. The cuts begin at his chest and spiral outward. The gray skin of his leg, cooked clean by the hot spring, looks like old paper with cursive writing from another language scrawled on it. Intricate lines and loops and swirls.

Chives ends his call and walks toward her with his back hunched and his hands shoved deep in his pockets. Years ago, when they first started working together, whether they were in the field or the office, he would always make an effort at pleasantries, asking about her day, about her family, before they switched over to business. But that was before. Ever since Mia went missing, ever since Nora divorced Jack, there is nothing to discuss but shell casings and blood spatter. He goes out of his way to be generous in other ways, but he's always quiet about it. A Hallmark card on her desk for her birthday. A bottle of wine, its neck wrapped with a glittery bow, at Christmas. An invitation to dinner with his family now and then, always with the expectation she'll say no. All these things and a dozen other kindnesses, despite the fact that she never offers any reciprocal gesture or even a thank you.

Chives watches her study the body for a minute before saying, "Found his wallet. No credit cards. Some small bills. And an expired driver's license. Nat Campbell. Twenty-eight. Few priors for vagrancy, trespassing, and assault."

"Tell me about the assault," she says, still gazing at the body.

"Some mushroom-turf thing. Got into it with another picker about a year ago. Broke the guy's nose and arm. That seems to be what they were doing out here. Harvesting. Bins on the trailer are full of paper bags, parchment paper, a beat-up pocket guide called *All the Rain Promises and More.* A few specialty knives too. Curved four-inch blade on one end, brush on the other."

Her hand hovers over the dead face and makes a scooping gesture over the empty eye.

"Yep. Pretty much." Chives coughs and says something about the smell and digs into his pocket for a small jar of Vicks. "So." He rubs a smear beneath his nose. "What do you think, boss?"

"You suspect that our perp is female."

"Whoever he was sharing that sleeping bag with, yeah."

"I'm sure you already noted he was killed by a single stab to the heart. And there are no lacerations to the hands."

"He didn't feel threatened," Chives says. "He didn't put up a fight. He didn't see what was coming. She was able to get real close and end him real fast."

"And because no clothes appear to have been cut or pulled off him, you're guessing he was naked at the time of the murder. Tucked into his sleeping bag. Perhaps because he and his partner were about to be intimate? That's what you think, anyway."

"Exactly." He cocks his head and narrows his eyes as if to see her better. "But it sounds like you don't think the same?"

"I'm still working out what I think."

"You've got that line scrunched up between your eyebrows, Nora. The one that means you're constipated about something."

"Several things, actually."

"What's the first?"

"The boots," she says.

"What about the boots?"

"Maybe she has another set. But that seems doubtful, given their circumstances. The fact that the boots — not to mention her bike and all the rest of her gear — were left behind . . . that doesn't track with the theory she killed him."

"Unless she's dead too."

"Oh, she's undoubtedly dead."

"Undoubtedly, huh? I got Bowers and a few others sweeping the woods. Called in a few cars too. They're patrolling the streets surrounding the park. You're thinking maybe murder-suicide?"

"No."

"No?" He gives a little laugh. "Do you ever say anything that's not decisive?"

"She didn't kill him. A woman wouldn't have done this."

"You don't think a woman can —"

"Of course I think a woman will kill. You know I think that. But you must realize that this was no lovers' quarrel. It's a ritualized killing. In all but the most exceptional cases, that kind of psychopathic behavior is not in my gender's hardwiring."

"I know," he says and wipes a hand across his face. "I know it doesn't fit the standard profile, but —"

"But what?"

"I don't know. Maybe we're dealing with a new profile? You like everything neat and tidy, but human behavior doesn't always, like, compute perfectly."

"Except that it does," she says. "It always does."

Chives's eyebrows are bushy, and they rise now in a silent question.

"Behavior is not random. There is always a reason someone does something. There is always an equation that informs a choice. There is always a wound that gives rise to troubled behavior. A wife shoots her husband because she is sick of him abusing her. A grandmother poisons the dog next door with a meatball because it attacked her grandchild. A troop leader molests a Boy Scout because he himself was molested."

A girl goes missing . . . and the impossible grief makes it impossible for the parents to stay together, she almost says.

She and Chives do not raise their voices. This is how they talk. Gently challenging each other. Sussing things out. He operates more on feeling. She deals in calculations.

"Okay, boss," he says. "Are we ever going to get around to talking about the elephant in the room? The real reason I dragged you out here? I know it's a lot to ask, but I kind of expected a *Holy shit* or a *No fucking way* out of you."

They look at each other for a long moment before she traces a finger along the thigh of the corpse, following the design intricately crosshatched into the skin that must have taken hours to carve. Her eyes rise from the body to Chives's tired, puzzled expression. She says, "Crotter."

"Yep."

"But he's been incarcerated for a year."

"So he either escaped or we got a copycat." He heaves a shrug. "Unless you got any other bright ideas? I sure don't."

"You're not wrong."

"I'm not wrong?" He barks a laugh. "I love how you'll never say I'm right."

"The blinded eye and shaved skin are consistent with Crotter's victims, but the body art is puzzling."

"No Bible verses this time."

She doesn't respond right away but stands and stretches out the kinks tightening her legs. "BTK was inspired by Son of Sam. He even modeled his own special signature after the one Berkowitz included in letters addressed to the press and police. And BTK modified the design just as he modified his murders to suit his own needs."

"So you're saying this is a modification? A sick riff off what Crotter was doing?"

"A modification or evolution of what he started. Yes. Instead of Bible verses carved into the skin, we have . . . a pattern."

"But what's the pattern? What does this stuff mean?" Chives says and waves a hand over the body. "It's just a bunch of crazy lines."

"It's not just a bunch of lines," she says. "Something is being communicated. We just don't know what it is yet."

"So you think we'll find the woman—whoever she is—cut up like this as well?"

"I think we'll find her dead, but I don't know that she'll be dead in the same way."

"Because?"

"Crotter focused his attention exclusively on males. Those who reminded him of himself. By punishing them, he was punishing himself by proxy. Anyone else he murdered was usually a witness. Collateral damage."

"So this one, wherever she is, she's as good as collateral damage."

"I suspect so. Yes."

"Jesus H." His cell rings and he fishes it out of his pocket. "Yeah?" he says, and a length of silence follows before he says, "We'll wrap things up here and head your way." He ends the call and stares at the dark screen.

"They found her?" she says.

"Yeah."

"Where was the body dumped?"

"You might be right ninety-nine percent of the time, boss, but not today."

Nora doesn't respond except to peel off her gloves, neatly rolling them inside out and into a tight ball.

Chives has no satisfaction in his voice, only exhaustion when he says, "They picked her up walking along Fifty-Ninth. Covered in blood. Wearing nothing but a T-shirt and panties. Knife in hand."

3

Kincaid Hall, on the University of Washington campus, is a brick building shadowed by fifty-foot evergreens. Their branches glisten with rain and sway with the wind, scraping gently at the windows of a third-story classroom where Jack paces back and forth in front of his students. He remarks on the rain and tells them a story.

In 1812 a volcano erupted in Indonesia. The event — seven thousand times more powerful than the 1980 eruption of Mount St. Helens — sent two million tons of rock, ash, and sulfur into the air, disrupting the global climate for years to come, resulting in blighted crops, snowy summers, fires, widespread famine. This lasted well into 1816, when Lord Byron, John Polidori, and Mary and Percy Shelley vacationed in a villa on the shores of Lake Geneva hoping to escape the constant storms and gloomy weather that still lingered. To keep themselves occupied, they challenged one another to a ghost-story competition. Polidori wrote *The Vampyre,* the first novel about bloodsuckers and the precursor to *Dracula,* and Shelley wrote *Frankenstein.* So you could say that the two primary texts of the horror genre were born out of a time of explosive forces and intolerable weather.

Jack taps at the rain-dappled window and says, "Who knows what monsters will erupt from this period in history?"

Five years ago, he reminds them, the meteor strikes packed a punch equivalent to many dozens of volcanoes erupting at once. They introduced gases, particles, and temperature fluctuations to the atmosphere that continue to disrupt weather patterns world-wide. The drought in the Pacific Northwest has only just broken. Just now. And the ten-day forecast looks good and gloomy. They should hope to continue to experience this lovely, delicious mix of delicate mist, light showers, and roof-drumming downpours that used to be the standard around here.

"Do you know why I'm so excited about this?" Jack says, clapping his hands together. "Because it's great news for all of us fungi fans!"

He hated how hollow his voice sounded. There was a time when he would have delivered this information with sincere enthusiasm. There was a time when he considered teaching to be a theatrical performance or even a religious experience, one he prepped for by writing out all of his lectures and practicing their delivery in front of the bathroom mirror. There was a time when he would put his whole heart into the classroom, because he truly gave a shit about inspiring others to love nature, to worship with him at the same soggy chapel built of spores and mycelia. But that time has passed.

Twenty-five sophomores and juniors are on the roster for his Bio 414 seminar, and five weeks into the semester, he can't name a single student. They're all the same fleshy blur of concert tees, beanie caps, nose studs, Apple watches, and Doc Martens. More often than not, he is what he once despised — the professor who seems to be phoning it in, droning through his lectures without any real sense of electricity or connection.

But he gulped a four-espresso Americano before class began, trying to fire up his nerves. And he arrived early to make sure his PowerPoint presentation was functional. And he wore a tie and ironed his shirt and shined his shoes and triple-checked his fly. He needs to make an extra effort today, because he's being observed as part of his tenure approval.

Associate professor Robert Gordon currently sits in the back row with his legs crossed. He is fat-bottomed with a small chinless face dominated by his nose, so Jack thinks of him as "the Tapir." On the tip of Gordon's nose, tortoiseshell glasses are perched, and his eyes wander between Jack and the notepad on which he is busily scribbling. He wears a sport coat, pleated corduroys, and boat shoes with argyle socks.

Jack has despised him from the first moment they met, and he's certain the feeling is mutual. The AAAS conference is an annual gathering for the sciences as well as a clearinghouse for academic job interviews, and seven years ago, Jack traveled there fresh out of grad school, wearing a borrowed suit. He had put the flight and hotel on his overtaxed credit card, and he hadn't slept much the night before. This was one of seven interviews he had lined up, all of them in the San Francisco Marriott connected to the conference center.

He walked into the hotel room crowded with professors on the UW hiring committee. They were all seated in a ring of chairs except for the Tapir. He was lying on the bed, twirling a Montblanc pen in his fingers. He asked only two questions of Jack. The first—"How would you describe your pedagogy?"—was generic and easy enough to field, but the second was intended to throw him: "You went to an Ivy League university for your undergrad. You then attended a—how shall we say it—*second-tier* regional school for your graduate education. Can you explain the . . . downgrade?"

He was referring to Princeton and Eastern Washington University. Some of the other professors tutted and scolded the Tapir and told Jack there was no need to answer the question, but he chuckled and waved off any offense and happily cited financial support and the strength of the program. He then pivoted to his love for the state of Washington and how he hoped to stay there, which allowed him to sneak in a reference to his wife, a detective with the Seattle PD, and their child. He wanted to keep close to home. He was interviewing with Stanford and Brown and Rice later that afternoon, but UW was honestly his top choice, because it was his backyard. Not only did he want to continue living there, but he wanted to continue researching there. The Pacific Northwest was his laboratory. He knew—legally—the committee couldn't ask about a candidate's personal life, but he also knew that offering up his family and his preferred zip code would help his chances, since single young academics were notorious for job-hopping, and if somebody left a department in this uncertain financial climate, there was no guarantee the position would remain.

The Tapir had tried to stab him but had inadvertently helped him. That didn't stop Jack from replaying the moment over and over in the hours and the days and then the weeks that followed — all the way through his eventual campus interview and finally the job offer — remembering the small smile tugging the corner of the Tapir's mouth.

And now, here in Kincaid Hall, the Tapir is once again twirling his Montblanc pen and judging from a distance as Jack speaks at the front of the room. "Did you know over one-quarter of the biomass on this planet originates from fungi? Two point two million species and counting." He clicks through green and gray microscopic images on the screen and talks about how the fossils of terrestrial fungi date back some four hundred million years. "And guess what? Some believe their earliest form might reach back a billion and a half years. A billion and a half!" He throws up both arms as if to elicit a cheer from them. "Though that's difficult to ascertain since fungi do not biomineralize. Oh, and get this — fungi may have been the dominant life on Earth until around two hundred fifty million years ago!"

Here he pauses for dramatic effect, and in the silence that follows, rain patters on the window and a student checks a text on her phone. The Tapir blinks at him a few times before scribbling another round of notes. He licks his finger and flips to a fresh sheet.

The thing is, as hard as Jack might be trying now, he realizes it's probably too little, too late. His first two years at the U, he was a standout. He volunteered for every committee. He aggressively pursued his research and presented at four conferences and published two papers in peer-reviewed journals. He worked for the university's extension program. He worked in the lab. He worked in the field. He was known for his hustle. His student reviews were universally positive, and the university awarded him the young faculty achievement award. Most of his colleagues were gray-hairs who had comfortably settled into their routines. He was—many of them said—just the blast of nitro their department needed. A good candidate for chair a few years down the line.

Then the sky fell. And everything changed.

Large swaths of electrical grids and cellular networks went dark. Waves rolled in clotted with dead fish, sharks, and whales, and the beaches hummed with flies and wasps. Fires sparked in Northern California and Colorado, and hundreds of thousands of acres blazed. A strange ghostly green glow was reported in the Louisiana bayou. Birds and butterflies suddenly seemed confused in their migration patterns.

Impact sites were reported everywhere in the world, but U.S. news was dominated by northern Minnesota, where meteor strikes caused massive destruction and a quarantine perimeter had been established with rumors swirling about radioactive metal deposits. The light show in the Pacific Northwest had been magnificent—the sky busy with green and yellow flares—although nothing substantial appeared to have touched down in the region.

But Jack was barely aware of any of this. Because Mia had disappeared. She had disappeared, and everyone seemed too distracted and awed by the meteor storm to care. When he called the police to the scene, when he beseeched the rangers to send out search teams, he felt like someone complaining that his house was flooding while a hurricane raged.

He didn't shower or shave. He hiked the woods by day and by night, subsisting on granola bars and filtered water. He called out her name until his throat was raw. He would start in the same spot, sometimes working outward in an ever-expanding circle, sometimes patterning the search into grids. She had mentioned a hole —hadn't she?—a big hole. He was almost certain of it. She was worried about it, and he had dismissed her, and he wished more than anything he could go back and revise that moment. When she asked about the hole, he would have said, *Show me.* When she asked if they could go home, he would have said, *Sure.*

No matter how many times he toured the forest, he could find no hole and he could find no Mia. There was nothing. She was nowhere. After two weeks, he was as afraid of finding her as he was of not finding her. There was more than one occasion when he mistook the pale glow of a mushroom for dead flesh. When he slept — in fitful patches — he curled up in the cab of his pickup, the windshield fogged over from his barking sobs.

He tried to blame the cops. But the cops were his wife. Though Nora wasn't allowed to work directly on the case, she was consulting on it, and she assured him every *t* was being crossed, every *i* dotted. Given her bossy perfectionism, he believed her. But even so, he couldn't help but scream at her. He reacted by being overly emotional, and she responded by buttoning down all feeling. To him, her face was an expressionless mask, unmoving except for the tic she developed in her cheek. When he tried to apologize, when he pulled her into a hug, she stiffened — and so he shoved her back. "What's wrong with you? Don't you feel anything?" he said, and she calmly asked him if he thought her grief was any less than his own. Was she one to ignore details and let things slide? No, she was definitely not. He believed her, of course. There was no one on this planet more particular than she. This was the woman who used a timer when brushing her teeth, who vacuumed carpets into neat stripes, who showed up ten minutes early to everything, who organized the apps on her phone in alphabetical order, and who had diligently taught Mia to read, add, and subtract by the time she was three.

Nora didn't suspect him — despite all the questions he faced — but she blamed him. How could she not? He blamed himself. Probably their marriage was already doomed — they had been fighting off and on for some time — but this certified the end. There was no recovering from a lost child. Being together only reminded them of what they'd lost. She filed for divorce, and he signed the papers without protest.

In the time that followed, he regularly missed classes and office hours and faculty meetings. He often neglected to grade the homework he had assigned. Late one night, in the campus lab, he drank too much and fell asleep on the floor; a grad student discovered him in a puddle of his own urine. His teaching ratings plummeted.

For several years his research was nonexistent, and he didn't publish any articles. He tried to blame it on the weather. The long drought made fieldwork pointless. His service to the university was lacking as well. When he was asked, one semester, to serve on a course-catalog committee, he stared at the professor and said, "Put my name down if you have to, but if I show up, I won't say anything, because I frankly don't care."

He came to hate the sun. The mocking light of it. It burned the clouds from the sky and cooked the fungi from the forest floors. And it made him want to retreat into the burrow of his bedroom. But now, at last, the hard rains have come again, and the sky is a welcome gray. The ground is so parched, you can almost hear it suckling greedily at every drop. And Jack feels similarly. He isn't over the loss of Mia — he never will be — but he no longer feels dead himself. He feels thirsty for recovery. He feels ready to live again.

He realizes that his mind has wandered away from the classroom when a student with purple bangs raises her hand. The room is silent except for the rain and the hum of the computer and the scribble of the Montblanc pen. Everyone is looking at him. He clears his throat. "Where was I?" He glances at the screen. "Right. The Great Oxidation Event! It started with ocean-dwelling cyanobacteria. You stir that up with some iron, some volcanic and tectonic activity, and boom — you've got the first squirts of oxygen. Soon after that, things get slimy. It started when algae slicked the shoreline. Then this algae began to slowly evolve into things like mosses, lichens, liverworts. These were responsible for boosting organic carbon into sedimentary rocks, which in turn became a primary source of oxygen. Oxygen levels went up and stabilized the atmosphere that supports our lives today. Without moss, in other words, none of us would be alive. Not you, not me, not your cousin Susie, and not your dog Baxter. Plants kick off new life cycles." He licks his lips and finds a new way to phrase this and really drive it home. "Plants will determine the future of our lives."

The student with her hand up begins to wave it back and forth. "Excuse me? Professor?"

"Yes!" he says. "Chrissy, right?"

"Missy, actually."

"Missy!" He smacks his palm against his forehead. "Of course. What is it you have a question about?"

She points to her wrist even though she's not wearing a watch. "No offense, but I'm going to be late to my next class."

He then notices the students have their backpacks in their laps or already looped around their shoulders. The wall clock reads five to two. "Sorry to keep you. I was just so caught up in the lesson that I lost track of . . . you know what? Let me just give you the homework real quick." He uncaps a marker but before he can write more than a few letters on the whiteboard, the students pop out of their seats and shuffle from the room. "Or how about I e-mail you the homework!" he calls after them. "Be sure to check your e-mail!"

The Tapir caps his pen, stands up nimbly, and joins the exiting current of students. He glances Jack's way, giving him that familiar smile. An executioner's smile. Then he reaches out a hand. And shuts off the lights.

When the room is empty and the door clicks shut, Jack stands dumbly in the gray light of the afternoon. Then he shoves a desk and yells, "Shit!"

He settles his breathing and tucks his laptop into his shoulder bag, then walks into the hall. He's scheduled for office hours but doesn't want to risk running into the Tapir, whose office is three doors down, so he takes the stairs to the ground floor and steps outside into the chill. It's not raining so much as misting, and the air smells like briny black dirt. As he follows the walkways, puddled and yarned with drowned earthworms, he keeps his head down and thinks about the end of his teaching career. Maybe after he's denied tenure, he can get a job working for UPS. That's always seemed appealing to him. Driving around all day, listening to the radio. Staying in shape by hoisting boxes and tromping up porches. He would have no real boss and everyone would be happy to see him, because the UPS man was like Santa in brown shorts.

Yes. That's what he'll do. He'll become a UPS man. It's decided. The only thing that could possibly save him from this fate is magically winning a Benjamin Franklin Award or suddenly stumbling onto a scientific breakthrough.

Just as the rain starts back up again, he arrives at the new Life Sciences Complex, a massive, two-hundred-thousand-square-foot windowed building with an attached greenhouse, where his lab is located. He's officially in charge of two grad students, but aside from signing their forms and allotting them grant money, he hasn't done much for them. He's been trying to make up for that lately by offering to coauthor a paper and personally taking on more field assignments when calls come in from the university's extension office.

One of the projects they're currently pursuing concerns a monster. Most people think that the blue whale is the largest organism on earth, but it's actually a fungus. A vast pathogenic fungus that takes up 2,384 acres in the Pacific Northwest and is estimated to be over eight thousand years old.

On the surface, the yellow-capped honey mushrooms pop up, but beneath the soil, the rhizomorphs slowly finger their way outward, filaments that weave tighter and tighter together, eventually forming a kind of mat. The digestive enzymes that it secretes kill conifers. Individual units are known as hyphae, but the larger network is called the mycelium. These are identical cells that communicate and coordinate for a common purpose. Botanists have tried to find its edge but given up. One of the goals of Jack's lab is to map it completely, expose its limit.

He knows that studying fungus isn't exactly cool, but giant mushrooms excite even the most scientifically disinclined.

The building is cold with air-conditioning, brightly lit with fluorescence, and still smells like fresh paint. He follows a branching series of hallways, his shoes damp and squeaking, until he arrives at the lab. He is the principal investigator, so his name is on the door. The sight of it fills him with a mix of pride and guilt. He key-cards his way in with a bleep. Inside he finds Darla, one of his grad students.

"Hey," he says. He flops off his shoulder bag and collapses onto a chair in front of a computer. "What's the latest from the field?"

He's so distracted that it takes him a moment to realize she isn't responding.

"Darla?"

She's in her late twenties, a Berkeley grad. She keeps her hair short and wears long, dangly earrings made of fruit or feathers. He guesses she recently came back from a survey, because she's wearing boots and jeans with mud still speckling them, and dirty sample vials are spread out across the table. She is tall and lanky, so the bow in her back appears especially dramatic, a spinal parabola. From her posture, he initially assumed she was hunched over a microscope, but now he hears her breathing fiercely — in through her nose, out through her mouth — and recognizes that she is doubled over in pain.

"Everything okay?" he says and gets up to approach her. "Darla? Anything I can do?"

He can see now that her eyes are scrunched shut and her hands balled into fists. He thinks about touching her back, but his hand hesitates in the air a few inches from her. He can hear now the static pop and gargle of her breathing, a pneumoniac thickness.

"I don't," she says. "Feel so."

He looks around for a trash can and scoops it up and holds it out for her just as she shoves her face into it. It's hard to tell if she's coughing or throwing up. The sound is in between, as much hacking as heaving. A disgorgement. There is a thick, heavy splatter. He looks away as she retches and gags and wheezes for a good minute. Then she wipes the back of her hand across her mouth and whispers, "I'm sorry."

"It's okay."

"I'm so embarrassed."

"There's nothing to be embarrassed about." He almost mentions the time two years ago that she nudged him awake with her foot as he lay snoring on the floor of the lab but refrains.

She walks unsteadily to the sink and runs the water and drinks from the faucet and swirls the water in her mouth and spits. Then she soaps up her hands and rips off a paper towel and pats herself dry. She is moving at quarter speed, so all of this takes a very long time.

"I've been feeling bad all morning. But I just went from bad to . . ." She blows out a steadying breath. "I don't even know."

"It's flu season. Better head home. Rest up."

"Yeah," she says. "Better."

"Do you want a ride? Or can I call you an Uber?"

"No," she says. "No, I've got my car. I'm just a short drive away."

"You're sure? I'm happy to —"

"I'm sure," she says, but her voice is weak and raspy as she gathers her purse, leaving behind her backpack and the mess of field samples. She pauses in the doorway, resting against the frame. "Can you . . ."

"Whatever it is, yes. Just say the word."

"Extension called. They need someone to . . . there's a tree farm in the Olympics . . . and . . ."

"They're requesting a fungal consult?"

"Yeah."

"Done."

The extension office, a branch of the U, offers free classes and consultations and presentations to the state. Through them, his lab has fielded requests from sources as varied as museums, farms, and nursing homes. "The call sheet with the date, time, and address is on the . . ." She motions toward the bulletin board beside him, and he pulls down the notice.

"Got it." The address on the sheet instantly catches his attention. "Shit."

"What?"

"Nothing." Not nothing. Not really. But he's not going to get into it with her. "Now go. Go. Get better."

But she's already gone, the door clicking shut.

He runs his thumb along the address and smears the ink. He hasn't been back to that neck of the woods for a long time. Not since the U.S. Forest Service auctioned off the parcel of land where his daughter had vanished. A tree-farm company has moved in since, harvesting the mature timber and planting rows of noble and Douglas firs in the clear-cuts for the Christmas market.

The air in the lab is sour with the smell of bile, and he goes to the trash can and peels the bag off the rim. He can't help himself—he studies gross things for a living, after all—and chances a look. Something gray and viscous slimes and splatters the bag's bottom.

4

◎

The Seattle PD is located just off the 5 in downtown Seattle. The high-rise is mildew-rimmed and the same slate color as an overcast sky. Squad cars crowd the lot, and mountain bikes dirty the hallways. It might be past midnight, but the office still hums with activity. Phones ring with complaints about a barking dog, a loud party, a suicide attempt, a hostage situation. A shipment of omnimetal headed for China has been stolen off the docks. Computer monitors glow. Printers churn out reports. Someone orders a pizza. Someone complains that the bathroom is out of toilet paper. Someone drags a handcuffed perp through the office for processing. Two flat-screens are mounted to the wall. One plays CNN on mute; the other displays dispatch information listing where officers are located and what beat they're assigned.

Nora's desk is the only one in the office that isn't heaped with paperwork. She keeps it bare to the wood. This same compulsion drives her to respond to or archive or delete every e-mail, so at the end of the day her in-box registers a clean zero.

She can feel tiredness pulling at her, and if she's going to sharpen up and last through the night, she needs a jolt of caffeine. She refuses to drink from the burned-bottomed carafe in the lounge. In one of her deeper drawers, she keeps a portable espresso maker along with pods and bottles of purified water. She makes a hot, black, sludgy cup and pulls back her mask to take quick sips of it.

Line one buzzes and she answers by saying, "Ready for me?"

"Got her in the chair."

"On my way." She picks up a pen and a yellow legal tablet and heads to the interrogation room.

At this hour, it's difficult to wrangle anyone into helping, but she managed to catch a narcotics detective named Peter Jenkins working late. He's waiting in the hallway for her. He has a white beard that can't hide his double chin and always keeps a cigarette tucked behind his ear. "I don't know how much you're going to get out of this one, Abernathy."

"What do you mean?"

"You'll see," he says and heads into the adjacent room, where he'll sit on the other side of the one-way mirror and cue up the recording equipment.

Maybe he's implying that Chives is better at this sort of thing? It's true. Her partner knows how to ask baseline questions, how to read eye activity and facial expressions and body language, how to interrupt denials, how to keep the suspect's attention, when to offer sodas and treats. He'll even go so far as to touch a hand or a shoulder. He's the good cop who earns their trust. She's the bad cop who machine-guns them with questions and doesn't offer tissues when they cry.

But Nora is good at what she does. She's broken down plenty of suspects before Chives can even crack open a Coke and set a doughnut on a napkin for them. This suspect isn't requesting counsel, so they need to get her talking while she's still fresh, muddled, and without a lawyer.

Nora steps into the room. The light is low, the temperature meat-locker cold, the color gray except for the blue stripe bordering the walls. The woman—her name is Ashley Harlow—is seated on the opposite side of the table. She might be five foot five and weighs maybe a hundred pounds, and the orange jumpsuit fits her like a collapsed tent. White-girl dreads. Hemp necklace. Tribal plugs in her ears. Her fingernails are bitten down to bloody nubs. Her hands are cuffed and linked to the bolt on the table.

Usually this is when the suspect makes some smart-ass remark about Nora's gender, her race, or her mask, trying to unsettle her and make a desperate grab for power. But Ashley doesn't look up when Nora enters the room, or when she pulls up a chair, or when she clears her throat and introduces herself. It's as though neither of them is there.

Ashley sways in her chair. Her eyes are wide open but far away, the pupils dilated, possibly indicating methamphetamines, mescaline, ecstasy, cocaine. But she has no scabs on her arms and her nostrils aren't raw, so who knows. She whispers under her breath in a way that sounds like someone penciling something swift and sinister.

"Ashley," Nora says. "Ashley?" Again and again and again, with no reply: "Ashley?"

Nora tries variations on "Did you love him?" and "Did he hurt you?" and "Maybe you were acting in self-defense?" Anything to provoke a response. "You don't have any priors except a DUI from five years ago," she says. "I see you're originally from Medford, Oregon. What brought you here?" she says. "I hear people can be pretty protective and even violent about their plots when mushroom hunting," she says. "I hear it's its own little industry. I hear that since the drought has shorted supplies, morels are going for thirty a pound at some of the high-end restaurants? That right? Was this about money?"

Nothing hits. Nothing works.

Nora crosses her legs and rests the pad on her thigh and pretends to be taking notes but really she's drawing neat, tiny grids and then blacking out every other square, a thinking habit she has maintained since she was in elementary school.

"I told my partner you didn't do it. I told my partner that when we found you, you'd be dead. A victim, just like your boyfriend. He was your boyfriend, right? Then you showed up with a knife. Blood all over you. Now my partner, he thinks he's right and I'm wrong. But I'm rarely wrong. I don't think you're a killer. Can you help me prove that? Can you help me understand what happened? I know you know something that will make *me* right and *him* wrong. Anything you want to talk about, I'm here to listen. What do you say, Ashley?"

Ten minutes pass. Fifteen. Here and there Nora punctuates the silence with a barrage of questions. She looks to the one-way mirror and knows that Jenkins is likely dozing on the other side of it.

Maybe Chives is right after all. Maybe Ashley did it. Given the right circumstances, everybody's capable of killing. It doesn't matter if you're a cross-stitching grandma or a five-year-old boy with candy-stained fingers. It doesn't matter if you're God-fearing or flinchingly passive, if you've got a PhD or you're ten or two feet tall or your eyes are fogged with glaucoma. Everybody, anybody might be guilty. Nora has worked the job long enough that she knows this for a fact. She has seen everything the human nightmare is capable of.

Usually the math is pretty simple. Sometimes it's a will or life insurance that makes a daughter nudge her father off a sea cliff or a son puncture the gas line while his family is sleeping. Sometimes it's an affair that makes a wife stir thirty Tylenols into a bottle of wine to shut her husband's liver down. Sometimes it's a promotion. Sometimes it's religion. Sometimes it's revenge. Sometimes it's pure dumb rage.

The point is, everyone has stared hard at somebody and imagined a chalk line around that person's body. Everyone is capable of slashing a knife or pulling a trigger. Probably you're not going to, but you could—you can.

If Ashley did it, Nora wants to understand the why. She's getting nowhere, so she tries to think of what Chives would do. And Chives would talk. Blabber, even. Go on and on and try to get the suspect to feel that he was relatable, that whatever crime had been committed was completely understandable, even forgivable.

"You probably don't remember the World Trade Organization protests," Nora says. "You would have been too young. But maybe you know about them? The Battle for Seattle?" She fills in another few grids on her pad before continuing. "It's hard to imagine, but downtown was a war zone. Now when people watch the news and see crowds chucking bricks and flipping cars and getting beaten by batons, the typical response is 'I would never do that. Not in a million years.' But whoever is saying that is not in the streets. They are eating spaghetti at the kitchen table or they're springing the footrest on the recliner in the living room while watching TV. Do you know what I mean?"

Nora tries to determine if Ashley is listening to her. She still isn't making eye contact, but her breathing is less panicked.

"A riot — like the WTO riot — works like so: One guy gets angry and screams. The screams make someone shake a fist. The fist makes someone chuck a bottle. The bottle bursts, and all of a sudden somebody thinks it's a good idea to go wild. A window shatters. A fire catches. Someone who would *never* normally do such a thing sees dozens of people running out of a looted store and then feels justified in snatching a box of diapers, a two-liter bottle of soda, or a wide-screen television. We all have our threshold, Ashley. We just need permission and a little encouragement to push past it. And then we're participating in the unthinkable."

Again Nora says, "Do you know what I mean?" and waits for a response beyond the soft rasp of breath, the rattle of the handcuffs.

Nora is not a talker, but she forces herself to keep talking. Sermonizing. Engaging in a call-and-response. That's how you get the congregation to lean forward, right?

"Murder's unthinkable behavior. That's why everybody acts surprised when their coworker, their student, their neighbor ends up cutting their fiancé's throat or emptying a Glock into a crowd of people. 'He seemed like such a nice guy,' everybody says, and you know what? I bet he was. I bet he was a genuinely nice guy until that moment. He just crossed the threshold. The same threshold that makes nice people riot. Let's say this murderer got fired or he got bullied or whatever and that's what made him snap. I'm not scared of that guy. And I'm not scared of you. Because I *understand* that guy, and you know what, Ashley? I bet, if you talked me through what happened tonight, I could understand you as well."

This is true. Nora isn't afraid of people, no matter what they've done, because their actions usually make sense. On a normal day they would have done X, but on this day they chose Y instead. And they chose Y because of Z. There is a logic to misbehavior, no matter how twisted. The math works out and that makes criminal behavior comprehensible to her. That's what she wants. The XYZ of it all.

There are exceptions, of course. Every once in a while she comes across somebody for whom the math doesn't work out. These people have no thresholds. She doesn't know what to call them — sick, evil. But they're wired differently than the rest of us. They're the ones hardest to pin down because there's no causality, no straight line, no cause-and-effect reasoning. The clues they leave behind are less like a trail of bread crumbs and more like a dozen jigsaw puzzles scrambled up in a windstorm. That's who Nora's scared of.

People like Albus Crotter.

So far she's held off on mentioning his name. She's still not sure she's ready to go there. Although it feels like the first thing she should have asked, she can't help but push it to the last. So she eases into the possibility by calling up some photos on her phone. The photos of the corpse. Close-ups of the cuts crosshatched into the victim's skin.

She scoots the cell across the table, the screen giving off a white and red glow.

"So I've been talking, and now I think it would be great if you did the same. Maybe you could start by telling me about these markings, Ashley? What do they mean?"

Something happens then. Ashley blinks rapid-fire. Then her face creases and she cries out and shoves away the phone two-handed and it clatters to the floor. "No," she says in a small, rusty voice.

Nora retrieves the cell and finds Ashley looking at her, truly looking at her for the first time.

"No," she says again.

"His name was Nat Campbell."

"No."

"You were sharing the tent. You appeared to be sharing a life. Can you describe your relationship?"

"No."

"One eye was carved out. His mouth was hewn open. And his skin was etched with markings. And you were found carrying the knife that did all this."

"No."

"Can you tell me what happened? Just a few quick details."

"No."

"Did you do this to him, Ashley?"

"No."

"Then tell me who did."

"No."

"Have you ever heard the name Albus Crotter?"

At this Ashley stops breathing for a good thirty seconds. Then her eyes search every corner of the room and she says, "Do you hear that?"

"Hear what?"

Her eyes continue to dart wildly about. "The whispering."

Nora inclines her head. The air ducts faintly whoosh and the lights buzz, but otherwise, she hears nothing, and she says as much.

Ashley tries to bring her hands to her ears, but the chain on the cuffs stops them short. So she leans forward until she meets them, her palms crushed flat against the sides of her head. Her voice comes out as a damp sob when she says, "That doesn't help." She claps her hands against her ears again and again, and the chain rattles and chimes with the movement. "It doesn't help!"

"Forget Albus Crotter for a moment. Let's go back to Nat. How about you tell me—"

But before Nora can finish the thought, Ashley's head slams into the table with a meaty thud. At first it appears she has fainted, but a second later she whips herself upright, her dreads tentacling the air. A rashy red mark begins to spread across her forehead.

"Ashley. Are you okay?"

Thud—her head drops again, this time with enough force to

split her eyebrows open. For a moment bone peeks out from the two rough vertical slits. Then the blood gushes out, filling her eyes, tracking down her cheeks.

"Jesus Christ. Don't." Nora rises from her chair and hurries around the table. "Stop hurting yourself." But she's not fast enough.

Thud — Ashley's face hits the table again, and there comes the sound of crunched cartilage. She swings her body back into an upright position. Her face is a mask of blood and her nose is bent sideways with a fleshy tear at the bridge.

"Ashley!" Nora grabs at her with one hand and bangs at the one-way mirror with the other. "Help! Jenkins!"

Thud. Splintered teeth mash through her lips.

Thud. Her jaw cracks.

Nora tries to hold her back but can't. She is reminded of the other day when she opened the door of her car and a hard wind forced it from her hand. This feels like that. Elemental.

Thud.

The door crashes open and Jenkins rushes in and only then are they able to contain Ashley, who continues to rasp and dribble the words "No, no, no."

5

◎

Five Years Ago
The Green Man

saac Peaches wore khakis and button-downs even on the weekend. He never ate or drank too much. He made it a priority to get a solid eight hours of sleep and always had a mild smile on his face and took pride in trying to look on the bright side of things. When his head of blond hair began balding in his early twenties, he was relieved at the money he would save on shampoo and the time he would save combing it. When his girlfriend from college said she liked him — she would always like him, he was impossible not to like — but he was too submissive to feel any passion for, he said he understood and then considered how he might take up a hobby like hiking or woodworking with his newfound freedom.

He was hired out of college as a genome engineer for a major agrochemical company, and for ten years it never occurred to him that he could do anything else. He made good money, though he was never sure what to spend it on. He had great benefits, though he rarely got sick and didn't dream about retirement.

Then the sky fell, and normal didn't make sense anymore. He watched the news with increasing alarm and wasn't sure whether the planet had dodged a bullet or swallowed one. He started thinking more about the life he had built for himself. A safety-padded, seat-belted, air-conditioned routine. He built programs that genetically modified seeds for a massive corporation. His bosses often clapped him on the back and occasionally treated him to happy hour at Buffalo Wild Wings for creating antifungal and low-hydration strains of seeds that defied drought and increased growth yields. Superseeds, the admins called his inventions. He was the Superboy of superseeds.

Sometimes he wondered if he ought to ask for a raise, given all that he had accomplished within the company, but the thought of asking made him so uncomfortable that he decided he was paid more than enough.

Then one day he came home from work to find an SUV parked in front of his house and a woman with a big head of hair and a powder-blue power suit waiting for him. She held out a hand — perfectly manicured and glimmering with rings — and said her name was Annabelle Ricketts and that she was terribly interested in his work.

"Are you a scientist?"

"No. But I help scientists. I fund them and I coach them, I suppose you could say."

"Where?"

"Ostensibly I work for the Department of Defense."

"Ostensibly?" he said.

"Let's put it this way — they decided we deserved our own corner of the office. We're a special program, and I'm one of the regional directors." Her eyes were unblinking, her teeth a marvelous white, and her voice was honeyed with a Southern accent when she said, in this time of need, they could very much use someone like him.

"Like me?" Peaches said and gave a small chuckle. "I'm just a laptop farmer."

"Oh, I hear you're a lot more than that. The folks at Pioneer and Monsanto say you've been behind some of the biggest breakthroughs in the industry."

"I have?"

"You're not one of those people who's always deflecting compliments are you, Isaac? Because you should really take credit for what you're capable of."

He didn't know what to say, so he just opened and closed his mouth several times.

"I hear they call you Superboy?"

"I—yeah." He felt his cheeks coloring with a warm blush. "Yeah, they call me that."

She took a step closer, clicking the asphalt with her heels. She smelled like one of those shops in the mall that sold all the lotions. He couldn't tell how old she was, maybe thirty-five or maybe fifty-five. But she looked at him with such penetrating eyes that he felt jellied in her presence.

"How'd you like to be a Super*man* with us?"

"I would—I think—I like—that could be—sure—yeah—okay—neat."

She motioned toward his house. "I hate to be a busybody bother, but maybe you should invite me in? We could have a Diet Coke and get acquainted. I think you'll find the opportunities we offer to be just as lucrative as the private sector, but you'll be serving your country instead of a corporation, and wouldn't that be nice? Especially in this time of global uncertainty? We need all the good soldiers we can get."

"Yes," he said, nodding his head until he thought it would fall off. "Yes. Yes. Yes."

An hour later, he had said yes again by signing the contract she produced. And he was glad to escape a job that, as Director Ricketts put it, seemed intent on screwing over farmers and polluting waterways and seeding cancer—until he wasn't.

For the next year, he worked on a campus of what he thought of as gray Lego bricks—windowless, featureless office buildings made from concrete. Level-four security clearance. Bordered by fences, patrolled by drones and guards, hidden away in the moss-draped woods southeast of Seattle, the toothy peak of Rainier rising in the distance.

In the time before, scientists estimated that 86 percent of life's species had yet to be fully described. Now that number has swollen. They were a long way from fully understanding what was growing in their own backyard, let alone the bottom of the ocean or the depths of the Amazon. The meteor shower had dropped its seeds and the U.S. government had collectors roaming the globe for samples. There were other DOD campuses stationed throughout the country, but this one specialized in the alien flora introduced by the comet.

Isaac spent his days at the computer, cycling through data, while researchers in white coats flowed past him in his peripheral vision as if in fast-forward, and he heard a babble of intersecting words like *phylum* and *hyphae* and *zygospores*. They studied slides. They used droppers. They ran cultures. They jotted results onto charts. They made small talk about plant pathology while drinking coffee in the break room. They were all once professors at research institutions or scientists at Syngenta and DuPont and BASF and Monsanto. They had published papers and they had filed patents for biochemical sequences. But now they were doing something different. Now they were studying the otherworldly.

Several times a week a helicopter would touch down on the landing pad or an armored semi would pull in through the gates and unload a fresh specimen. There was a new species of tree in Central Park that grew taller than any skyscraper. There was a translucent flower that thrived in salt water and had the look of a petaled jellyfish. There was a purple fern exclusive to Antarctica that was snatching, poisoning, and consuming penguins with its fronds.

Director Ricketts oversaw Isaac as the administrative head of the facility. She called him in for private meetings now and then. Unlike the industrial sparseness of the larger facility, her office felt crowded with comfort. There was a fake fireplace, an Oriental rug, fleur-de-lis wallpaper, glittering sconces and candles, pots of potpourri, wingback chairs, and a massive burl-mahogany-and-gold-leaf executive desk.

On this desk she had the standard arrangement of a keyboard

and monitor, notepad and pen pot. But she also had a curious rod that was shaped like a thin tuning fork. It was the size of a wand and made of omnimetal mined in Minnesota. She would flick it with a fingernail or rap it softly on the side of the desk and a humming energy would pour off it. You could feel it as much as you could hear it. She would bring it close to her ear and get a faraway look in her eyes and move her lips as if speaking to someone. Sometimes, when she was in such a trance, it took her a minute or two to realize Isaac was waiting at the door to her office.

She would tell him to have a seat. She would offer him a Diet Coke and he would say no, thank you, and then she would pout her lips and say, "You're not going to make me drink alone, are you?" He would then agree, and she would pull two cans from her mini-fridge and pop straws in them and set them on floral coasters.

They would drink their Diet Cokes—he estimated she consumed a dozen every day—while discussing his latest findings. She would nod her head and offer him many compliments and communicate requests that often translated to weaponization. Could the new strain of cellulose be developed into a bark blade? Could the pronounced alkaloids be distilled into an untraceable poison? Was there a way for this sponge to absorb sound, and if so, could it be used for surveillance? What about chitinous armor? Or bullets that could seed growth inside of their targets? And let's not forget the symbio prototype. Yes, let's especially not forget that.

The higher-ups had a pronounced interest in the idea of convergence—splicing and threading genes—so that humans (read *soldiers*) could host alien matter. She often referenced a man named Dr. Thaddeus Gunn, the principal director of their program. She rarely blinked, but whenever his name came up, her eyes snapped shut for a moment, the thick black eyeliner sealing them.

"I haven't quite cracked it yet," Isaac said. The symbiote discussion had begun following the discovery of a capuchin monkey in Brazil that had green tendrils subcutaneously rooted and threaded through its fur. It could unleash vines from its arms and legs, employing them like spider silk to swing from branches and net prey.

When the monkey was captured and dissected, scientists found what appeared to be a floronic bond that responded to neurological stimuli. The monkey and the plant shared a body and a mind. "I'm trying to be careful."

"On the one hand," she said, "I appreciate that. I appreciate you being careful. On the other hand . . . why?"

"Well," he said, "science demands patience and skepticism. That's why. During the pandemic, no health expert would say anything definitive about whether a vaccinated person could still spread the virus. Even though there had never been a vaccine that prevented infection but not transmission —"

She cut him off. "But that was stupid of them. They undersold the vaccine as a result and people were hesitant to get it."

"That's one way of looking at it. But they didn't know, and when you don't know, you shouldn't pretend to be certain."

"Wrong. They should have said the vaccine was one hundred percent effective so go out and get it and save the world."

"Maybe."

"There are other countries trying to do what we're doing. Do you know what that means? It means we're in a race. And winning that race means saving the world."

"What if we're not careful and we unleash something that accidentally ends the world?"

She nodded and made a *Hmmm* sound. Then she rose from her chair and walked over to where he sat and stood behind him. For a few seconds she rested her hands on his shoulders. Then she seized one of his ears and twisted until the heated pain there was the only thing he knew. "I need you to hurry. Do you understand?"

"Yes," he said, his voice cracking. "I understand."

"I am facing pressure from above and I am passing some of that pressure on to you. Do you understand?"

"I understand. I understand!"

"Good," she said and released him. "I'm sorry to be such a B-word."

"It's okay." He put a hand to his ear and touched it gently, making sure it was still attached to his head. He never complained, even when she drew blood or called him a weak pathetic piece of slime, which happened on occasion. They both enjoyed themselves in their own way.

She told him that he could go, and he scurried from his seat. But her voice chased after him, calling out, "Oh, one more thing."

He bent his back as if bracing for another blow, but she said only, "Be a dear and leave the door open on your way out?"

"Of course, Director Ricketts," he said. "Thank you for everything."

One day, a man entered the building and everyone went still in his presence. He did not look particularly formidable. Short and round and spectacled, he wore a tweedy three-piece suit. But as he surveyed the lab, walking up and down its rows with his hands clasped behind his back, people noticeably shrank from him.

He approached Isaac where he sat on a stool, half-studying a laptop screen while biting at the tip of a pen. "You're Isaac Peaches?"

"I am." Isaac stood from his stool and stuck out the hand with the pen still in it. "Oh, sorry," he said and tossed the pen aside, but the small man ignored his offer to shake.

"I'm Dr. Gunn," he said and raised his eyebrows. "I assume you know who I am."

"Yes!" Isaac said. "Of course! Great to meet you, sir." And then he babbled on for a moment, motioning to his laptop and hurriedly talking about some of his current work with fungal pathogenesis.

"That's all fine and well," Dr. Gunn said. "But you know why I'm here."

"The symbio prototype?"

"Indeed." Dr. Gunn removed his glasses and polished them with a handkerchief pulled from his breast pocket. "Why haven't you tested it on humans?"

Isaac said, "Only mice and pigs and monkeys so far, but the results have been super-encouraging."

"That wasn't the question. The question was why *not* humans?"

"Because." Isaac cleared his throat. "We're not quite ready yet."

"We need to be ready *now.*"

"Oh. Okay."

"Fetch it for me."

"I'm sorry—what are you asking?"

Dr. Gunn's voice took on the tone of a parental lecture. "I would like you to show me the symbio prototype."

Isaac was taller than Dr. Gunn, but there was something about the man's presence that made him hunch over, making himself smaller, as if in apology. At a fridge he withdrew a specimen jar that contained a slimy green tangle, like something pulled from a clogged drain. He held it up and the muck slithered from one side of the glass to the other. Then it whipped a tendril toward the cap and dragged itself up and out of sight.

"I've been reviewing your lab reports and it appears that the prototype fails in most of its hosts."

"Yes. That's the thing. We're not sure what makes for a good match yet. Whether it's blood type or some genetic marker or—"

"Excellent," Dr. Gunn said. "Now, follow me, please."

They departed the laboratory together. The rest of the scientists studied them in silence.

Isaac and Dr. Gunn spent the next ten minutes moving through security locks and taking elevators that required key cards until they came to a series of cells. "Wow. I've never been down here," Isaac said. "I didn't even know these existed."

"Now you know," Dr. Gunn said. He walked swiftly for someone with such short legs.

The cells were made of glass, not metal, and brightly lit. One of them was smeared with black mold. Another fluttered with moths with red eyes on their wings. Another held a man with skin that appeared gray and cracked and elephant-like, and as they passed by, he peeled off a long dry strip from his arm and ate it. Another contained a teenage girl with purple-flowered branches growing out of her heels and knees and spine and elbows and shoulders. In the last they found a man who appeared to be dead. Flowering vines spilled out of his open mouth and reached across the floor and along the wall, splitting into smaller and smaller shoots like green capillaries.

"Oh, shit," Isaac said as Dr. Gunn trained his eyes on him. "Oh, shit, sir. What happened to him?"

"What happened to him? He died. He's compost. That's what happened to him."

"Right. But . . ."

Dr. Gunn gestured at the body and said, "This is a member of the Iranian military. He parachuted onto an American naval vessel in the Persian Gulf and killed twenty men before he was overpowered and detained. Do you understand what that means?"

"I — no."

"It means Iran has developed its own symbiote."

"Oh. Damn. Wow."

"This soldier was shot ten times. We tried to keep him alive. Unsuccessfully. And now — as you can see — the floronic half of him remains our prisoner. It's like a garden without a proper patch of dirt in there."

"That's good news, then. I can take some samples off him and —"

"No more samples. No more mice and no more pigs and no more monkeys. No more hundreds of tests to be certain of this or that. The old rules of science no longer apply. There's no FDA to worry about. This is a *race*."

"Then what do you want me to do? How can I speed things up for you?"

"Let me show you," Dr. Gunn said. And with that he swiped a blank badge to open the door to the dead man's cell and motioned for Isaac to step forward.

"I'm sorry?"

"In you go."

Isaac, who outweighed Gunn by fifty pounds, allowed himself to be pushed into the cell. He said, "Dr. Gunn, come on, I —" and then the door shut and the locks engaged. Isaac did not throw his body against it. Or beat at it with his fists. Or beg. Or shout. He was in disbelief. Any second now, Gunn would let him out. This was just a prank. Or a mistake. A misunderstanding.

"They call you Superboy, yes?" Dr. Gunn said. "Now's your chance to prove them right. Go on. Be super."

The vines rustled and whispered. One by one they uncurled and tested the air and then, scenting his heat, they slithered across the floor, moving toward him. Isaac flattened his body against the wall and looked about him, though he knew there was no escape.

"You can either ingest the symbiote sample yourself," Dr. Gunn said, his voice steaming the glass with little puffs of moisture, "or you can allow the floronic invader to merge with you." He pulled out his pocket watch, glanced at the time. "Either way, I'm very curious to see the results. I certainly hope, for your sake, this experiment works out. Director Ricketts says you're such a promising young man."

6

◎

Now
A Time of Growth

Jack's not asleep and not awake. He's in that in-between place that feels swimmy and misty. At first he knows only cold. His whole body is shuddering with it. He reaches for his blanket and snatches nothing but air. He tries to roll over and instead takes a step. The world rearranges itself. He's not lying down but standing upright. He's not in his bed but on his driveway.

He's outside. He's standing outside — outside his condo — in his boxer briefs and nothing else. His skin appears milky and silver. His feet are soaked through with a chill, nearly numb. When he tries to stamp some warmth into them, they feel like bricks. Something flashes in his hand. The moon. The moon is in his hand? Reflected on the blade of a knife. The Wüsthof butcher knife that Nora bought him for Christmas a thousand years ago. He is gripping it so tightly that his hand aches. He pries open his fingers and the knife falls, clattering on the concrete.

He turns in a circle, orienting himself. The streetlamps glow, but the houses are all dark. A dog barks a few blocks away, but otherwise it is quiet. "What the hell," he says. "What the hell is going on?" He retrieves the knife and walks stiffly through the open door of his condo.

In the kitchen, the oven clock burns red with the numbers 3:47.

He slides the blade carefully into its slot in the butcher block. As he does, something fits into place in his mind. A tattered image. From the dream that possessed him when he sleepwalked outside. The more he tries to pin it down, the more it unravels. Before it escapes him fully, he hurriedly opens a drawer and pulls out a pad and pen and scratches down what he can remember.

Then he flips the light switch and blinks hard in the yellow wash of the kitchen and sees the tiny, detailed loops and swirls he scratched onto the paper. It looks so familiar and alien at the same time. Like handwriting in a foreign language he should be able to recognize. It meant something a minute ago, and now? Nothing.

He wavers over the pad with his pen poised, and when nothing comes to him, he heads for the stairs. And then circles right back to the kitchen. He's black-brained and exhausted but jittery enough that he knows sleep won't come without some help, so he digs through the cabinets and pulls down a bottle of Dewar's, splashes a coffee cup full, and drinks.

There was a time in his life when everything felt like an addition. He was gaining more muscle when he went to the gym. He was gaining more credibility when he sat in a classroom as a student and gaining more money when he later stood at the front of it as a teacher. He was gaining more knowledge when he tromped through the woods or hunched over a microscope in a lab. He was gaining more love when he married Nora, when they had Mia. As if his life were ever-expanding. As if his purpose were getting fuller, bigger.

That ceased to be true after their daughter vanished. That day on the calendar felt like a fulcrum point when everything sharply tipped. Life is now about depletion. If he posts on social media, he does so with a mild disgust and the feeling he's lost a few particles of his soul. If he drinks — which he does every evening — he counts, with every sip, the brain cells lost.

That's what he's doing right now. Sip. A hundred brain cells gone. Sip. A hundred more. Sip. A lesson from calculus washed away with a swallow. Sip, sip, sip, sip. A memory of a treehouse, of an actor's name, of a hike along the coast, of a sushi dinner at Kokkaku. But the pain washes away too. The pain of loss. So he drinks. Every day is now a drink. Life is subtractive.

He is relieved to wake up on the couch. His head might give an electric throb when he sits upright, his mouth might taste of bile, and his lower back might be bunched tight like a fist, but that's better than him wandering off into the dark in his underpants.

He swings his legs off the couch and massages his temples with the heels of his hands. His mind is dizzy and his joints bee-stung when he makes his way to the bathroom. He doesn't feel hungover as much as bruised by a restless night. His piss stutters out thick and orange, and he tells himself — for what must be the thousandth time — to drink more water and less whiskey and coffee. But later, later, because right now he needs some caffeine if he's going to function.

In the kitchen he bangs through the cupboards searching for a fresh filter before giving up and using yesterday's grounds. The coffeemaker burbles and sputters, and he fumbles for his phone and finds the home screen busy with e-mail and calendar alerts, one of them reminding him of his UW Extension appointment this morning. The fungal consult at the Hemlock Hills Tree Farm in the Olympics. "Shit."

It's ten now, and he's supposed to be out past Griswold by eleven, which isn't happening. He tries dialing the number on the call sheet, but it rings and rings without going to voice mail. So he skips the shower and breakfast, hustles on a flannel shirt and canvas pants, stuffs his rain gear in a pack, fills his thermos, and heads out to the truck; his field kit's already in the cab.

The concrete of the city soon gives way to an evergreen blur as he rounds the southern shore of Puget Sound and heads toward the Olympics. The water is the same churning gray as the sky. The mountaintops are lost to clouds. He turns the radio on and cycles through the stations and sings along briefly with Hank Williams before tuning in to the news that a Seattle-based tech company is lobbying for the creation of an omnimetal roadway that would power the city with the kinetic vibration of the traffic on it. He sees the omnimetal Teslas gliding through downtown and he knows about the Bullet monorail that just opened a Sea-Tac station, but he prefers to live low-tech and happily drives his old truck and would chuck his phone and laptop into the Pacific if he could get away with it.

He exits the 5 onto 101 and from there gets onto a country highway fenced by firs and blackberry thickets. The speakers in his truck are old and tinny enough to make his ears ache, so he punches the dial and settles into a silence broken by the occasional logging truck roaring by. He tips back his thermos and empties the last drops from it. There's something about the sleepy gray of western Washington that makes ground Colombian beans as essential as oxygen.

Fog thickens as the grade of the road steepens. White tendrils wisp along the ditches and then swirl up to soak the forest. As he travels through this phantom zone, minutes haze by and his mind wanders. He glances at the passenger seat and lets out a gasp because a child sits there—his Mia. Then he blinks hard and the vision of his daughter dissolves into his backpack.

She's always there with him, but he can escape his grief more easily than Nora, because he is farther from the reminders. He moved into a condo, but his ex-wife still lives in their old place and keeps their daughter's room tidy, the carpet vacuum-striped, her clothes and stuffed animals sealed in Ziploc bags so they won't get musty, giving the space the feel of an evidence locker.

He once suggested to her—during one of her deepest sadnesses—that she might have an easier time if she sold the house, if she sought out a fresh start elsewhere. She gave him a look of disgust and said, "This isn't supposed to be easy."

It's not easy when he turns onto the road—the same road he took five years before, the last road he and his daughter ever traveled together. Sometimes when he's drinking, when he's accounting for the brain cells lost with every sip, he worries that she might be erased. He would forget the pink and white tiger she curled her arm around every night. He would forget the tiny dimple on her left cheek that appeared when she bunched her face into a smile. He would forget the way she splatted ketchup on everything she ate. He would forget the way she collected coins — found in couch cushions and parking lots — and called them wishes and tucked them between the bark plates of the ponderosa pine in their backyard, so that it flashed in the sun. He can't remember the sound of her voice, but he can remember the way she mispronounced words — *cashews* were "cow shoes," *napkins* were "mapkins," *cinnamon* "cimmanon," *turkey* "churkey," *bananas* "balanas," "ka-prise" instead of *surprise*.

He remembers the time they camped in Coeur d'Alene. Mia was four, and all she wanted to do was climb. In the living room she would be on top of the couch instead of on the cushions, and at the playground she would shimmy her way up the pole to balance herself above the swing set. He and Nora woke up one morning to find the tent flap undone and Mia's sleeping bag empty. The sky was blushing with dawn when they raced outside in their underwear, calling her name in a panic, only to hear a giggle overhead. They looked up to find her waving from the uppermost branches of a juniper tree. When they ordered her to come down, the girl realized she couldn't and began to cry. So Jack and Nora had to calm her down and pull on their hiking boots and scramble up the tree. Jack was in his boxers and Nora in a T-shirt and panties, and when they reached the top of the tree they were scratched up and sticky with sap and spiderwebs and they couldn't help but laugh. Nora hooked an arm around Mia and thumbed the tears from her cheeks and said, "Shh. It's okay. It's all right."

But when Nora shifted her feet, readying to climb down, Jack said, "Hold on a minute. When's the last time you were up in a tree?"

"Twenty years?"

"Who knows if it'll ever happen again, right? Might as well enjoy the view."

So they sat up there as the sun rose, pinking the sky and sparkling the lake. "You saved me," Mia said. "Thank you for saving me."

· · ·

The road splits and splits again, going from asphalt to gravel, and steeply inclines. His shocks whine and squeak as his tires shudder in and out of hardened, treaded ruts. Trees flit in and out of the fog like black wraiths. The road bends and Jack notices the SUV parked up ahead just barely in time to stomp his brakes. The pickup skids to a rocking stop.

It's a black Chevy Tahoe that wouldn't look out of place except for its government plates. A man climbs from the cab. He's tall and wears a cornflower-blue collared shirt and khakis, and his waist is so thin that his braided leather belt is tightened to its farthest notch. He looks to be in his early thirties but his blond hair has receded into a downy horseshoe. He smiles and gives an apologetic wave as he approaches.

Jack drops his window and the cool moist air pours into the cab and the man says, "Sorry about that."

"You trying to turn around?"

"No, no—I'm parked like this on purpose. Road's closed, I'm afraid."

"Sorry?" Jack squints as if to see past the Tahoe, but the fog is too thick to reveal much. "But you don't look like Bureau of Land Management or Forest Service."

"Right?" The man laughs and pats his head. "I should get one of those Smokey the Bear hats, huh? To fit the part?"

"So you are with the Forest Service?"

He holds out his hand and tips it one way, then the other. "Basically. Government."

"Basically government?"

"Yep." The man is still smiling, but the smile twitches at the corner.

"Look, I'm supposed to head up this way. I work for the U—so I'm *basically government* too—and the Hemlock Hills Tree Farm gave UW Extension a call, asking for a consult."

"Huh. Weird. I don't know anything about that." His eyes turn down the road, where another engine can be heard grinding up to gear behind them. He gives Jack a little two-fingered salute and says, "Be right back."

In the side mirror Jack watches the man trot down the road to greet a sedan, ill-suited for these roads, as it brakes and pulls off into the brush. A big guy in a suit is driving, but he stays seated. The rear door opens and a woman gets out. Her hair is sprayed and styled like a winged helmet—auburn with a bold streak of white running through it. She wears high-waisted gray slacks and a pink silk blouse and heels. She and her skinny friend confer quietly for a moment and then she marches toward Jack's pickup. She doesn't stumble in her heels; she spikes her way across the uncertain surface of the dirt road as if it were level hardwood.

A thick cloud of perfume accompanies her. Her cheeks are bright with blush, and her mouth is a red bloom of lipstick. "How are y'all doing?" she says with the brightness of a country star taking the stage and adjusting the mic.

"Doing good." He points up the road. "Except that I need to get through."

"You came all this way, and here we are gumming up the traffic." Her mouth bends into an exaggerated frown. "That's so frustrating, isn't it? But I'm sure you understand."

"Not really, no," Jack says and puts his hand on the gearshift like a threat. "I was told to come up here. It is my job to come up here."

"Any chance you have the wrong address?"

He almost argues with her further, but given the uncertainty of his mind lately, he might as well double-check. Maybe he saw the wrong location in the same way that he saw his daughter seated beside him. "It's right here." He digs into his backpack and rifles through it and comes away with nothing but a pair of Gore-Tex gloves, a water bottle, some topographic maps. "Or not. Must have left the call sheet at home."

"Sometimes our eyes deceive us."

"I'm ninety-nine percent sure."

"Be that as it may. As my colleague Agent Peaches already explained, the road is closed."

"*Agent* Peaches?"

"Yes," Peaches says and hurries over to join them. "Hello. Hi. That's me. Isaac."

"And I'm Annabelle Ricketts."

"What agency are you with?" Jack says.

Peaches looks to Ricketts as if for approval, and she nods. He digs into his back pocket and pulls out a badge that reads DEPART-MENT OF DEFENSE.

"DOD? I don't understand. Why would—"

"I'm so sorry," Peaches says in an apologetic voice. "But that's classified."

"We wish we could tell you," Ricketts says, and her smile widens to show all of her teeth, "but we're a bunch of boring old rule followers."

"I—" Some movement catches Jack's eye and he looks ahead to see several figures in hazmat suits emerging from the fog. They stop thirty feet away, silent and watchful. The clear plastic masks reflect the white whirl of the fog, making them appear as if they are filled with weather.

"I do apologize about the confusion," Ricketts says. "I can tell you're ready to punch the steering wheel and yell the S-word!"

"I guess."

"I hope the rest of your day turns out to be something special to make up for this frustration."

"Hrrm" is all he can manage as a goodbye. He drops the gearshift into reverse and creeps backward down the hill until he has space enough to turn around. Then he bumps down the road another mile before finding himself facing another Tahoe. For a moment he wonders if he has somehow circled back the way he came. Then the SUV flashes its lights, and he realizes he is the one blocking the way. So he pulls over to the edge of the road and lets not one, but two, three, five, eight, twelve vehicles pass. SUVs, trucks, and vans, and though their shaded windows don't reveal much, he spots inside them several more people wearing hazmat suits.

7

Nora changes the sky-blue sheets to the sunflower-yellow sheets. She tightens the corners, fusses with the symmetry of the fold. She plumps the pillow and lays down the quilt and runs her arm along the length of the mattress to erase the wrinkles. In a Ziploc bag is Tigey — Mia's pink and white tiger — and she places it upright at the head of the bed. Rain patters on the window. Out of it she can see children in raincoats walking to the bus stop, tortoised by the weight of their backpacks. She watches them until they're out of sight.

Things had gotten worse after Mia disappeared. But they hadn't been great before. Nora always had to read the newspaper in a particular order. She would meticulously peel the strings off a stalk of celery before eating it. She couldn't leave the house with dirty dishes in the sink. But there was something about her marriage to Jack — and about parenthood even more so — that forced her to give up control. Jack refused to read instructions. He was never on time. He forgot obligations. He threw his clothes on the floor at night and sniffed them before putting them back on in the morning. He often said, "Good enough," or "Close enough," when inadequately sweeping out the garage or guessing the measurement on a recipe. At first this is what she liked about him. That he could drive by a theater and say, *Hey, want to go to a flick?* instead of buying reserved seats three days in advance. She thought maybe his flexibility would be contagious, and he seemed to bemusedly enjoy the structure and checklists she brought to his life.

They first met when she almost busted him. Dispatch reported a guy creeping through the backyards of a West Queen Anne neighborhood. Nora was a patrol officer at the time and took the call. The old lady with the slippery dentures who'd made the report claimed the man had a knife and was crawling in and out of the woods. "Like an animal," she said, tucking her teeth back in her mouth. "A wild animal. Who knows what he might do!"

The houses here all ran up against the greenbelt, a thick strip of woods that buffered the houses from the interstate. There were several homeless villages tucked away inside it, and it wasn't uncommon for Nora to answer calls about people digging in trash cans or sleeping on stoops or breaking into cars. But Jack was nothing like the image she had in her head of the man she was looking for. She found him in the woods kneeling next to a stump as if in prayer. He wore canvas pants and a flannel shirt beneath a down vest and carried a backpack with him. He was muddied up but looked more like a weekend camper than someone living in a tent.

"Hello?" she said.

"Oh." He started at the sound of her voice and then flashed a smile and waved a hand. A hand that held a knife that gleamed silver. "Hi. What's up?"

She put a hand on the butt of her pistol, still uncertain what kind of person she was dealing with. He was handsome in a scruffy kind of way, but most of her attention was focused on the blade. "I'm here checking up on you."

He seemed genuinely confused. Classic white guy. No fear at the sight of an approaching cop. "About what?"

"About you creeping around in people's yards with a knife. You're making folks nervous."

"Oh. Right. Sorry. I've been trying to stick to the woods, but I thought I spotted some oysters in a lawn a few plots back."

"Oysters?"

"Oysters are mushrooms. I'm collecting mushrooms. This greenbelt is a treasure trove!"

"You some kind of druggie?"

"What? No. I'm some kind of scientist."

He invited her over to study a porcini the size of an elephant ear. And before they parted ways half an hour later, he had harvested it and convinced her to let him prepare her a mushroom and risotto dinner. "Perfectly paired with red wine. It'll be the best thing your tongue ever tastes."

"I find that hard to believe," she said.

"I like to make big promises."

"Hmm."

She couldn't believe she'd said yes. She couldn't believe she enjoyed herself. Just as she couldn't believe, in the months to follow, that she took him shooting in a gravel pit or he took her hiking in the Cascades. He lived in Spokane, where he was working on his doctorate, but he drove back and forth to the Sound constantly. "For research," he said and then bobbed his eyebrows to imply he might have something other than fungi on his mind.

Her job was an unendingly stressful catalog of nerve-shredding arrests and mind-numbing reports — and he was an antidote to that, always so good-natured and curious, an exclamation point or question mark springing from the backs of his sentences as he pointed out funny things like the call of a rare bird or a constellation in the night sky.

She was focused on the practicality of the day-to-day — groceries, oil changes, bills, securing her detective license — while he constantly spoke of a future that didn't exist, like going surfing in Australia (even though he didn't know how to surf) or starting a horror movie club (even though he didn't know who he would invite to it). In a way, he drove her nuts, but in another way, it felt like a good kind of nuts. A new and easier way of encountering the world. Sometimes she joked with him, saying how nice it must be to go through life with the dreamy optimism of a white dude, but the barbs were always softened by the understanding that he was his own unique brand of weird.

He never stopped surprising her with questions. *How do you keep your posture so straight? How do you put somebody in a choke* hold? Do you want to take salsa lessons? Who is your favorite writer? Do you like it when I touch you like this? What is the greatest love song ever written? How do you make a New Year's resolution that you actually follow through on? What kind of lotion do you want me to use when I'm giving you a full body massage? How do you solve a crime? Do you ever feel bad for the people you bust?

For all his questions, he never asked the ones she hated most: "Can I touch your hair?" and "What are you?" *What are you?* is the queen bee of white-people questions. They never seemed to realize how soaked it was with the implication of otherness. *You don't belong, so how do you fit?* She got hit with it on a weekly basis and had finally bitten back at enough of her colleagues that they knew to shut the fuck up. Her lighter complexion apparently confused people, and given all Jack's obsessions with categorization, she felt certain the day was coming when he asked an unforgivable question.

They were at Constellation Park, wandering among the tide pools, crouching down to run a finger along the rippled leg of an orange starfish or the fleshy purple belly of an anemone, when it happened. He said, "Maybe this is an annoying thing to ask," and her finger slipped into the poisonous bloom of an anemone, so it shrank, contracting its tentacles into what looked like a puckered mouth. She stood and sighed and readied herself for what was coming, and said, "Go ahead." But he surprised her by asking a different question, one that unbalanced her enough that her foot slipped on some seaweed and she dropped calf-deep into the water: "Why did you become a cop?"

She could never find the right words in response to this question. It was like trying to explain the impossible ingredients that went into a medicine. The batons and the pepper spray and the bullets and the tear-streaked faces she saw on television and social media made her feel sick enough to puke poison. Taking some of that power back with a badge of her own seemed like its own kind of cure. To serve and protect a community instead of beat it into submission. But alongside all the heavy but honest moralizing, there was also a simple explanation. Simple and silly: she was obsessed with mystery novels and detective shows.

Her mother had been strict with her as a child, making her go to Bible study and volunteer at the food pantry and maintain perfect grades and finish a daily list of chores. Nora's busyness and discipline and severe behavior hadn't helped her social life, so reading was her constant escape. She visited the library weekly. Some of the best friends of her childhood were Sherlock Holmes, Hercule Poirot, and Easy Rawlins. The tidiness of their plotted structure appealed to her greatly. Every mystery began with a mess and concluded with the mess getting cleaned up. The math and predictability of the storytelling made sense in a way that life never did.

She and Jack made a mess together, a beautiful mess, when she got pregnant. Marriage seemed like the best way to clean it up, but still she hesitated. When she said they came from different worlds, she didn't just mean that they lived hundreds of miles apart. Then there was the professional problem. She had just been named a detective, and he was finishing up his doctorate. Presumably he would be going on the job market soon and applying to postdoc gigs across the country. But he told her not to worry. He would move to Seattle, and they would figure things out. He would apply to local institutions, no problem. As long as they had each other — that's what mattered. "Why do you have to be such a sweet idiot?" she said to him when he improvised a ring out of a long blade of grass and tied it around her finger.

When Mia was born, the balance of their differing personalities served them well. Yes, Nora could schedule naps and measure formula and pack the diaper bag with butt cream and wet wipes and children's Tylenol, but she couldn't keep every onesie clean of stains or remember where to find the binkie when a colicky infant was screaming in her ear. Jack couldn't keep track of what temperature the bottle should be, but he helped Nora let go of worrying over every little thing, and he also had the magical ability to calm Mia down, tickling her feet until her cries turned to giggles or rocking her in his arms and shush-shush-shushing her until she fell asleep. The baby whisperer, Nora called him.

Being the parent of a young child is all about survival. In those early years, Nora and Jack relied on each other—if one wanted to get some sleep or a shower, the other was there. But when Mia grew older, she didn't need them as much, and as a result they didn't need each other as much. They began to annoy each other more and more—and after Mia was gone, nothing seemed to bind them together, and they both slid into the extremes of their worst behavior.

In the middle of Mia's bedroom stands a vacuum cleaner. It roars to life and Nora backs out of the room, erasing her footprints from the carpet as she goes. She does this for two reasons. The first is simple orderliness. The second is she dislikes the pulse of hope she feels every time she enters the room and spots tracks and wonders for a moment if her daughter has at last come home.

She closes the door slowly—then leaves the house and drives swiftly downtown to the station. Chives is waiting for her, sitting on the edge of her desk and drinking from an oversize mug that reads HUSBAND DADDY COP HERO. His eyes are dark-circled and his posture slumped.

"What?"

"Got news," he says.

She shoos him off her desk. "What?"

"Open your e-mail."

"What, what, what?" she says as she rolls her chair forward, shakes the mouse, logs in, and calls up her in-box.

Chives pulls the string of his tea bag and dunks it up and down.

"Normally you only drink tea in the afternoon," she says.

He blows the steam off his mug and takes a sip. "Didn't know my drinking habits were of such interest to you."

"Why aren't you drinking coffee?"

"Didn't sleep so good last night. Feeling a little under the weather."

"So you're not only sitting on my desk with your dirty ass, you're polluting my airspace with your germs?"

"Just open the e-mail."

She and Chives are copied on a message from a detective stationed out of Bellevue. The subject line reads *Look familiar?*

The body of the e-mail comes with a link that invites them into a time-sensitive drop box containing several folders. She opens the one labeled REPORT #06-4927 and then clicks on the top sheet, filed at three a.m. She speeds through the description, reading it aloud. "'The victim, Linda Susan McNally (fifty-five years old), was found in her living room after a neighbor reported hearing screams. When officers (PJ Mendes and Sanford Greene) arrived on the scene at thirty-one thirteen Madison Street, they discovered the front door open, and after announcing themselves, they entered the residence and immediately noticed signs of distress, including a knocked-over lamp, a broken picture that had fallen from the wall, and bloody footprints and handprints. The living-room carpet was soaked through with blood and the victim's body'—"

With some impatience she clicks over to the photo folder and dashes through image after image of a heavyset black woman with her eyes carved out, her head shaved, and crosshatched lines engraved in intricate spirals on her skin. "This happened last night?"

"Time of death was estimated to be eleven p.m."

She clicks through a few more photos and then says, "What about the husband?"

"No husband. Lives alone."

"Any suspects?"

"They're doing knock-and-talks in the neighborhood right now."

She spins her chair around to study Chives. "You know what this means?"

"No, actually," he says, pulling out the tea bag, shaking off the excess liquid, and dropping it into a nearby trash can. "I have no idea what the hell any of this means."

"It means I was right. Our perp didn't do it." She stands up from the desk so quickly that her chair rolls back a few feet. "There's somebody else out there."

"Where are you going?" Chives says.

"Records."

The clerk who works in the basement is a cotton-haired man named Victor who used to be a beat cop. He has sloping shoulders and a potbelly that seems to drag him down as he leans tiredly on the counter with the sports section of the *Seattle Times* spread before him. "Detective Abernathy," he says and folds the paper shut. "What can I do for you on this fine, soggy morning?"

"You're taller," she says. "By an inch or so. Did you get new shoes?"

He has meaty jowls and they curtain his smile. "You and your details." He motions for her to look behind the counter, where he stands on a thick silicone mat. "Wife got it for me. She was sick of rubbing my sore damn feet every night." He bends and bounces his knees a few times. "But here's the thing I'm wondering. If they can make omnimetal batteries that charge themselves, why can't they make some shoes comfortable as this mat?"

"I need all the files on the Blind Prophet."

His smile fails and the jowls droop. "Crotter, huh?" He turns to look behind him at the rows and rows and rows of packed shelves. "All of it?"

"All of it."

He knocks the countertop with his knuckles. "Gonna take some digging. Gonna be a lot to carry."

"You're asking for my help?"

"You're the one who's going to need help." He shuffles over to the corner and rolls out the squeaky hand truck. "Come on, then."

When they head down the corridor of shelves, the motion-activated lights buzz on. "You on a nostalgia tour or something?" he says. "Digging up your greatest-hits graveyard?"

"Got a copycat."

This stops him and he looks over his shoulder at her. "Copycat, you say?"

In a windowed conference room, she heaves the five storage boxes off the hand cart and onto the table. She flips the tops off and begins to lay down the files one by one in a chronological display from the top left to the bottom right. The photos and reports account for several years of police work, some of it her own.

Albus Crotter began his killing spree soon after the meteor showers five years ago. He was nicknamed the Blind Prophet by the press because he carved an eye out of all his victims. He then shaved their bodies bald and gouged Bible verses into their skin. He mostly preyed on prostitutes and hitchhikers and the homeless, the vulnerable who wouldn't be missed. He usually killed with a knife but sometimes strangled those he could overpower. Most of the bodies were found in the woods. One was discovered in a storage container, one in the trailer of a semi, and one in the tunnels of the Seattle Underground. Places where he could be alone with his meticulous work. But dark places too. Places where bad things grew.

Nora was brought on as a detective because she was known for seeing through the mess of a case — the ten thousand irrelevancies you collected for every crime — and homing in on the causal patterns. She started with scripture. They knew their suspect was religious because he etched Bible passages onto the skin of his victims. There were the standard mentions of plagues and pained multitudes and trumpets and fire. But Revelation 3:20 was his constant refrain. "Here I am! I stand at the door and knock. If anyone hears my voice and opens the door, I will come in and eat with them, and they with me." He also occasionally dropped an "Ask and ye shall receive; knock and the door will open," from Matthew 7:7. In both instances the words *the door* were always written in oversize, capital letters. The emphasis mattered — of this she was certain — which led to a revelation of her own.

Everyone else on the investigative team had commented on the gouged-out eye. Sometimes the left, sometimes the right. They guessed he had some deformity that compelled him to blind his victims. But if that was the case, why not both? Then she studied the autopsy photos and noted that in addition to scooping out the eye, he also carved a triangular notch below the cavity. It was the shape, she pointed out, of a keyhole. He must see himself as a kind of key. But where the door led, she didn't know. Heaven and hell, she supposed.

The sarge had instructed the detectives to focus on faith. Contact local churches to see if they had any extremist members they might be worried about. Scour social media and all the Jesus-y message boards to see if there was anyone who seemed particularly . . . apocalyptic. The trouble was, since the meteor strike, evangelism was on the rise. Churches of every denomination were booming with new members who wanted some way to make sense of a world whose rules were suddenly shifting. And the fastest-growing religious group was known as the Roofless Church. Some called them a doomsday cult. Some called them metal-eaters. They worshipped — and consumed — omnimetal. Their eyes glowed a starry blue and they ended every prayer with "Metal is."

Nora had experienced her own crisis of faith. Every Sunday she spoke to her mother, and the conversation always began with a question: Had she been to church? No, the answer had been for many years. No, she hadn't. The response was always a weighty sigh. Sometimes they moved on, but sometimes her mother laid into her about the power of prayer and how they were never going to find little Mia without the good Lord's help.

Nora understood why people belonged to congregations. It was the same reason they cheered on sports teams: they wanted to feel like they were part of something bigger. But she has never experienced anything other than a disconnect in church. She just wasn't hardwired for it. She operated on evidence. She liked detective novels, not fairy tales. But you can't simply forget eighteen years of Bible study. The hymns still echoed in her head, the taste of Styrofoam-cup coffee still lingered on her tongue, and when her eyes caught the light, the orange starburst of color around the pupils reminded her of stained-glass windows. She had never actively spoken against religion — until now.

The loss of Mia made her feel more embittered about any discussion of a benevolent God. If someone said, "She's in a better place now," or "Trust in His plan," she wanted to scream her throat bloody about the facts. She encountered them every day in the wife with the swollen, purpled eye or the kids in week-old diapers or the dead body rotting in a dumpster. The universe was cold. The universe didn't care whether you lived or died or prayed or raged. If you wanted justice or reward, you had to seek it out yourself. Judgment came with a badge, not a Bible. Her work was her religion and she was committed to finding and stopping the Blind Prophet because she knew he was causing a pain and loss all too familiar to her. She would be his reckoning. She couldn't save her daughter, but she would save others and damn a murderer and defiler in the process.

So she studied the evidence as she used to study scripture, and she changed the course of the conversation completely when she recognized the simple pattern of geography. Forget about the messaging of the churches and their parishioners for a second and focus instead on the location of the altar itself. Look at where the prophet was choosing to do his work.

The crime scenes had clearly been scouted in advance, and they were all isolated but near roads. She guessed the killer had a job that not only brought him to such places but protected him, cloaked him. He worked alone because his anger and doctrines and — possibly? — a crippling insecurity didn't allow him to function around others. And he drove something that would go unnoticed.

She noted the common proximity of cell towers, all within a few hundred yards of the bodies. Not only that, but a few phone calls revealed that each of these towers had recently been retrofitted with an omnimetal booster antenna that enhanced its signal range fivefold. She rightly guessed that their suspect was the technician.

His windowless van — with the cell phone company's logo painted on its side — had been used to transport the bodies. He had killed over thirty people by the time Nora, Chives, and six other officers pulled up, their lights flashing, to a tower he was working on.

They circled the structure and called up with a bullhorn, telling him to climb down. He did not respond for the longest time, only watched them from a height of some two hundred feet. She secured a pair of binoculars and glassed him from below. Her colleagues had been wrong about his profile. There was nothing special about his appearance. He didn't have wild eyes or long stringy hair or devil's horns or face tats or burn marks or scarring or anything that distinguished him. He was in his forties, brown-haired, beginning to bald, soft around the edges from too many cheeseburgers. Completely unexceptional. She knew something terrible roiled inside the man, but she didn't know the source. His lips were moving, not constantly, but intermittently, as if he were in conversation with someone, something.

"Please climb down now," the sarge shouted through the bullhorn. "Climb down or we're coming up after you."

Crotter's lips stilled. He nodded and hesitated only another moment before jumping. Nora pulled the binoculars away from her eyes just as his body momentarily eclipsed the sun and threw a cool shadow over her face during his few, long seconds of flight.

He landed with a meaty smack. The ground was grassy and marshy enough that he lived. But he fractured his spine and fissured his skull. The ambulances didn't arrive for twenty minutes and she spent that time kneeling over him, talking to him, trying to keep him alive, because she wanted an explanation. "What is the door?" she asked him over and over and over until a single bloody tear escaped his eye and the corners of his mouth trembled and he said, in a whispery voice, "The door . . . is opening. And God is waiting on the other side."

Then his eyes fluttered shut and he descended into what the doctors referred to as a vegetative state.

This was one year ago. He now spends his days drooling in a chair or a bed, overseen by both guards and nurses, at the Black Creek Correctional Facility's geriatric unit.

. . .

The door opens and Chives enters the room, giving a low whistle. "Look at that." He picks up a photograph showing Romans 6:6–7 scratched into the flesh of a rib cage and tosses it back onto the table. "What are you going to do when the department goes digital? Can't do this with a laptop."

She readjusts the placement and squares the lines of the photo he just dropped. "I will remain stubbornly analog." She stations herself at the center of the table and scans the whole of it. "How do you feel?"

"Like shit." And indeed his breath wheezes. "You going to talk to Ashley?"

"That's what I'm getting ready for. And I was planning on you coming with me, but maybe you should go home? Have you even taken any medicine?"

He gives a noncommittal nod and clears some crud from his throat. "She's all healed up?"

"Long way from healed, but she's bandaged. She lost several teeth. Seven stitches on her lip. Another five on her forehead."

"Jesus."

"I put in a call with provisional detention and they'll escort her to interrogation in a half an hour. Chief said to make sure a lawyer was on hand this time, so there's a suit in our way now. Things started off ugly and he doesn't want anyone thinking we're the reason she's roughed up."

He gestures at the tabletop of evidence and says, "What are you looking for here? Anything in particular?"

"Everything in particular."

Chives circles the table, cocking his head this way and that, and says, "It's like one of those Magic Eye books."

"What are you talking about?"

"You know what I mean, yeah? In those books, there's like a page of squiggles or dots or geometric shapes or drippy designs, but if you kind of make your eyes go unfocused, an image pops out. Like of a train or a snake or whatever."

"Mmm," she says, not really paying attention to him.

Chives coughs a few times into his fist and she says, "Do that into your elbow, please." He continues to cough and she takes a few steps back from him, imagining the germs floating through the air like the black fluff of a diseased dandelion. "Chives. What the hell. When you cough into your hand, you just spread disease by touching everything. Didn't COVID teach you anything?"

He clears his throat and pounds his chest. "Yeah. Sorry. Ugh." He wavers in place and puts a hand on a chair to steady himself.

She picks up a composition notebook, one of dozens taken from Crotter's home. In it, written in the same tidy small script carved into his victims, are recitations and meditations on Bible verses. *The door, the door, the door* keeps springing off the page and knocking at her mind. She's seen all this before. What she needs is to notice something new. She reads and rereads pages, skimming over them, and it's only then that her eyes blur — just like Chives said — and she notices a hidden pattern. The handwriting is typically neat. Straight lines. Compact lettering. Like the circuitry he worked with as a technician. But then, every other page or so, the penmanship dissolves into illegibility, almost like static pops interfering with the message. She has always dismissed this as a product of exhaustion. Crotter's hand and eyes must have grown tired. But now she sees — in the letters coming apart — something that appears almost filamented. Something that looks like the lines etched onto the victim from the other night. A new translation.

Chives coughs again and distracts her. "Seriously, man," she says. "It's disgusting. And selfish."

"Sorry. Sorry! You want me to go? I'll go."

Her cell rings. A number inside the building. She answers and listens to the guard in provisional detention tell her in a shaky voice, "I'm sorry, but Ashley — I can't —"

"What? Is the lawyer running interference?"

"No," the guard says. "She's gone."

"What do you mean, gone? Where the hell did she go?"

"No," he says. "I mean dead. She's dead. She hung herself."

• • •

She and Chives hurry over to detention and find a cluster of guards whispering in the cellblock. A shoebox-size window is cut into every cell door, and each one is darkened by the head of an inmate. They press their faces up against the glass, trying to see. Their voices are muffled, but they speak loudly, asking what's happened. Some of them pound their palms against their doors, and the air throbs with their noise.

Nora pushes past the guards and steps through the open door and takes in the sight of the cell. She isn't sure where to look at first.

The nurse had bandaged Ashley's head heavily with gauze and medical tape that the young woman had peeled off and twined to fashion a makeshift noose. She slumps beside her bunk with her neck bound against the top corner post.

But Nora gives the body only a glance before taking in the walls and floors and ceiling, all of which are marked with spirals of blood, roughly finger-painted in a filamented design that is now familiar.

She walks the perimeter of the room, studying the red matrix, and then approaches the body for a second look. Ashley's legs and the floor are damp with what is presumably her vacated bowels, but there is a gray mucus-like quality to the mess. Her face is a swollen scabrous mask — hardly recognizable — and the same kind of gelatinous material oozes from her eyes and her nose and her mouth.

Nora pulls a pen out of her pocket and reaches it to one of Ashley's eyes. There is a squelching sound when she prods it. The pen pulls away with a thick damp string attached and wobbling from it.

Up to this point Chives has remained in the hall, talking to the guards, but he enters the cell now. "Nora?"

"Contact the chief. I want to fast-track labs on her, and we'll need his priority sig."

"I don't understand. She — you don't think she hung herself?"

"There's nothing that makes me think she didn't."

"Then what are you looking for?"

"There are answers in her blood."

8

ack at his condo, Jack finds the UW Extension call sheet where he left it, on the counter. The paper is browned and wrinkled from where he spilled coffee on it but still legible. He double- and triple-checks. He was in the right place. He pulls out his phone and tries the contact info again, and this time the line doesn't even ring. An automated voice says, "I'm sorry, but this number has been disconnected."

He opens his laptop and plugs *Annabelle Ricketts* into Google Scholar and the UW library's search engine. He scrolls through the hundreds of results. There are thirty different people who are some version of *Anna* or *Ana* and *Ricketts* or *Rickets* who work in paleontology, in feminist studies, in comparative literature, in electrical engineering, but there is only one Annabelle Ricketts; she's listed as a coauthor of a paper titled "The Biology of Nationalism." The lead author was a professor of international studies at Texas A&M, and the article abstract indicates she argued that humans are inherently tribal, and when people bond over common appearance, myths, and sense of place, they historically have the greatest odds of survival and success. He doesn't have time to read it, but it sounds like an anti-globalist stance that could be used as a justification for everything from eugenics to closed borders.

He seeks her name in a general Google search and turns up a few possibilities of military service, a Pentagon post, and a fuzzy photo from a political gala in China, but nothing conclusive.

He realizes then that he is coughing. A tiny itchy hack punctuates each breath. He goes over to the sink and drinks straight from the faucet. He pounds his chest and calms his breathing. His throat rattles with crud, so he decides on a hot shower to clear his thoughts and his lungs.

The water needles his face and he takes in big gulps of steam and coughs again and spits out some greenish-grayish flecks he catches only a glimpse of before they vanish down the drain. Maybe he caught something after sleepwalking last night or maybe he picked up the same bug as his grad student.

That reminds him. He should follow up with Darla. After he stumbles out of the shower and towels his body dry, leaning against the sink to rest for a moment, he fetches his cell phone. He dials her number and listens to the line ring as he walks around his bedroom picking clothes off the floor and smelling them for freshness. The walls are bare, but the carpet is obscured by heaps of dirty laundry. Not for the first time, he thinks he should do something about this — hang some pictures, dust and vacuum, at least try to perform the part of a civilized grown-up. By the time he decides on a shirt and a pair of pants, Darla still hasn't answered and the call goes to voice mail. "Hey," he says. "Just checking in to make sure you're okay. Let me know if there's anything I can do. I've . . . got a question for you. About the fungal consult at the tree farm? So, yeah, hit me back when you can. E-mail or text is fine."

As soon as he ends the call, his phone buzzes in his hand and he nearly drops it. The number comes from the university and he answers by saying, "Darla?"

A rough male voice calls out, "With you guys, I swear. Half the time I don't know what to clean up and what not to clean up."

"I'm sorry — what?"

"You professors — you're always leaving your crap lying around like a bunch of spoiled-ass kids, and then I get into trouble when I clean it up. People whining about experiments and the like. Well, I don't know. How am I supposed to know what the hell's an experiment and what's just a damn mess?"

"Who is this?"

"It's Earl in Custodial, and I'm calling because I just walked into your lab. And I don't know what to tell you, but I'm not cleaning whatever that is up. Do it yourself. Understand?"

"I—" But before Jack can ask him anything else, the caller hangs up.

Years ago, when he was still married, he returned from a three-day conference to find a surprise from Nora. His office was not as he'd left it. The furniture the university provided—a dented desk, a cheap roller chair, metal bookshelves, metal filing cabinets with gashes and sticker residue on them—had been replaced by furniture from Ikea and Pottery Barn. The white walls had been painted slate gray. His heaps of papers had been filed and his books alphabetized. Several maps and fungal charts had been framed and hung on the wall. Later on, he would feel at once grateful and mildly resentful that she needed to control even his workspace. But at the moment he stood at the threshold of his office, he simply gaped for what might have been an entire minute. Blinking. Slowly processing that he was not in fact in the wrong place.

There is a similar feeling of disorientation when he keys open the door to his lab. The dimensions are the same, but the familiar sight is gone. The air is thick with humidity and the smell curls his nose, an earthy sourness that you get from a dank cellar or a moldering bag of potatoes. The overhead fluorescents are off, but the light from the hallway is enough to show him that something has grown in his absence.

It is hard to know what to call them, tendrils or roots or tentacles, but they run across the floor and along the counters and on parts of the walls and ceiling. They are of varying length and thickness. They split and split again and then somehow seem to thread back together. The skin of them has a slimy pallor. Here and there he notes a kind of broccoli bloom, a tumorous sprout knuckling upward. And when he looks closer, he thinks he sees a bent arm here, a long-toed foot there, a knobby knee, a screaming mouth, the glossy sheen of an eye. But then he blinks—hard—and everything looks like one big, messy organic tangle. He steps fully into the room and lets the door close behind him and reaches for the light switch. He knows what he is looking at, even though he has never seen anything like it in his life. Fungus.

9

Nora sits at her desk with her hands clasped neatly in her lap. In front of her is one of Crotter's composition notebooks. She finds in it mostly excerpts of John 3:16 and Romans 3:23 and Proverbs 3:5, but he also writes occasionally about how God is talking to him. He says he hears Him best when climbing the cell towers, because they focus the connection. His voice comes between the signals. His voice comes through the antenna. There are no words, only a feeling. A feeling like darkness gathering. A feeling like tentacles reaching. God is coming. And Crotter is but a servant of His hunger. These are often the places on the page where his handwriting frizzes apart, like split threads, becoming something unreadable.

She stares straight ahead into the dead screen of her monitor. Everything else has faded to a blur. She isn't aware of the room buzzing all around her, of the wall-mounted television playing coverage of a plane that mysteriously vanished while en route to Alaska, of the people who occasionally glance her way and say, "Looks like Abernathy's gone fishing."

That's what she calls it when she's deep in the zone. Fishing. The sensation is equivalent to floating on a boat in the middle of a calm black lake. But *nothing* is a better word for it. She was in the nothing. Nowhere. If she's still enough, quiet enough, something will rise to the surface and dimple the water. A realization. A connection. She learned the move from Sherlock Holmes, who referred to it as his mind palace, and she supposes it's a form of creative meditation. Sometimes she goes to the nothing to crack a case. Sometimes she uses it to calm herself.

The lake is where she went after Mia vanished, and more than once she thought she saw the shape of her daughter faintly below, a pale surge that sizzled briefly with bubbles and then was gone.

She can sense something now. Stirring in the deep. Darting beneath the surface. There are the meteors falling from the sky, and there is Crotter falling from the cell tower. There is Crotter writing furiously into his notebook an apocalyptic translation he can't quite manage, and there is a body found in a park with a similar cipher etched onto its skin. There is Ashley slumped in her cell, and there is death fouling the air, and there is Crotter falling from the tower, and there are the meteors falling from the sky, and there is the connection that for now remains unknowable.

Then she blinks — and, with a disorienting lurch, finds herself at the station once more. Her desk phone is ringing. She suspects it has been ringing for a long time. She snatches the handset from its cradle and clears her throat. "Abernathy."

"Yeah, you're the one who priority-tagged the bloodwork on — um, what's her face — on an Ashley Harlow?"

"Yes."

His voice is rusty and high-pitched. "You need to stop doing that. You're always doing that. Do you know how busy we are? I'm backlogged months on toxicology, fingerprints, DNA. Nearly a thousand deep right now in unreleased specimens. If the chief hadn't signed off on this, you'd be waiting months."

"Exactly."

"'Exactly,' she says. 'Fuck me,' I says." From the high volume and theatrical inflection of his voice, she suspects he is the type of person who talks with his hands, and she imagines one of them karate-chopping the air now. "You're cutting the line! And you're making me look bad doing so."

"Do you have the results or not?"

"Yeah, I got the results. Why do you think I'm calling?"

"The blood was contaminated?"

"Pfft. You can say that again."

"By what? LSD? Meth? Mushrooms?"

"Mushrooms," he says, and his voice drops to a lower register. "But not in the way you think."

"What are you talking about?"

"No psilocybin or psilocin."

"Then what?"

While she waits for an answer, she sees on her office phone one, then two, then three other lines blink red with incoming calls.

10

◎

Sometimes, when Jack and Nora were first married, his wife would lie in bed with the blankets cocooned thickly around her and refuse to speak or eat and she'd rise only to use the bathroom. These dark moments lasted for days and came once or twice a year, usually after the holidays, when the wind carried ice in it and daylight grew scarce. He tried to be there for her, bringing her water, rubbing her back, asking if there was anything he could do, but over time he grew impatient, resentful, and exhausted. She was exhausting. The same could be said for her everyday anxiety. He couldn't understand it except in the abstract. *Just snap out of it,* he wanted to say. *There's no reason to obsess or worry over this,* he wanted to say. *Who cares if I mixed up the ordering of the pint glasses and the juice glasses in the cabinet? Who cares if I bought the regular bananas instead of an organic bunch? Who cares if the lawn hasn't been mowed in two weeks?*

"I guess we're just too different," she once said.

"I didn't say anything."

"You don't have to say it for me to sense it."

"How am I supposed to even respond to that?"

"We're just too different, and you can't take it, and I told you that was a risk from the moment you proposed."

"Whoa, whoa. No. That's not what you ... when you said we were too different ... that has nothing to do with ... as if this shit between us has anything to do with race? No. Definitive no."

"We don't match. We don't fit."

"Stop that."

"Stop what?"

"Stop trying to pick a fight. Stop trying to push me away. Just stop." He always fumbled his words at times like these, when she looked at him like he had pink feathers instead of hair or paws instead of hands. "Sometimes I feel like I don't understand you sometimes. That's all."

"You shouldn't have married me. I shouldn't have married you."

"It would just be . . . so much easier if you didn't get so uptight about everything."

"That's who I am."

"Or at least you could stop—"

"Go on and say it."

"Getting so down. Being so sad sometimes. It would be so much easier. For both of us. Things aren't that bad. You don't have to be that way."

"It's not a goddamn choice, Jack."

Then Mia vanished and he finally understood. He suddenly had a vacancy inside his chest that couldn't be filled, not by booze or work or companionship. It was more than emptiness. It was as if emptiness had its own gravity. There was a black hole at the core of him that sucked everything in so that his muscles felt bruised and his bones in danger of cracking as his body slowly collapsed in on itself.

Five years ago, he felt so separate from his wife in their marriage—but now that they're officially apart, he feels like they might be the same after all. He's never seen a therapist, but he can diagnose himself just fine. He's clearly got what she always had: a big old dump truck spilling over with depression. At his cruelest, he wants to blame Nora for infecting him. At his most generous, he wishes he had shown her more compassion. In the time before, his emotional range had been limited to happy, sad, or angry, and now he realizes there's a whole range and depth of notes he never knew before. And the emotional and physical are very much entwined in a way he had never experienced. Symbiotic.

There hasn't been a minute of his life over the past five years when he hasn't felt a low-grade anxiety buzzing through him. He doesn't know how best to describe it; it's very much its own terrible thing. Maybe it's like standing below an electrical tower for months until your veins feel zapped and frayed. Maybe it's like standing on top of an ant pile and having them crawl up a hole in your foot and gnaw their way through your body, nesting in all your dark hollows. He can be sitting at a traffic light or reading the Sunday paper and feel sick and worried for no reason at all. He half-does a lot of things. He'll take his empty bowl of cereal to the sink but leave the glass rimmed with orange juice on the kitchenette table. He'll start an e-mail response on his phone but then get distracted by a weather alert. He puts on his jacket but doesn't step into his shoes.

And now? Now he has every reason to worry, so he feels barely functional. He stands in the lab for what might be ten minutes unable to settle on an action. He is at the threshold between believing and not believing what he sees. When he finally does back out and close the door, he opens it again immediately, just to make sure he didn't imagine it all.

On the one hand, he wants to cry out *Holy shit* and take a million samples and post photos online and call everybody in the department and tell them to get their asses over here on the double because he's discovered something new, something impossibly amazing, something that might, just might, save his fight for tenure after all.

But on the other hand — and here's where the anxiety kicks in — if he shares what he's found with others before he even knows what he's looking at, he'll lose any claim on it. They'll effectively steal it out from under him.

And on a darker note, the expansion rate and growth pattern are more than troubling — they're scary. Only twenty-four hours have passed since he was here last. Yes, the lab is climate-controlled, a kind of spacious petri dish meant to encourage fungal habitats, but what he's seeing is an unprecedented form of metastasis. He remembers something that happened to the department secretary a few months ago. One Monday, she sliced a deep paper cut into her finger at the copy machine. On Tuesday, she had fever and chills. On Wednesday, the cut darkened to black and blue. And by Thursday, when she finally went to the doctor, she learned sepsis had infected her joint and gotten into her bloodstream and she had to have her index finger surgically removed. Things that spread quickly scare him.

And here's where his thoughts swing hard in another direction entirely — this moment doesn't belong to him alone. Darla, his graduate student, brought the samples in. As part of his research team, yes, but she has some ownership as well. This will help her on the job market as much as it will help him secure his golden handcuffs as associate professor. And frankly, he needs her, because he remains clueless about so much, including the habitat she sampled.

He tries calling her, without success, so he logs on to the department directory and finds her address, only a mile from campus. He starts down the hall a few steps and then circles back. Out of his valise he pulls a legal tablet. He uses a Sharpie to scrawl a message: *Experiment Under Way. Do Not Enter! Thx. Dr. Abernathy.* He rips out the sheet and hangs it from the clip anchored to the door.

Rain spits from the sky. He pulls up his hood, steps into the gloom of the day, and hurries along at such a pace that he barely notices his phone buzzing in his pocket. He fumbles it out and discovers it's not Darla calling but . . . Nora?

He can't remember the last time they communicated. Over a year? She texted him a photo she had found of Mia tucked in a hollow log, poking her head out of its shadows and grinning one of her gap-toothed smiles. He didn't know how to respond. He resented her for sending it, but he was also grateful she'd sent it. Was it better to forget or hang on to what they shared? The first was easier, but the second was more important. He began and deleted a dozen different versions of *God, I miss her,* and he imagined Nora looking at the message and waiting for him to finish typing. In the end all he could manage was a heart emoji.

And now she's trying to contact him. It's not that he doesn't want to speak to her — just not right now. His mind is too loud and her voice will confuse it further. So he declines the call, but before he can even get the cell back in his pocket, it rings again. They used to play this game when they were married. She would keep calling until he relented. He answers with a "Hey. Can I call you back later?"

"Something important has come up," she says. "I need you to —"

"I don't have time," he says, nastier than he intended. *Need?* She *needs* him to do something? Of course that's the only reason she'd reach out to him. Because she needs something. Probably some book she'll claim is hers. The demanding tone she took always felt like a tightening leash that made him want to yank back in the opposite direction.

He ends the call and opens up Settings and punches the icon for Do Not Disturb before she can try him again. But he still hears a whispering — some trace of a voice ghosting the air — and he pauses and looks around to see if he is being followed.

Ten minutes later, he stands outside Darla's address, a two-story Arts and Crafts home split into two residences. Blinds whiten the windows. The roof is shingled with moss. A Subaru crowned with a roof rack and plastered with bumper stickers is parked in the gravel driveway. He climbs the porch and finds both mailboxes full. The street is empty, so he pulls an envelope out of one to see the name. A medical bill. *Dolores Jensen,* it reads.

Just then the door beside him creaks open and an old wrinkled face peers out "Stop right there!" an old woman says. In her fist she grips a black cylinder, probably pepper spray.

"I —" he says and raises his hands. "I'm not — it's not —"

"I said stop! Stop!" Her long hair is up in a silver topknot and she wears big round glasses and a faded floral muumuu. "I'll spritz you good! You stole my package yesterday! Does that make you feel good, robbing the elderly? Hmm?"

"What? No. I —"

"And you're back today for more! Oh, I'll pepper you black for that!"

"Please." His hands remain up and he releases the envelope, which flutters through the air between them and lands on her bristled welcome mat. "I'm here to see Darla Noble."

"Oh, so you stole her mail too!" She gestures threateningly with the pepper spray and he takes a step back.

"I work with her. I'm her professor."

"You don't look like a professor. Don't give me this *I'm a professor* business. No, sir, and no, thank you. You're not a professor."

"Some of my colleagues feel the same way."

Her mouth hikes up in confusion, revealing a yellow-gray ridgeline of teeth.

"She's sick," he says. "Darla. I'm coming to check on her. That's all."

"You're the sick one," she says and that's when he realizes he's coughing between his words.

"Listen, I'm sorry I looked at your mail. I was just double-checking who lived where so that I rang the right bell."

Her eyes narrow. "Hrrm."

He hurries a hand for Darla's buzzer and a distant ring sounds. Though he means to help the situation, to call her down to clear everything up with the neighbor, the sudden movement startles the old woman. "I said I'd squirt you, didn't I?" She steps fully onto the porch. "Well, here it comes!" She punches the trigger and a jet of liquid shoots out and splatters the porch railing.

"Oh, shit." He hurries backward so quickly he nearly falls down the steps. Already he can smell the skunky pungency of the spray, and he dives onto the lawn and sprints down the sidewalk as the woman cries after him, "You're no professor!"

He's too exhausted and jacked up on adrenaline to make good choices, but that doesn't stop him. He takes his time circling the block and then returns to the house and sneaks up the steps and hits the buzzer again. The air still has a funk to it from the pepper spray and he tries not to breathe, not wanting to set off his cough. It's then he notices that Darla's door isn't fully latched, and when he gives it a nudge, it swings open with a whine.

He pops inside and closes the door as softly as he can. He walks along the edge of the staircase, where the wood is the least warped, trying to keep it from creaking. The rain drums outside. Gray light seeps through a window on the landing. Shoes jumble the floor here. Flats and sandals and sneakers and the mud-caked set of hiking boots she was wearing when he saw her last. Some dizziness bothers him so he grabs the railing, worried for a second that he might faint. Whispers tease his ears and again he looks around for a hidden speaker.

Another door waits for him, this one locked. But through a leaded-glass window he can see into the apartment's living room. The furniture is the standard mismatched assortment you see in every academic's home: Ikea mixed with antiques captured from garage sales and thrift shops. Books fill shelves, and a bird-identification poster hangs on the wall. The couch is nested with blankets and the TV is on but muted. He gives the door a soft rap with his knuckles. Then knocks again, louder this time. Then he thumbs on the cellular service for his phone once more. When he calls her, he spots her own cell buzzing on the coffee table. The TV throws its changing light across the room and makes everything uncertain. He knocks again and then rattles the locked knob. "Darla?" he says. "It's me. It's Jack."

He hears a high-pitched whimper, what sounds to him like someone in pain. "Darla?" The lock holds when he twists hard, but there's no dead bolt and the door is old enough that it takes only a nudge of his shoulder to crack through.

"Darla?" he says. "Hey!" Shouting makes him cough so hard his ears buzz. "Anybody? Darla?"

He takes a few steps into the apartment and his shoes stick to the floor. There is something disrupting the grain of the hardwood.

A glistening tackiness. He crouches to examine it. He can see little slivers in it now, what appears to be hair. And it's everywhere. Not a specific trail, but a larger mess. What could be blood.

The whimper sounds again, this time rising to a yowl. He startles, because it seems to come from all around him. "Darla?" he says, and his eyes settle on the shadows below the couch. Something is moving.

Out of the darkness, it slithers more than crawls. All teeth and blood and muscle. Like something born too early. He doesn't understand it to be a cat at first. Not until it opens its mouth to hiss. Some of the hair has been roughly shorn from its body. And hatch marks redden its bare skin. One of its eyes is jellied in its socket. The cat flashes by him and raccs, with a yammering cry, for a secret space deeper in the apartment.

From here he can see the length of the layout. All the way through the dinette, kitchen, to another door that likely leads to a shared basement. A hallway branching off the kitchen must lead to the bathroom and bedroom. And it's here that he goes, his feet syrup-sticky, calling out to Darla and trying to muffle the chest-shaking coughs that bother him all the way.

The bedroom consists of a bed and a bureau. She's not as messy as he is, but close, with heaps of rain and snow gear lying about, a pair of cross-country skis stacked in one corner, a snowboard in the other. A backpack rests on its side like a black pupa. A beige bra dangles from a doorknob. The cat mewls and growls beneath the bed, as if it can't decide whether to give in to pain or rage.

"Darla?" he says again when he tries the bathroom, the door half-shut. He pushes it open and finds the sink and toilet splattered with the same mess she left behind in the lab's trash can.

A window is open and the rain sizzles outside. A breeze blows through, and the shower curtain breathes it in and out. He can't be sure if he hears someone whispering on the other side or if it's the sound of wet tires on the road. He creeps closer and reaches out a hand to tug aside the curtain, but before he can, the wind shifts and the fabric eases back and takes the shape of a face pressed against it.

The eyes appear as gray hollows and something wet soaks through where the mouth is.

"Oh, Christ," he says, and then the ghostly shape lunges forward. The curtain tears from its rings and billows around him and he stumbles back in a weighted tangle. His head thuds against the toilet and his mind blackens briefly in confusion. When he finds his focus again, he can see teeth gnashing through the fabric, chewing holes in it, trying to get at him.

He curses and pushes the body off him and scrambles back into the hallway, and the curtain sloughs partially off to reveal Darla. Her arms reach for him wildly, her fingers bent into claws. What looks like gray oatmeal mushes from her nose and mouth along with a garbled, barking noise that could be words or could be coughing.

He retreats until his back bashes the wall in the hallway and she follows him, slugging along, half draped in the curtain. He kicks at her hands and then at her face — once, twice — and she gives a shuddering gasp before slumping over.

He blinks a few times and reminds himself to breathe before dragging himself upright. He isn't sure what to do, check her pulse or call an ambulance or run away. The decision is made for him when he hears the thudding boom of a fist at the front door and a voice calling out, "Police! We're coming in!"

11

n the Olympic National Forest, the air appears thick with ghosts. A creamy fog drifts along and the evergreens knife through it. The old shaggy trees give way, in clear-cut patches, to the young noble and Douglas firs of the Hemlock Hills Tree Farm. It's here that dozens of men and women gather wearing hazmat suits. The moisture in the air carries sound strangely, making things seem both up and down, far away and nearby, so the shuffling of fabric could be the wingbeats of birds and the tromping of boots could be the drumbeat of an elk herd on the move.

The road is blocked, and they have established a perimeter. Guards are stationed along it in case any hunters or hikers or foragers should wander by. The scientists among them construct temporary greenhouse labs with air locks. They collect samples. They consult their tablets. They send up drones. They fire up generators, unspool cords, arrange stadium lights, and snap photos that light up the fog in quick bursts like a thunderhead.

The FAA reported the formation to them. A Delta pilot en route from Seoul to Seattle was readying for her descent when she spotted something bulging out of the clouds. She described it as an upright UFO. Instead of a saucer or cigar on its side, it was a vertical formation. It would have sounded crazy except for the shaky cell phone video that accompanied it. The clouds were thick and the shape phased in and out of view, seemingly stationary but never entirely visible. She estimated its height as somewhere between five hundred and a thousand feet. "It was already weird, but then it got weirder," she said. "When it came out of the clouds for the last time, I swear I was looking at a face."

The DOD met her and her copilot at the airport and confiscated her cell phone before she could share the video with anyone else, then escorted them to a room below the concourse where they were interviewed and frightened into signing NDAs. All flights were diverted away from the area, and a containment squad immediately set off for the Olympic Peninsula.

The owner of Hemlock Hills did not live on-site but visited twice weekly for trimming and pest control. "That's the nice thing about Christmas-tree farming as opposed to dairy farming. You can leave the trees be. Their teats don't get swollen." His name was Red, and he was seventy-two years old and favored camo and denim. He sported a gray beard stained yellow from all his smoking. It had finally started raining again in earnest about a week ago and he'd decided to tromp around the acreage and see how his trees were holding up. He found the ground bulging and cracked in places. From these points of inflammation grew fleshy white stalks, some of them as big as him. "No, I don't own a goddamn cell phone, and I never goddamn will," he said. And no, he hadn't taken a photo, but he had called in the problem to both the UW Extension and his insurance company, because this could obviously effect his bottom line. "I'm supposed to be retired, you understand? This was supposed to be easy money, tree farming. But between the damn drought and now this damn fungus, it's turning out to be a genuine pain in my asshole." He was offered a check then, one that was the equal of all future profits. He was happy to give up the land to them for what he called "Hawaii money."

Since the last time Red visited the land, those young stalks have grown swiftly and exponentially. They form a ring approximately a hundred yards in diameter, and though the team has yet to excavate and study what lies below, the radial height of each stalk appears to be six hundred feet or so. Their conical caps are porous and ridged, and though it's difficult to see from the ground, drone footage indeed reveals something resembling a face in each, like some version of the Easter Island monoliths.

The scientists speak of glucose, yeast nitrogen base, incubation, optimal growth, rhizopus spores, conidia commencement, germination, hyphae elongation rates, and possible growth curves for the filamentous fungi.

But there is only one person here who has an answer that reaches beyond the data. And he is also the only one present who doesn't wear a hazmat suit. Isaac Peaches.

He positions himself at the center of the formation, with Director Ricketts standing attentively beside him. He breathes in the chill loamy air, while she breathes through a hissing filter. "Ready?" she says. He nods, and she unclips a walkie-talkie from her belt and says, "Clear the circle."

The command is repeated dozens of times all around them as everyone marches away and escapes their range of view and he and Director Ricketts are left with only the Christmas trees and the swirling porridge of fog.

"Better?" she says. And he says, "Much."

He unlaces his shoes, peels off his socks, and tidily places them aside. Then he digs his pale pink feet into the black dirt of the forest floor and closes his eyes and takes a deep breath.

There is a sound that follows, like the sudden turning of many earthworms. His feet tickle as the soles open — and filaments tongue out of his flesh and burrow downward. With his eyes closed, other senses take over. A conversation with rock and dirt and plant, with ant and fungus. The understory of the forest. The information flows from root to root like nerve impulses travel from neuron to neuron in the brain. His intelligence becomes collective. Five minutes pass or maybe fifty. A moth lands in his hair. Spiders scuttle up his ankles and into his pants. When he opens his eyes again, they are threaded with red and green capillaries. He can see this reflected in the plastic of Director Ricketts's face shield. She is watching him.

Her carefully penciled eyebrows rise and her head inclines as she awaits his response. "Yes?"

"It's a door," he finally says. "A gray door."

She was never Annabelle to him, only Director Ricketts. She has kissed him only once. It happened the day Dr. Gunn locked him in the cell.

He had unscrewed the cap on the specimen jar and knocked it back into his mouth, nearly gagging on the marshy flavor. He could feel it surging in his throat like a live toad as he swallowed it down. He tried to avoid the vines that snaked across the floor, dashing from one side of the room to the other, but in the end there was nowhere to go. They tangled around his legs and then his torso and finally found his mouth, nose, and ears and probed their way inside him. He remembers suffocating on foul pollen. He remembers hearing grubs and worms twisting in the ground. He remembers his vision going kaleidoscopic with ultraviolet light. He sucked in carbon dioxide and gasped out oxygen. He tasted the sour rot of mildew on his tongue. He became an experiment in his own lab. He spoke to the dirt and the dirt spoke back.

He was certain his symbio prototype—a genome splicer—would negotiate the bridge between flora and fauna. And it did. But his sense of self gave way to a collective intelligence, the phenology. He was and wasn't Isaac anymore—he was something else, something bigger and extrasensory.

He would remain in his cell less than a day. The door was locked, and the facility was guarded heavily, but the rear wall was not reinforced or alarmed. And why would it be? It was one foot thick and some twenty feet belowground. He could hear the roots on the other side of it—the long, strong roots of a Douglas fir more than a hundred years old—and later that night he put his hand flat against the concrete and called them inside.

First one crack reached across the wall, then another, then another—making a crinkling noise, like a fistful of cellophane.

The fissures continued to multiply and widen until all at once they spilled forth a rush of dirt with fat roots snaking through them. Isaac held out his arms in welcome, and the roots wrapped around him and pulled him into the loamy passage they had dug.

His hand broke through the crust of topsoil, then his arm and head followed as he pulled himself up and crawled into the night air and let out a choking, incredulous laugh. But the laugh was cut short by a familiar voice saying, "I always knew you were special."

He started at the sight of Director Ricketts. She was alone. Her mouth was arranged in a smile and her hands were clasped at her breast. She rarely blinked, and the whites of her eyes gleamed in the moonlight. "Now we can be special together."

He stood upright, wavering for a moment, uncertain whether he should run to or away from her. There were no guards. She had no weapon. Her smile widened as she took a step forward and he tried uselessly to compose himself, brushing a palm through his hair, shaking some dirt clods off his torn clothes. He coughed out a spumy cloud. Fireflies rose from the grass and alighted upon him like jewels.

He held out a hand spangled with their green-yellow light, and she took it and squeezed it. "I know you're afraid," she said. "I do. But I can protect you. I can take care of you. As long as you promise to be loyal to me, I'll be loyal to you."

He looked over his shoulder at the beckoning dark. A wind hushed through the trees and shook their branches like welcoming hands. "I don't —" he said. He didn't what? He didn't want to? He didn't know?

She answered for him. She always did.

"You won't ever have to see Dr. Gunn again. After what he did to you, I gave him a talking-to. I scolded him raw. I told him to get the H-word out of here, and let me tell you, he ran off with his tail tucked."

Because he wanted Isaac locked up and experimented on. As a proto soldier. "But that's cruel and cold and positively stupid. Why would we punish someone who has given us so much? Why would we let one of our most valuable assets collect dust when he could be out on the front lines?"

"I—" Isaac said. "I want to be with you."

"You're so sweet," she said.

She leaned in then and paused for just a moment, inches from his face, to say, "Your eyes—they're green now." Then she kissed him. Her mouth was hard and hungry. He allowed her to do what she wanted. She ended the kiss by sucking his lip into her mouth and biting down on it. He made a little yelp of pain and pleasure, and she released him. He could see his blood on her teeth. It gave him some satisfaction to know that he was in her, and from now on, he would imagine them in this way: interspliced, bound together, mixed. Anyone who studied her cells beneath a microscope would find his face smiling back. A team. A couple. A they.

Now he pulls on his socks and nudges his feet into his shoes and says, "We'll need to gently excavate this area. Let's say a ten-meter perimeter from where we currently stand. No shovels. Trowels and whisks."

She says, "It goes without saying that all the soil should be bagged."

"It goes without saying."

"How deep?" she says.

"Not very. Less than three meters."

In the space of a few minutes, they establish a grid with stakes and string that looks equivalent to an archaeological dig. Layer by layer, the excavation continues through the topsoil and subsoil. The deeper they dig, the fuller the mycelium network, veins of gray and white that are woven together more and more thickly. What at first is as thin as a strand of yarn becomes as swollen as a thigh. They stop cutting through it and instead brush and blow away the soil, revealing the larger fungal web that grows out of a central axis they finally expose deep in the night. It looks less like a door and more like a sarcophagus.

Peaches and Director Ricketts stand at the lip of the pit looking down on what has been unearthed. "Besides you," she says, "this is our most exciting discovery."

"Yes," he says, feeling at once pride for her approval and a nibbling anxiety at the threat of what they have uncovered.

"Of course you know what I'm thinking?"

He says, "You're thinking, *What is the science? What is the data? What are the rules?*"

"Because once we know them, we know how to break them."

12

Nora's ear is hot and numb from pressing the phone to it, and her fingers are dirty with ink from scratching down notes.

There is a case in Tacoma. An employee of the Golden Dragon Chinese Restaurant biked to an apartment building to deliver a late-night order of wontons, chop suey, and Mongolian beef. He was buzzed in and climbed the stairs to the third floor, but before he could knock, his feet squelched and he looked down to see a pool of blood oozing from beneath the door. It opened a second later, and he was dragged inside.

There is a case in Shoreline. A woman was out for an early-morning walk with her golden retriever when the dog broke away from her. It didn't respond to her commands, bolting around the house of a neighbor. In the backyard, she found Boo Boo sniffing and mewling at the corpses of a family of four, all of them shaved and etched with markings.

There is a case on Bainbridge Island. A father called 911 and said he wasn't sure whether he needed an ambulance, the police, or a priest, but there was something wrong, desperately wrong, with his daughter. She's not herself, he said. She hasn't been herself. Before he could elaborate, he cried out in pain and the line went dead, and when the cops arrived, they found the driveway entirely covered with crosshatched markings made with sidewalk chalk, a cipher that was replicated in blood inside the home.

And more. How many, she isn't sure, because she's now calling different departments and asking for an account of all violent crimes reported over the past few days.

Some appear to have been murdered by familiars, others by strangers. Some are wealthy and others barely scraping by. They are men and women, young and old. White, Black, Asian, Hispanic. Some have criminal records, others don't. Some committed suicide. Some are unaccounted for. And some are in custody and exhibiting symptoms of what she can only describe as a collective psychosis. The pattern seems broken, but there is always a logic system. If only her brain didn't feel like a defective calculator that couldn't process the algorithm. She has requested blood tests on all, but labs won't move as fast as she needs them to.

If only her selfish, reckless idiot of an ex-husband would call her back, she could get some verification on her suspicions.

Instead she keeps hearing from the wrong person. Three e-mails and two voice mails from a reporter at the *Seattle Times*. Nothing has so far run in the paper, and she has to get out ahead of them. Because once this is out to the public, the case will no longer belong to her. A task force will be arranged. The FBI will get involved. There is nothing she hates more than losing control. But it's more than that.

She can't even get support from inside her own office. She told the sarge she might be onto something — she had a hunch — and if the hunch was right, it would result in a citywide quarantine. Here he cut her off and said, "Don't you tell me that shit. Don't you even start." Seattle had been a launchpad for COVID in the country, and even with all the warning signs out of China, the city was impossibly slow to respond, reluctant to admit the threat. "How do you think they'd handle me telling them you've got a hunch? And no clear data to back it?" he said. "Denial. That's how. So I hope you're wrong, Abernathy."

"I do too," she said. "But I'm not the only one with a hunch. The *Seattle Times*—"

"No, no, no. You keep away from the press, you understand? You don't say one fucking word to one fucking reporter or it's my head in the guillotine."

"Okay. For now."

"For now? For now, my ass."

Even with the phone off the hook, her desk is no longer a place she can get anything done. A police station isn't a place where you can hide and think. So she heads off for a walk to the Sound, where the open water offers at least the illusion of solitude.

The clouds are thick and the sidewalks are damp, but the constant rain of the past few days has paused for a moment. The sun is setting over the distant Olympics and below them ferries chug through the water, carrying people from the city to the many island communities that spot the inlet. A few people glance at her, suspicious of her mask, as if she is the one who is sick. They don't like to be reminded of the pandemic. She's a walking memory of darker times. But they — she wants to yell — *they* are the ones who could be infected and not even know it. She knows this is an affliction most police suffer from — constant paranoia, suspicion of danger around every corner — and it feels more real than ever right now.

A waft of fryer grease hits her and only then does she realize how hungry she is. It's the dinner hour, and as she walks by a diner, she looks through the windows at the brightly lit space where forks clatter, knives scrape, and people toast with beers and laugh their way through conversations. How can life continue so normally when so much fucked-up shit is going on just up the road? It was a thought she often had in the months after Mia went missing as well. Why wasn't everyone feeling what she felt? A man at a window table is cutting up a steak covered in mushrooms, and when he brings it to his mouth, he catches her eye and pauses his chewing.

She starts down the sidewalk again. Around the corner comes a dog, a mutt maybe eighty pounds, broad-backed with a boxy face, and brown fur dappled gray. There is something clearly wrong with it. Its gait is unsteady and its head glances off a telephone pole and then crashes full-on into a parked car. It wears a collar, but when she whistles, when she says, "Here, boy," she realizes she won't be able to check the tags because it goes still at the sound of her and wrinkles its muzzle and shows its teeth. They are red with blood and clotted with flesh. A growl rumbles the air, heavy enough that she can feel it. The light is fading, but she sees now that its eyes are rimmed and oozing with what appears to be fungal growth. Mushrooms sprout tumorously from its nose and ears.

The growling sharpens into a bark. She retreats one slow step at a time. The muscles in the dog's legs spasm, and she can't tell if it's trying to hold itself up or readying to lunge.

Then a car alarm sounds across the street — with a *honk, honk, honk* — and the dog swings toward it. Something oozes from its chops and dampens the concrete as it lets out a snarl. Then it bounds off the sidewalk into the screech of traffic.

She doesn't wait to see what happens next but hurries into a minimart on the corner. The clerk gives her a look, and if he even thinks about following her around the store — which happens too damn often — she might be in enough of a mood to flash her badge and scare him. In the candy aisle, she pulls out her cell and texts yet another message to Jack. *I don't know what this is,* she writes. *Please.* She isn't supposed to release crime scene photos, but fuck it and fuck him. This is the only way she'll get him to pay attention to her. She attaches several images of Ashley dead in her cell, including close-ups of the fungus spilling out of her eyes and nose and mouth. The same fungus she's pretty sure she just spotted on the dog.

She almost never says *please.* Or *sorry.* They're meaningless if you say them constantly, wasted words. She saves them for when they matter. They matter now. And she knows Jack understands that. *Please,* she writes again. *I need you.*

Not thirty seconds later, her phone rings. His voice is raspy but familiar on the other end of the line, saying, "I need you too."

Inside the entry to his condo, she finds a mess of unread mail and newspapers on the floor. "Jack?" she says. "I'm here." He told her over the phone to come on in. She can hear the shower running upstairs, so she takes the opportunity to snoop around. His television is balanced on a filing cabinet, and his couch has a broken leg, its corner propped up by several books. The kitchen is busy with beer cans, unwashed coffee mugs, and bowls of sludgy milk and cereal. A piece of paper catches her eye. On it he has scribbled a filamented design, the cipher she has grown familiar with. She folds it and tucks it into her pocket. "Jack?" she calls out.

The bedroom is worse than a college dormitory. A mattress on the floor. Bare walls. Piles of clothes and gear. Not for the first time, she wonders how she was ever married to a person like this. "Disgusting."

She knocks at the bathroom door. "Jack?"

She might hear a muttered response and puts her ear to the door to listen before calling out his name again. The hollow-core door is damp, as if the water has been running for hours, as if the tub has overrun and filled the bathroom to the ceiling. "Jack, are you okay?"

The door shudders as a blade spikes thorough it. The splintered gouge is only inches from her face.

She doesn't scream. She simply takes two steps back, withdraws her pistol from the shoulder harness, and kicks open the door. It slams into his body and sends him tumbling.

A cloud of steam oozes into the hallway. She finds him curled up on the floor, naked and shivering. His hand is bleeding. His eyes are far away. His chest hitches with a cough.

"What the hell is wrong with you?" she says, and all he can say is "I'm sorry. I'm sorry. I'm sorry."

And then the coughing takes over and something gray and gelatinous ejects from his mouth onto the floor.

"Oh, hell no," she says quietly. "Not you too, Jack. Not you too."

He tries to tell her something. Something about escaping from an apartment. He doesn't enunciate, the words coming out drizzly and murky when he says, "I ran. I opened the window and I jumped onto the roof and then hung from the gutter and dropped onto the lawn and I ran. And I came here. And it happened again. I woke up and I had a knife. And the whispers. The whispers told me—"

"You're not making any sense. Slow down or shut up."

"I'm not safe. I'm not safe."

He coughs again, every tendon and vein standing out from his skin. "I'm not safe," he whispers.

She studies him for a long time. "Well, I'm not afraid. So you're safe with me." Then she unclips the handcuffs at her belt and tosses them at him with a rattling clank. "Now put those on."

He picks them up incredulously. "Where," he says. "Where are we going?"

"I'm taking you home."

13

◎

This isn't the first time Jack has woken up confused. But instead of a whiskey headache pounding behind his eyes, he feels deeply rested. Instead of standing blearily in his driveway, he is lying in bed. Instead of midnight air chilling his naked skin, a band of sunlight warms his face and goldens his vision when he flutters open his eyes.

Outside the window a magnolia tree blooms and birds flutter among its white fist-size flowers. He knows that tree well, but he hasn't seen it in years. And the window is on the wrong side of the room. The walls aren't blank but filled with neatly arranged framed prints of Mondrian and Miró. His body is naked and the bed is stripped down to a plastic mattress pad. All of these details come to him in a disoriented rush, and he tries to sit up but can't, his wrists rattling with the handcuffs that link him to the bed frame.

His right arm hurts when he flexes it, and he sees then that a catheter burrows into the soft basin of his elbow and attaches to an IV drip on a pole. He wears a mask that makes his breath hot and suffocating and bites into his skin with its bands. His voice is muffled when he shouts out, "Hello? Hello! Help!" He swings his head around in a panic and then finds the anchoring detail he needs: the photo of Mia on the night table.

Over the huff of his breathing, he can hear footsteps approaching. Nora enters the room wearing a mask, goggles, and latex gloves. She pauses six feet away. "How do you feel?"

"I feel—I don't—how?" He rattles his handcuffs. "Very fucking confused is how I feel."

"What's the last thing you remember?"

His mind is muddied when he tries to bring up any sort of chronology. "I was on campus and . . ." There seem to be things in his head—an apartment, a billowing shower curtain, the police, a knife—that don't belong to him. "I was sick?"

"You were very sick."

"How long have I been here?"

"Two days," she says, but there's a part of him that wanted her to say five years. That the past five years have all been a fever dream.

"You had an infection. I've been treating you with an echinocandin. It's an—"

"Antifungal."

"Yes."

He says, almost to himself, "I was sick," because more memories are coming back and threading together. "I wasn't myself. But why didn't you—"

"Hospitals are death traps of secondary infection. They wouldn't have known how to treat you and you would have infected others. I believed I knew what to do, and I was right. After you moved out, I had the house sealed up and the ducts cleaned. I installed a top-of-the-line HVAC that is considered the Mercedes-Benz of air purification. No germs, pollutants, fungi, or mildews can survive inside. I am living in a clean lung. For the past forty-eight hours, I've cranked up the dehumidifier and kept you hydrated with an IV to keep moisture levels as low as possible. This—along with the echinocandin—appears to be effective."

His handcuffs rattle again when he tries to reach for the mask. His feels like he's breathing through an exhaust pipe. "Can you please take this mask off me?"

"I think so," she says but makes no move to do so. "That was for me more than you. To keep all aerosols contained." Her eyes roam the room. "I'm going to let this room sit for a few days before I do a deep clean. The pad is hypoallergenic and waterproof, but I still may toss the mattress and box spring. You might have noticed that I had the carpet removed and replaced with a hardwood laminate. So that's good. For cleaning away any contaminants, I mean."

"You changed a lot of things since I left."

"Yes."

"I'm amazed you let me in."

"Frankly, so am I."

"Why?"

"Why?" she says, as if the word has an unusual flavor.

"Why did you help me? Why did you let me sleep in your bed?"

She doesn't blink, but her eyes go someplace far away for a few seconds. "For a long time, Jack, I realized I had two choices when dealing with you. Be mean and chew away all the weakness so that only the strong stuff is left. Or be kind and hope that this brings out the good. For a long time I've employed the former strategy, but I decided to give the latter a try for a change."

"Thank you. I think."

She reaches into her pocket and removes a key and finally approaches him. "I also need your help." He can tell that she's wary; she's studying him carefully, as if he might kick at her. "Will you help me?"

"How come we never did this before, huh?" He manages a smile. "The handcuffs? Could have been fun."

She narrows her eyes, and because her mouth is hidden from view, he can't tell if she's smiling. Even though she was mostly humorless, never making jokes herself, he used to be able to startle a laugh out of her. She twists the key and he shakes off the cuffs, then rubs his wrists. "I still can't believe you let me sleep in your bed."

"It was the only place I could securely handcuff you. Besides the toilet."

His body is stiff when he swings his legs off the bed. "I know I'm probably pushing my luck on charity, but can you get me something to wear? And eat? I'm starving."

A minute later, he is pulling on a robe and taking in big gulps of clean cool air, then he follows her out of the room and down the hall. But he stumbles to a stop in front of the next bedroom even as she continues on to the top of the stairs. She turns to watch as he sets his hand on the knob — and then startles back as a needle of static electricity shocks him.

He doesn't ask for permission but looks her way. She gives a nod. He pushes open the door and a blast of sunlight hits him and makes him throw up an arm to shade his face.

He steps inside. The carpet is recently vacuumed, the shelves dusted, the bed tightly made. His attention focuses on Tigey. Mia's pink-and-white-striped stuffed animal is tucked into a Ziploc bag and propped up against the pillows. His hands reach for it and tremble before picking it up. The plastic ripples and bulges as he squeezes it. He hurriedly unseals the bag and pulls out the plush animal and brings it to his face and takes a deep sniff. All these years later, it still smells like her. Grassy. And sour-sweet, like milk poured over Cheerios.

He feels Nora's hand on his shoulder. He prefers to think it's a comforting gesture rather than a warning. But he tucks Tigey back in its bag and with two hands delicately arranges it on her pillow once more.

Downstairs, he eats four fried eggs splatted with hot sauce, two pieces of wheat toast smeared with butter and raspberry jam, a pile of veggie sausages, a banana, a cup of blueberries and yogurt; he drinks a short glass of orange juice and three mugs of coffee. He feels hollow. He can't ever remember being hungrier. "Man, these eggs. The yolks. They're so orange. They're so good. Is this that free-range shit or something?"

"Yes."

"Damn."

Nora continues to bring him food, and this, more than anything, makes him wonder whether this is just one more level of the dreamscape he has been lost to. "I never thought I'd be here."

"Here?" She takes a pan to the sink and scrapes some grit off it. "As in, your old kitchen?"

"Here more generally. The two of us, you know, just talking. Without some kind of wall between us, I mean."

"I guess there's something about you having had a psychotic break and waking up handcuffed and naked that makes this easier."

"Yeah. I guess so."

She dries her hands on a dishtowel and watches him as he speaks between smacking bites and slurps of coffee. "You know . . . when I was a kid . . . I had this recurring nightmare. I would wake up — but I was still dreaming; the waking up was part of the dream, understand? — and I would go downstairs for breakfast. But there were small things different about the house. Like a new rug. Or framed photos I had never seen before, like of me playing baseball when I had never played baseball. Or me standing in front of Old Faithful when I'd never been to Yellowstone. My parents were in the kitchen, puttering around like they always did, washing dishes and poking at something frying in the pan, but they were older. A little fatter and more stooped. A little grayer. I had lost time." He sops up the last of the yolk with his toast, pops it in his mouth, and shoves his plate away. "I can't help but feel like that's where I'm at."

"You're back now. You're good again."

"When I'm talking about lost time . . . I don't just mean the past few days."

"I know."

He leans forward and rubs his face in his hands and looks at her through the gate of his fingers. "I hurt you."

"You *tried* to hurt me. I'm the one who hurt you. You had a knife, I had a gun." She pulls a chair away from the table and sits down opposite him. "If you're looking to apologize, don't bother. You weren't yourself. I don't mean that in the normal way. I don't mean that you were blackout drunk or crazy-exhausted or any of that. I suspect you were literally not yourself."

"I want to hear more about that. I do. But to be clear, when I said I hurt you . . . I wasn't talking about two days ago. I wasn't talking about when I was . . . infected . . . or whatever we're calling it. I was talking about before."

A ripple passes over her face like wind over water. "Trauma is an infection too. Grief is an infection too."

"Yeah," he says. "Well . . . just know that I'm sorry."

There is a beat of silence. "Since you seem to be doing better, I think it's time that we get to work."

"Yeah. Yeah, sure." He picks up his coffee mug and sets it back down roughly. "I am doing better, I think. After eating, I'm feeling a little more with it now."

"That's good," she says and stiffens her posture. "Then let's stop with the Hallmark crap. You tell me what you know, and I'll tell you what I know."

"You show me yours, I'll show you mine?" he says, but her face registers no humor. She's in full detective mode now. Whatever warmth or vulnerability she displayed a moment ago, her shields are back in place.

He stands up from the table and paces back and forth. "Okay." He tells her about the samples his grad student collected, her illness, his sleepwalking, the mess he found when he returned to the lab, and the horror he discovered when he visited her apartment. The police had come. He had panicked and climbed out the back window, skidded off the roof, clung to the gutter, then dropped into the sodden backyard and ran. He says it out loud as if trying to convince himself, then nods. *Yes. That's what happened.* But everything after that was a gray haze. "I realize it all sounds nuts, and for all I know I've had a psychotic break. I honestly have no idea what to think right now. I don't know if you even believe me. But there it is —there it all is— I've unloaded on you."

A long minute passes and he can tell from her gaze that she is calculating.

"I believe you."

His words come out as a sigh of relief: "Thank you."

She pulls out her phone and calls up a photo of a prison cell, the floors and ceiling of which are dirtied with bloody ciphers. She sets it on the table and then removes a piece of paper from her pocket with something on it that he recognizes. He drew that. With a pen. The looping swirl of a design he dreamed about when he woke up in the driveway.

"This pattern. What am I looking at?" she says, prodding it with her finger. "What does it mean?"

"I think it's mycelium," he says, and she looks at him blankly. "It's the fungal network. It's their communication system, their infrastructure, their language. The instructions of the underworld."

14

Going green. That's what Peaches calls it when he lets the other part of himself take over. The symbiont.

A normal mind is like a mansion, one that's always under construction, with a new wing or garage being added. Some of the rooms you visit regularly; others, not so much. Every room has dressers and cabinets and end tables, and all of them have drawers or shelves. There are things filed away in them, like papers and books and photos that aren't referenced often and collect dust. You surprise yourself sometimes. You go down a hallway you forgot existed and visit a room threaded with cobwebs and remember the faint smells, textures, and faded voices that linger in the air.

And this is necessary. We need to compartmentalize. To categorize. To file. We have too many moments. We've eaten too many meals and had too many conversations. If we remembered it all — all the time and all at once — we'd go crazy.

Going green is a little like going crazy. Because the mind of the forest knows no limit. Imagine if every door of the mansion was blown open and every light flickered on and every drawer spilled its guts? And you could be in the master bath and the dining room and the garden at the same time?

He always has trouble cutting it off and coming back to the constraints and limitations of the present. It's a little like waking up from a heavy nap or deboarding an international flight or pulling off a mask and tank after scuba-diving for several hours. You still feel the previous world clinging to you even as you engage with the new one.

It used to be that going green felt like a dream, but more and more it feels like reality. The roots still tremble beneath his feet and the woods still whisper in his ears, as if calling to him, asking him to come back, *come back,* even as he blinks hard and nods along to whatever Director Ricketts is saying to him. Yes, they should continue to excavate the area. Yes, they should transport the gray door off-site. Yes, he will personally accompany it, just in case anything should happen along the way.

The web of connective tissue is severed—and Peaches feels something like knives shrieking together, a sharp pain from below —and then a hammock of ropes is arranged beneath the growth and it is hoisted out of its crater with a small crane. Its shape is roughly that of a cocoon or sarcophagus, its weight comparative to an upright piano at four hundred pounds.

They place it inside of a windowless trailer hauled by a Tahoe. A DOD agent will drive, with Director Ricketts and Peaches riding along. Two vehicles, one in front and one behind, both armed, will escort them. "Well, I don't know about you," Director Ricketts says as they slam shut their doors and the engine growls to life, "but I surely am excited to cut that thing open and see what's inside."

Isaac grew up in Boise, raised by a single mother. Agatha worked as a receptionist at a dental office, and though she loved him, the love sometimes felt like a hug that could suffocate. They lived in a small ranch home with plaster saints and gnomes in the garden and peach-colored carpeting covering every inch of floor—even the kitchen and bathroom—because she hated for her feet to be cold. Throughout the house hung photographs of him as an infant and a toddler wearing blue satin jumpers and red velvet suits she had sewn for him. He can't remember her ever taking a photograph of him after the age of four, and that's where he seemed frozen in her mind. She demanded, even when he was a teenager, that he sit on her lap in her living-room recliner or cuddle in her four-poster bed at night. She would stroke his hair and talk about her day, and often their conversations would bend toward the Bible. She wasn't strictly religious, but she did have a fondness for crosses and saints. There was one story in particular she loved to share about Saint Julian.

As the legend goes, Julian was hunting in the woods when he came upon a stag. He notched an arrow and took aim, but before he released the bowstring, the stag turned to study him. Julian saw wisdom in its eyes and lowered his weapon. The stag spoke to him, offering a sinister prophecy: he, Julian, would be responsible for his parents' death.

Because Julian loved his parents, when he reached adulthood, he tried to escape this fate by moving far away. But his parents were bereft and sought him out over many miles and many years, wondering why he had abandoned them. When they finally located him, they were old, weary, and terribly sick. They knocked on the door to his cottage, and Julian's wife answered. She hurried the elderly couple to bed and told them to rest while she ran off to fetch a healer. While she was gone, Julian came home and found two people asleep in his bed. He assumed his wife was sleeping with another man, and in a blind rage, he yanked his sword from its scabbard and stabbed them both to death, fulfilling the stag's prophecy.

Agatha told of a stone carving illustrating Julian's story that can be found hidden away on rue Galande in the Latin Quarter of Paris. It is said to be mortared onto a building about ten feet above the cobbled street, just around the corner from his namesake cathedral, Saint-Julien-le-Pauvre.

"Have you ever been there?" he asked his mother.

"I don't need Paris when I have Boise," she said and kissed him on the forehead. "I don't need the world, because you're my world."

"But what's the lesson of the story?"

"The deer is the devil. He never should have listened to the devil."

"How is the deer the devil?" he said.

"It has horns," she said. "Like a devil. He should have stayed with his parents. Then none of that trouble would ever have happened."

"But . . . wait . . . why is Julian a saint?"

"What's that, sweet pea?"

"If he killed his parents, why is he a saint?"

"Oh, don't go worrying about all the little details. I told you the part of the story that matters most."

He knew what she was trying to say, and the threat worked. He couldn't help but believe, through a combination of guilt, anxiety, threat, and superstition, that he was better off by her side. He couldn't help but see every temptation as a stag. When a brochure came in the mail for a two-week science camp, he discovered a deer in its pages. When he fantasized in the shower about a girl in his AP chemistry class, he saw her with horns branching out of her head. When an Ivy League college called to recruit him after he scored 1550 on the SAT, he could only imagine its campus existed in a sunlit forest surrounded by antler-locked gates.

He didn't attend the science camp. He didn't ask the girl out on a date. He didn't accept the scholarship to Dartmouth. He attended Boise State, which was just as good, his mother assured him, earning his bachelor's and then pursuing his master's in genetics. And in the end, she was the one who left him, when a bad case of flu led to pneumonia and shut down her lungs.

He buried her on a hillside cemetery in Boise. He visited her every Sunday and left a fresh arrangement of flowers. He received the job offer from Monsanto a few weeks before graduation and didn't even tell them he'd think about it. He just said yes. An enthusiastic yes. He had barely traveled out of his own city, and Washington State sounded like a great adventure. He left a plaster figure of Saint Julian on her grave when he said goodbye.

It is night when Isaac, Director Ricketts, and the agents depart the formation and drive slowly along the old rutted logging road, trying to keep their load steady. After about a quarter mile, a buck bounds out of the woods and hoofs to a stop before the blaze of their headlights. Its black eyes brighten in the reflection, and Isaac feels as if those eyes are burning into him.

Their driver brakes but then begins to ease forward, as if to nudge the deer out of the way. "Hold on," Peaches says in a whisper.

"I'm sorry, sir? What did you say?"

"I said hold on, please." The deer continues to stare. Its horns form a brambled crown. It lowers its head, maybe in deference or maybe to ready a charge.

"What are you waiting for?" Director Ricketts says.

"The stag," he says quietly, as if afraid he'll frighten it off.

"What?" She leans over the seat and toots the horn. "Let's go already!"

The deer flinches at the sound and scrambles for the side of the road; it leaps between two trees and vanishes with a swirl of fog. Isaac feels a pull, wishing he could follow. But he stays with Director Ricketts. Of course he does.

15

Nora stands by the window, watching the rain slap the glass and the trees toss in the yard. In the reflection, she can see Jack behind her in the kitchen as he fills the kettle and sets it on the stovetop, then cranks the burner. A ghost version of him — a ghost version of them — smeared through with raindrops.

A memory comes back to her. A storm from six — or was it seven? — years ago that sent gale-force winds howling through Seattle. She'd laid in bed that night, unable to sleep, listening to the house stretch in places it hadn't before, the wooden bones of it moaning and popping. She had never been an easy sleeper, and at the time, she couldn't help but imagine every creak was the footstep of an intruder.

There was a part of her that had known no one would break in on a night like that, and there was another part of her — the middle-of-the-night, rotten-with-paranoia part of her — that thought a storm might be the perfect cover. She knew plenty of people who wanted her dead. Courtroom screamers. Mostly the fathers and uncles and brothers of those she had put away. Her car had been keyed more than once, her mailbox ripped off its pole. Anonymous e-mails filled up her in-box, calling her every racial and sexist slur, threatening to hurt her in every way imaginable. Once she came home to find a dead black cat nailed to her front door.

Her getting hurt didn't scare her; Mia getting hurt did. That was the curious thing about having children. They soaked up all anxiety. Any way in which Nora might abuse or endanger herself

—not getting enough sleep or eating crap food or dodging into traffic or knocking on strangers' doors—became an obsessive point of concern for her daughter, as if all of Nora's raw nerves and flammable emotions had been puttied together into a little creature. Nora had been accused of being cold, removed, empathy-proof. Fine, fair enough, whatever. But her feelings for her child were another matter. A child was the ultimate exposure, giving Nora a feeling in her mind like the tenderness of the skin beneath a bent-back toenail.

On that long-ago night, she'd heard a thump downstairs. And then a creak. Jack snored softly beside her. Waking him would only create more noise, so she slid open the drawer of her night table and reached inside and found the grip of her Ruger. She padded across the floor and paused at the doorway, listening between the big gusting breaths of wind and the peppering assault of rain.

She crept forward farther. From the landing she could see a light below, seeping out of the kitchen. She moved slowly down the stairs, her back to the wall, peering over the railing until she saw the tiny figure standing in front of the open fridge. "Mia!" she said and her daughter spun around. She wore her pajamas and her hair was smooshed on one side from her pillow. "What are you doing up?"

"I couldn't sleep, just like you," the girl said before returning her attention to the fridge and pulling down a bag of bread.

Mia had a weird wisdom about her. She always seemed to know what her parents needed before they did, bringing them ice packs or chocolate or coffee. Rubbing their temples with her tiny fingers. Asking them if they wanted to watch some television to relax. In this case she had three plates on the counter and she was knifing peanut butter and raspberry jam onto bread slices. "I knowed you guys would come."

"You guys?" Nora said.

"What did you make me?" Jack said, entering the kitchen behind her. His voice was husky with sleep. "And why do you have a gun?"

Nora looked at the pistol and sighed, setting it on the counter. But it looked foolish there, so she tucked it hurriedly in the junk drawer before rubbing her eyes and saying, "We should all be in bed."

A fresh, angry wind blasted the house and Jack said, "There's no point trying to sleep with all that racket."

Then they gathered together and ate the sandwiches Mia had made them.

"These are perfect," Jack said through a full mouth.

"You know what would make them even better than perfect?" Mia said.

"What?" Nora said.

"Hot cocoa," Jack said.

"That's it," their daughter said. "That's exactly what I was think-ing."

But that was years ago. Now it's day, not night. It's two of them, not three. And it's coffee, not hot cocoa, that Nora and Jack have in their mugs as they file out of the kitchen.

They go into the living room, which looks more like a war room. Nora has collected all the information from the local precincts — the photographs, transcripts, and reports of the past week — and printed them from her home office. She and Jack then laid every-thing out in a grid on the floor, some of the pages still warm from the printer and smelling of toner. Small pathways allow the two of them to navigate the timeline.

At the center of the grid she has a map of Sea-Tac metro, and with a red marker she has neatly noted all relevant locations. When she takes a step from one section of the grid to another, she travels the equivalent of many miles. When she crouches down, she drops a thousand feet into a photograph of someone's backyard. She has a telescopic and microscopic view simultaneously.

Most people think of time as a straight line — you wake up, you go to sleep; you're born, you die — but she knows that time moves in many directions at once. This is why her wristwatch and bedside clock are analog, not digital. Digital clocks are a lie that show you stationary in a moment, fixed in time, but analog clocks never stop moving; they're a constant swirl, all the numbers visible at once. Her mind is a constant swirl of yesterday and today and tomorrow — and so is the floor before her, a confused calendar of violence.

She's been on sick leave for two days. She needed to look after Jack and quarantine herself until she was certain she wasn't infected. Sarge was as pissed at her as he was worried. Several more bodies had piled up, and the *Seattle Times* ran a piece that morning on the rash of deaths that hinted at the Blind Prophet's return. The press secretary at SPD had called the reports unsubstantiated, but the social media feeds had already lit up with speculation. All this time she's kept busy, monitoring her in-box and the news while adding to her diagram, but now she's ready to move. Instead of collecting damage, she needs to prevent it.

She reaches out to Chives, but his wife answers his cell. He's fallen ill. He's not acting like himself, his wife says; he's been closed up in the dark of his room all day, breathing raggedly, refusing to answer her questions, lashing out at her when she brings him soup. Nora instructs her to call Chives's doctor and demand echinocandin treatment for him. "Not later," she says, "now. And take some of it yourself as a preventive."

Jack will be her partner instead. It's a word that feels right, given their history. No longer spouses, but no longer separate either. Partners.

There have been twelve deaths so far. Twelve that they know of, at least. They can't trust the data to be definitive. How many bodies are waiting to be discovered? How many infections are waiting to bloom? The first twelve could be 80 percent or 30 percent or 1 percent of what's actually happening.

Jack says, "So you've got cases from the past mixed up with cases from the present."

"Maybe."

"You seem to think there's some sort of connection to Seattle's favorite serial killer, Albus Crotter."

"Maybe."

"Well, why don't you just go interview him?"

"Because a year ago he jumped off a cell tower, and ever since then, he's been staring at nothing and being fed through a tube."

"Oh. Right."

She hopes he'll be quiet now, because every time he talks, her thoughts break up and swirl away. Part of her wishes he had taken a little longer to heal, if only for the peace and quiet.

"Hey," Jack says with the beginning of a smile. "Do you remember how Mia was always scared of the dark?"

"Hmm," she says, trying not to listen.

"We'd shut off the lights at night, and they'd always be back on by morning. I tried night-lights. I tried glow-in-the-dark stars. I tried bribing her with candy and taking away screen time and everything else. None of it worked."

"Hmm."

"I was just thinking about something she said. About the dark."

Nora is often accused of being rude — but people are wrong. She's just focused on what matters, so she doesn't have time to accommodate everyone's feelings. Most people exist in a state of fluttery inattention, chopping up vegetables for dinner while watching the news while helping their kids figure out an algebra problem while answering texts while worrying about the bills. She prefers to do one thing at a time. And she gives that *one thing* everything she has. That's why she dislikes music except as a pure listening experience. How can she drive a car, focusing on the traffic weaving through the lanes all around her, while listening to the radio? She can't possibly take in the speed limit, road signs, turn signals, flashing lights, and congestion *and* analyze the lyrics, appreciate the harmony and melody, isolate each instrument, imagine it as sheet music, and compare the song's construction to a rare B-side from the late seventies.

If she hung up on you midconversation or failed to make eye contact or say thank you, that's because something more important is occupying her mind. If she were a superhero, her power would be the ability to concentrate, to go to a place of singular focus most people didn't understand.

Jack has always made this impossible. When they were married, he would drive her nuts: singing or whistling while doing dishes, reading aloud sections of novels or newspaper articles he found interesting, watching television while grading papers. He was a perpetual multitasker, always doing more than one thing at once, often poorly.

Now he's back at it again. "Did you hear me? Nora? Earth to Nora?"

She realizes two things simultaneously. She wants to hear more about Mia. And she won't be able to concentrate until he shuts up. So she gives him her full attention. "I heard you. What did she say about the dark?"

"There was a thunderstorm one night. She called out for us, and I ended up lying in bed with her for an hour." On his way to the couch he messes up a stack of paper that she immediately neatens. He plops down, sips his coffee, and creases his face at its bitterness. "I tried to calm her down by boring her. Making things less scary with science. I talked about how to calculate the distance of a lightning strike by counting from the sight of the flash" — here he raises a finger and wrinkles his forehead as if listening — "to the sound of the thunder. That got us into a discussion about the speed of light. She said she had a question about this. People were always talking about the speed of light, but what about the *speed of dark?*

"I laughed, but she was completely serious. And when I explained that the speed of light and the speed of dark were one and the same, she said no. That wasn't true. She saw proof of this every evening when I said good night and flipped the switch. 'Dark is faster,' she said. 'Dark is worser.'"

He's still smiling, but it's a sad smile now.

"Why are you telling me this?" she says.

He makes a sweeping gesture with his arm indicating the whole mess of casework on the floor and says, "I'm starting to think she was right."

In Capitol Hill, the police were alerted to a missing manhole cover. When they investigated, shining their Maglites down into the shadows, they discovered a woman curled up in a ball and whispering to herself. Her body was covered in blood not her own. An award-winning architect who had never had so much as a speeding ticket, she was suspected of murdering two of her neighbors and the doorman of her luxury condo. Each body had an eye gouged out, and one was shaved and etched with ciphers. When the officers descended the ladder and tried to coax her up, she attacked them and scrambled off into the dark. She remains at large.

In Bellevue, a family reported a break-in, and the responding officers located a man in their basement, dead, with mushrooms budding from his mouth. His hand was gripped around a box cutter clotted with the blood and fur of the family dog, Waffles, whose carcass was later discovered in the backyard.

In Renton, in an apartment building, water poured through the ceiling of a first-floor unit. When the landlord knocked at the door of 2F, he received no answer, so he entered with his key, thinking he was dealing with a busted pipe. In the bathroom he found the shower hissing, the tub overflowing, the room full of steam, and a naked old man who spoke in an unrecognizable language. The landlord said, "Maybe it was Russian or Mexican or something, but it didn't sound like it to me. It sounded like somebody trying to talk through a mouth full of mud." He had disassembled his shaving razor and was in the process of carving out his left eye when the landlord wrestled him down and called for help.

And then there was the case of Darla Noble, the graduate student at the University of Washington. After a complaint from a neighbor about a possible home invasion, the police explored her Wedgwood address. They found her on the floor of the hallway and described her state as initially catatonic, but when the ambulance arrived, as the EMTs were checking her vitals, she lurched suddenly to life. The report described the attack as animalistic. She bit and clawed and howled in a way that the officer believed meant she was suffering from some kind of psychotic episode or severe mental illness. She was cuffed and sedated and remains in critical condition at Virginia

Mason Hospital, being treated for what has been described as a systemic infection. Blood tests are pending.

This individual wouldn't even have been on their radar except that Nora requested her information specifically. There was nothing in the report about Jack or any male suspect. The initial suspicion of a home invasion was considered a misguided but ultimately helpful call; the senile occupant of the first-level unit was rightfully worried about her upstairs neighbor.

There were more cases, all unique but with an approximation of the same elements. Like people making up their own words to a half-remembered song. The filamented spirals. The blinding. The self-harm or harm to others. The inexplicable motive. The sudden violence with little or no history of criminal behavior.

"And a lot of them were found in dark places," Jack says. "Dank places."

"Go on," Nora tells him. "Do your fungus thing. That's what you're here for."

"You never wanted to hear me talk about fungus before. Now it's suddenly the most fascinating thing in the world. How times have changed."

"Don't be a smart-ass, Jack. Just hurry up and professor me already. As you're processing all of this, what are you thinking?"

"All right," Jack says, clapping his hands and popping up from the couch again to pace the living room. He tells her about some species of aspergillus, a mold, that can grow in the lungs and spread to other organs and make you wheeze and cough up swampy mucus and eventually drown you in a gargle.

He tells her about the drug-resistant yeast *Candida auris* that has been working its way through hospitals around the world, covering every inch of floor and ceiling tile, every mattress and gown seam, every monitor and tray and door and curtain, creeping into the wounds and airways of patients as they recover, feeding on them.

He tells her about *Ophiocordyceps unilateralis,* the rain-forest fungus that infects the bodies of ants and saps them of nutrients and pirates their minds. The ant becomes fully possessed over the course of a week, and during that time, it seeks out an ideal temperature and humidity for incubation — what turns out to be a height of twenty-five centimeters. Here it latches onto a leaf near its colony. A stalk of fungus then splits the ant's head and the spores spill down onto the other ants, infecting them.

Not only are there approximately 3.8 million different types of fungi in the world, but fungus finds a way to kill around 1.5 million people every year.

"But have you ever heard of a fungus that causes behavior like this?" she says, and he says, "No. That's why I need a sample to study."

"I can't believe we're talking about murder as a contagion," Nora says, and their eyes meet and settle into a stare. "We're saying that, aren't we? That murder is catching."

"Is it murder, though?"

She feels that old flash of annoyance at his question. It could be such a classic Jack throwaway comment, since he's so often like the jackass kid in ninth grade who's always trying to rile the teacher: *Can you actually cry underwater? Why does a round pizza come in a square box? Is soy milk just milk introducing itself in Spanish?* But his tone appears genuine, so she tries not to make her voice too biting when she says, "What else would you call this?"

"You're a cold person. Just think about it in coldly scientific terms."

"Oh, I'm a cold person?"

"Yes. That's not a judgment."

"How is that not a judgment?"

"Because a fact is not a judgment. Has a commercial ever made you cry? Do you ever ask if you can pet other people's cats or hold their babies?"

"Cats are creepy."

"Do you find Christmas annoying? Do you call friends to check up on them?"

"Who just saved your ass?"

"I'm grateful!" He holds up his hands as if she's aiming a gun at him. "I'm not saying you're not a *good* person. I just mean — let me rephrase what I mean. Forget the emotions behind all of this. Forget the so-called rightness and wrongness. Because morality is irrelevant to the natural world. Mistletoe siphoning nutrients off a balsam tree isn't wrong. A lion chasing down a gazelle isn't wrong. So neither is a fungus killing someone. It just is what it is. And if something has to die for something else to grow, then so be it. That's the law of the jungle."

"Maybe you're the one who's cold."

"Hey, I cry during commercials all the time. I will pet the shit out of somebody else's cat. And I fucking love Christmas."

"Well, you're still wrong," she says.

"Oh, am I? Please explain to me how I'm wrong."

"This thing isn't killing out of need."

"What if we just don't understand the need?"

"It's evil."

"You're anthropomorphizing. An avalanche isn't evil. A tsunami isn't evil. A killer fungus isn't evil."

"It is. There's cruelty at work here. There's perverse delight. This is sadistic behavior."

"Well, maybe that's the human side of the equation. Maybe it's triggering the id somehow. Darker impulses."

"How is everyone having the same impulse? The fungus is the common denominator, not the people."

He shakes his head and puts his hands over his face. "I don't know! I'm just throwing shit at the wall and seeing if it sticks."

"On every case, there's always a motive. Always. You just have to trace it back far enough. That's what we need to figure out now. Figure out the motive for this thing. Figure out the source that's making what happens *happen*."

He stares at the ceiling when he says, "Maybe we should be focusing on transmission instead? All these people here. All these victims and these perps. We need to figure out who they've been in contact with. Family, friends, cops, doctors, whoever. Contact tracing. We ask them to get tested. We suggest antifungals as a possible treatment and—"

"No."

"No? Why no? Are you arguing just for the sake of arguing? That is a perfectly reasonable—"

"If you look at the arc of a new virus, if you look at what happened with SARS or COVID, infection is unstoppable. We've got to think of this as the equivalent. We've got to think of this as a new kind of infection. One no one has resistance to. You said it yourself—fungus grows crazy-fast. We couldn't stop COVID. We could slow it down, but look how long that took. It was months before people even believed it was a threat."

"You've got to call the hospitals. You've got to call the newspapers. You've got to, at the very least, tell them about the antifungal thing you used on me."

"Fine. You do that."

"Me?"

"You're the fungus guy. You've got credibility."

"I have very little academic credibility, if you ask my department chair. But I'll do it. Sure. Okay. It's just one more extension assignment."

"But I'm telling you, Jack. Nobody—no politician or doctor or cop—will believe us. Not unless we have some core evidence, and even then they'll ignore it until it's too late. And it's already too late."

"What are you suggesting?"

She navigates the grid and steps onto the file of Darla Noble. "Take me to your lab."

On their way out the door, she hands him a mask. Without complaint, he fits the bands over his ears and snugs the filter into place over his nose and mouth. "I look like a bad guy," he says and makes his finger into a pistol. "Stick 'em up."

She pulls aside her jacket to show him her shoulder holster. "You first."

She drives. In the history of their relationship, he has driven only a handful of times. She likes the control, and he prefers to daydream, sightsee, or read. On the few occasions he did take the wheel, she yelled at him in an unrelenting stream of back-seat driving, so they stuck with what worked. When he leans back his seat and flops one foot up on the dash, she gives it a long stare but doesn't say anything. He has his cell phone powered up and he's tapping out an e-mail message to Virginia Mason Hospital.

"You know what this reminds me of?" Jack says.

There he goes, multitasking again. Typing and talking. She doesn't respond, despite the long silence, because she knows he'll tell her anyway. "You ever hum a song and you have no idea what its lyrics are or even what it's called?"

She doesn't hum or whistle or even sing. But she always remembers the lyrics.

"This is like that," he says. "The music's inside you even when you think you've lost it. You know what I mean?"

She knows. He's talking about them. Their relationship — maybe even their love — is still resting inside them. They know how to talk to each other and move around each other. They haven't forgotten what it means to be in the same room.

"We weren't terrible together," he says.

She laughs. She can't remember the last time she laughed, and it startles her enough that she claps a hand over her mouth.

"Okay," he says and continues to type. "I guess I'm wrong again."

It's cloudy but not raining, so the campus green is packed with students. They toss Frisbees, play guitar, kick Hacky Sacks, lounge on blankets. Many of them appear to be in denial about the weather. Fifty degrees with a chill wind, and only half the young men wear shirts. All Nora can think about is exposure. The way the students are all piled on top of each other, rubbing shoulders, sharing drinks, trading phones. When one young woman throws back her head and belts out the lyrics to a song playing on her phone, Nora can't help but imagine a geyser of aerosols expelled from her mouth, spreading at least ten feet and breathed in by at least seven others.

Could one of the students be infected? Could it already be spreading among them?

A lot of eyes are on Nora and Jack. At first she thinks it's because they're old, but then she realizes it's because they're both wearing masks. People hate to be reminded of the pandemic that stole more than a year of everyone's life. The big duffel bag Jack carries probably doesn't help. The two of them look like a warning. They look like they're heading into a shoot-out or robbery. And in a way, they are.

An older woman with dyed orange hair, a floral sweatshirt, and polyester pants walks toward them and Jack calls out, "Hi, Wendy."

The woman pauses, narrowing her eyes, not recognizing Jack with his mask on, so he pulls it briefly aside. "It's me."

"Oh, it's you, Professor Abernathy. I'm glad it's you."

"Jack. It's just Jack."

They pause on the same square of sidewalk and she says, "I'm glad it's you, because he's looking for you."

"Who?"

"Professor Gordon. He's been looking everywhere for you."

"Oh God. What does the Tapir want now?"

"The who?"

"Never mind. Why does he want to talk to me? Is it about my class? The one he reviewed?"

Nora dredges up an old memory and places Wendy as the department secretary, introduced over the cookie tray at some long-ago holiday gathering. She might have been wearing a similar sweatshirt then, decorated with snowflakes instead of flowers.

"I believe it's about the classes you *haven't* taught," Wendy says. "Over the past several days. Several students have stopped by the office to complain. Professor Gordon said he's left you several e-mails and voice mails."

"Oh, right. Yeah. I'm so sorry about that. I've been sick."

"Well, it's no good to be sick." She takes a step back. "That's why you're wearing the mask?"

"Yes. That's why I'm wearing the mask." He sets down the duffel bag to rest his arm, and it makes a clanking noise; Wendy looks at it curiously.

"But you see—everyone's quite upset," she says. "And then the janitorial staff put in a complaint about the state of your lab."

"That's actually where I'm headed right now."

"Good. That's good. You're going to clean it up, then?"

"No."

"No?"

"Tell everyone I'm on the verge of a big breakthrough."

"Oh?" Wendy's cheeks bunch up in a confused smile.

"Huge!" Jack says and throws out his arms. "World-changing!"

"Oh, that's good to hear. I've always liked you. I'm rooting for you, Professor Abernathy."

"Just Jack is fine."

She gives them both a little wave. Jack scoops up the duffel bag and they continue on. "Department secretary," he says.

"I gathered."

His head swings toward her a few times. "Why do you look so ir-ritated? Because I didn't introduce you?"

"You're working on something world-changing, are you? A big breakthrough?"

"Oh, that was just misdirection."

"Didn't sound like it to me."

"Well . . . so what if I see the opportunity in a moment like this? Isn't that what happened in Minnesota? All that metal fell from the sky and you know what? People got rich. I could at least get tenure."

"So you're actually thinking about your career right now?"

"Wouldn't I be stupid not to?"

She doesn't respond except to increase her pace.

He catches up with her. "Tell me you aren't thinking about your name in the newspaper if you crack this."

"No."

"Come on."

"All I'm thinking about is stopping it. Period."

They cut between two buildings, and a huge glass-walled facility looms up ahead. Jack turns onto a sidewalk that arrows them toward it. "We kind of do the same job, if you think about it."

"Not really."

"Being a scientist is like being a detective. We study the data and figure out the reasoning behind it."

"Except that you get summers off and grade lab reports while watching Netflix and complain about having to stand in front of bored teenagers."

"Ouch." He walks with his head down, silent for a good minute, maybe lost in thought but probably sulking and feeling sorry for himself.

When he talks about greedily collecting data, when he reveals that he's thinking about this as a possible step toward tenure and promotion, she is reminded of why she couldn't be married to him for a single second more. She might be cold or cruel, but he's always been selfish, and that's a worse crime.

She doesn't care about promotions or raises. She never sucks up to her superiors or pays any attention to getting press. She does what she does because the universe is a cold, indifferent place that doesn't give two fucks whether anyone lives or dies — but she does. They never got an answer to what happened to their daughter. She was just snatched up. Just like that. No answers. No justice. Nora's been trying to rectify that imbalance ever since, one case at a time.

He seems to sense her thoughts. "You've always been so impossibly rigid in your thinking."

"Oh? Do tell."

"You're right. Everyone else is wrong."

"They're only wrong if they disagree with me."

"Did it ever occur to you that somebody can do two things at once?" He switches the duffel bag to his other hand. "I can drive and listen to music. I can cut the carrots and carry on a conversation. I can help you investigate these murders and conduct scientific research."

"Research that helps you."

"You're so anal. About everything. The way you make a bed. The way you load a dishwasher. You even organized sex."

"It's good to keep a schedule."

"Ten p.m.? On Wednesdays?"

They are walking up the stairs to the building now, stomping their feet with every step. "It gives you something to look forward to."

"It's not sexy. It's not passionate. It's not romantic."

"I'm sorry if I don't like to have sex every time there's a thunderstorm."

He holds open the door, waves her through with irritation. "Thunderstorm sex is the best!"

A few students glance at them.

She marches down the nearest hall and he says, "You're going the wrong way." He points in the opposite direction. "It's this way."

"Then lead."

"You're not giving me the chance to."

They don't talk for a minute, but their feet batter the floor. He trades the duffel from one hand to the other and then back again, starting to breathe heavy from the strain. They pass door after door after door, all of them the same except for their numbers and placards. They turn a corner, and then another, and she loses all sense of direction. The building seems endless. Finally, he stops. He drops the duffel to the floor, catches his breath, and sets his hands on his hips. Clearly he's been formulating some sort of response. "You know that saying?"

"What saying?"

"About mirrors?"

"What saying about mirrors? Stop being so weird. Why are you always talking like somebody can see inside your head?"

"It was from a philosophy class I took in college. Something about how when you're looking in the mirror, you're looking at a younger man. Because of the time lag of the reflection itself, no matter how minute. You're looking at a younger man. You're looking at the past when you're looking at yourself."

"What does this have to do with anything?"

"I keep looking at us." His hand flaps back and forth in the air between them. "And seeing us in the mirror. And the mirror is cracked."

"I still don't understand."

"I'm going to try to stop looking at us that way. I think you should too. I think we'll get along a lot better. Let's just pretend there's no past."

"Pretend there's no past?"

"Yeah. That's what I said."

"Well, that's not what I meant. I'm not going to pretend we never had a daughter. I'm not going to pretend there's no such thing as Mia."

He can't help but flinch. "No. No, I don't mean that. Of course I don't mean that. I just mean . . . all the shit, all the baggage. Let's forget that for the moment and just focus on the future."

"Okay."

His eyebrows pop up. "Okay? You're okay with that?"

"I am completely okay with that. Let's concentrate on figuring out what to do with this time. Not the last time."

"Right. Yeah. That's a better way of putting it." He seems to have been ready for more of an argument, but she's tired and just wants to move forward. "Well. Good." He crouches down and unzips the duffel bag. "Since that's settled, I guess we better suit up."

Their goal is to retrieve the sample containers Darla brought in the other day. She would have labeled them with the date and location. Jack refers to this as a parent site — a primary source for germination — as opposed to the secondary carriers they've encountered at some of the crime scenes.

From the hall they can see black tendrils, like damp hair, reaching out from the edges of the door. "This is going to be bad," Jack says. The door is the weakest seal in the room. The vents, thankfully, are filtered for strict climate control and to prevent any cross-contamination between the labs.

It's late enough in the day that they haven't seen any students or faculty, but just to be sure, they raid a nearby janitor's closet and set up a cart on either end of the hallway with notes that read CLOSED FOR CLEANING. Then they shut off the lights so the only illumination is the Exit sign's red glow.

On the way to campus they swung by the police station and Nora swiped two hazmat suits out of the back of a forensics van. Now they step inside the floppy fabric and zip each other up. She loves the security of the final zipper tug, the knowledge of her vacuum. It's the same feeling she gets every time she puts on the mask, only bigger.

They also have a spray bottle of bleach, a few kitchen knives, and several Tupperware containers that will double as specimen jars.

"Ready?" Jack says, his voice hollowed by his suit, and she gives him a nod.

He pulls out his key card but doesn't bother bringing it to the sensor. The door is already unlatched. "Oh, shit," he says.

"What?"

"I locked this door. I left a note that specifically said no one should come inside. And now . . ." He gives the door a push, and it doesn't swing open so much as squelch forward. "No lock, no note."

What she sees inside is overgrown completely, no longer even faintly recognizable as a lab. They might be stepping into a damp cave or the stomach of a whale.

"Hurry," he says, waving her in. "We want to limit its exposure to the hall."

He tries the light switch, without luck. So they both click on the headlamps stationed in the visors of their hoods. She steps into the room and the floor feels slippery and loamy beneath her booties' cloth tread. It is hard to know where to look, so she focuses first on the air — thick with spores highlighted by the beam of her headlamp. She waves a hand and watches the spores swirl in its wake.

She's reminded of a long-ago investigation into the death of a beekeeper. His hives had been overturned and his body lay among them, so she had to wear a beekeeper's suit when visiting the scene.

The sense of protection it gave her was a delight as the honeybees buzzed and crawled across her body, their stingers so close. She feels something similar now with the spores snowing the air around her.

"Look at these formations," he says, crouching down to study what looks like an oversize gray cauliflower, one of many knuckling the floor, counters, and walls. When he takes a kitchen knife and pokes at it, a mucusy strand clings to the blade. Then the fruit of the fungus begins to pulse, almost as if it had a heartbeat. He leans in and Nora says, "I wouldn't do that." Before he can respond, it ruptures and spits a black cloud of spores into his face.

He falls back on his rear and wipes a hand across his mask. A sooty blackness has coated the plastic and it smears beneath his gloved fingers. "I don't know whether to say cool or gross," he says.

"Let's hurry."

"The jars were on the island counter," he says, but this isn't going to be as simple as snatching them and hurrying off. The fungus has grown thickly over every surface. There are fruiting bulges and hyphae strands. There are gray fibrous striations that look like muscle tissue or the twisted grain of an old tree. Finding anything in this room will require slicing and digging. An autopsy.

"I'll keep looking," he says. "You start filling up containers."

The gloves are clumsy and she has some trouble fingering off the lids of the jars and scooping gloppy samples into them. She tries to be as methodical as possible, taking different excisions from different formations in different parts of the room. There is a mass she pauses over, like a small hill on the floor. Its texture is that of many sticky spiderwebs woven together. She takes the knife and thrusts it into the fungus. She tries to saw it back and forth, but the blade resists. She pauses then, noticing a sudden redness along the metal. She pulls the knife out, and what is unmistakably blood begins to seep from the gash.

"Jack," she says.

His back is to her as he digs busily at the formation on the counter. "Hold on."

She now recognizes that this small hill is roughly the size of a person. When she studies its shape more carefully, she notes the belly bulge at its center, a half-revealed arm sleeved with thread-like filaments. "Jack."

"I think I've got it."

She sets down the knife and uses her hands to garden away, peeling back the gray and pink tangles, swiping away the muck glue, finally revealing an eye, then a nose, then a mouth.

"Jack!"

"Got it." He holds up a jar caked in goop triumphantly. And then he cocks his head at her. "What's going on down there?"

She gestures with her hand, indicating that he should see for himself.

He crouches opposite her as she peels away more layers, unshelling the body, stripping away a tacky, clinging membrane that feels almost placental.

"It's the Tapir," he says.

"What?"

"It's Professor Gordon. He must have come looking for me here and —" But before Jack can finish the sentence, an arm snaps up and grabs hold of him. The man's eyes peel open and he makes a noise like the gargling cry of the drowned.

16

◎

They call it Brigadoon, this island off the coast of Washington, because it is so often cloaked in fog. This is their new outpost, a kind of floating laboratory. Why build a fence when you can surround yourself with ripping currents and slate-gray waves that thunder the rocky shore? The campus, at the center of the island, is hidden by stacks of black basalt and spiked walls of evergreens. There is a landing strip and a helicopter pad and a cove for docking. Sometimes a crabbing or halibut boat will putter by curiously, but before it can get too close, a patrol boat armed with .50-caliber machine guns and a 25 mm Bushmaster cannon will direct it elsewhere.

There is no sign identifying this as DOD property, though even that would be misleading. There is nothing decorative about the facilities in the slightest. Brutalist in design, the buildings were constructed for strength, not style. You could say they are meant to withstand sea storms and the constant salt-toothed wind, but you could also say they are meant to confine what is hidden within.

One room contains a bank of screens that broadcast video feeds from Alaska. The cameras are stationed atop cell towers, water towers, and weather balloons in and around Fairbanks, where the sky has become its own special canvas. Faces form in the underbellies of clouds. Gray tendrils like the stingers of a jellyfish dangle downward. Some of the feeds go dark and never find their transmission again.

Another room is empty except for what looks like an open gate or door standing at the center of its concrete floor. The frame is made of black coral. It was harvested from a trench in the Pacific. What appear to be carvings are etched on it. There is a shimmering quality to the air within, like the vaguely rainbowed translucence of a bubble. Researchers once went into this room to study the gate, to send drones and even people with chains around their waists through it. They don't anymore. The entrance to the room has been welded shut.

One chamber goes below the island, circulating the tide into a series of salt-water tanks. In them are unknown life-forms harvested from the ocean by on-site remotely operated underwater vehicles: A glowing whale. A kind of krill that behaves like a single organism, coming together and solidifying into the shape of whoever stands before it. A shark that opens its mouth and unleashes black tentacles with teeth nested in them.

In a subbasement lab rests the fungal pod unearthed from the grove in the Olympics and transported here. In the center of a room that looks a little like an operating theater, the gray cylinder lies on a stainless-steel table. The air lock fizzes open—with a blast of UV light—as more than twenty people in hazmat suits file into the room. More wait behind a windowed wall, observing. Lights blaze down. Tools lie on trays. Photographs are snapped. Samples are sliced off. Sensors are jammed into it and taped onto it. Ultrasound probes scan the length of it but can't beam through the entirety of the thick chitinous husk.

"Strange as this may sound," one of the scientists says, "we might have a heartbeat."

Someone else says, "Are you sure?" They both study a rolling monitor, and after a long wait, a spike registers. "There!"

But no one can be certain what the slow spiked rhythm, which comes once every two minutes, actually indicates. Damaged plants and fungi send off electrical signals like wounded human tissue does. An organic alarm.

Isaac Peaches and Director Ricketts stand behind the window, observing. Her arms are crossed except when she leans forward to punch the intercom and ask questions or direct instructions. "Cut it open," she says, and the team members nod.

An oscillating saw with a blade the size of a sword swings down from the ceiling on an articulated metal arm. It bites into the hard husk and eats through a good ten inches of woody material before finding the softer gray tissue beneath.

There was a time when Isaac Peaches considered himself an indoorsman. Someone who spoke binary code and preferred blue light to sunlight, stale ventilation to fresh air. Now the opposite is true. He feels most alive outside where the earth hums beneath his feet. His skin prickles as if alive with ticks. Every nerve feels like a breeze-blown cobweb. He can taste leaf musk on his tongue, and his fingers dance constantly through the air as if conducting it.

Here, in the reinforced laboratory, he suffers a kind of sensory deprivation. He squints in the harsh light. He clears his throat and licks his lips, dried out by the HVAC. He feels dizzied by the movement of bodies all around him and unable to feel any sort of connection — cut off — which maybe makes him equivalent to the fungal pod removed from its muddy burrow. He feels sorry for it. He feels kinship with it.

When he is outside, he reads thermal variations, beetle-bitten leaves, lichen-stained bark. He breathes pollen and mold and the decay of cellulose. Snags and logs are the twisted dead veins and rotting bones of the fallen, and sword ferns and Oregon grape are the hair and fruit of the newly risen. His feet spring off moss and sweep through ankle-deep pine and fir needles. His heart is full and happy as he enjoys an awareness of the network living and dying all around him. Not just bear grass here and a liverwort there, but an interconnected thicket, an organism that most humans are oblivious to unless it erupts into a picturesque view. He sees what is invisible, he hears what is silent.

That's what Director Ricketts wants from him, to serve as a medium or translator. But the conversation is narrow. Just as some people look at a granite ridge and see a kitchen countertop and others look at a cedar tree and see a rot-resistant deck, she sees the potential for power and profit in alien matter. Weaponization. From their saltwater research, they have developed coral armor, jellyfish drones, krill camouflage, and oxygen-rich fluorocarbons you drown your lungs in so that you might breathe underwater.

So when the oscillating saw completes its lengthwise cut, when clamps are inserted in the incision, when the pod is torn slowly open, the gray hyphae yanking apart damply like the inside of a squash — when the core gives way to reveal a body, a human body, curled into a fetal ball, Director Ricketts turns her gaze on him and says, "Well?"

There are so many questions nested in that word. *Is this a case of replication or consumption? Are you excited or terrified? Are there more of these? How can we use this thing?*

"Well, well" is all he can muster as a response.

Even when split in two, the sarcophagus is too heavy for the researchers to manage, so they bring over a harness. With the help of a hydraulic lift, they hoist one half, then the other, away from the operating table.

There is a kind of gloppy shawl or placenta that surrounds the body. The scientists suction it off and now she can be seen more clearly. A girl. Or a young woman. Peaches would guess her a preteen or teenager. Her hair — the texture of seaweed — glistens down the length of her back. Her fingernails and toenails are as long and curled as talons.

They haven't slept in some time, and Director Ricketts opens what must be her tenth can of Diet Coke with a snap and a fizz. She drops a straw in and sucks until its length is darkly veined with soda. "When I say *well*," she says with a smack of her lips, "I mean, 'How in the H-word is this possible?'"

"That's a question so commonplace these days it might be considered a verbal tic."

"What are you thinking? I want to know what you're thinking. I can tell you're holding back on me."

He is thinking about how fungal networks — the billions of miles of hyphae strands in every acre of soil — don't just underlie a forest, they unite it. He is thinking about how they communicate information, alerting nearby trees of blight or beetle infestation or even the cut of a chain saw. He is thinking about how they trade chemicals and nutrients, killing arthropods and sapping minerals from rocks and transferring it all into the root systems of trees. He is thinking about how before Douglas firs die, they flood their silo of nutrients into the fungus cabling the ground to share with neighboring trees. He is thinking about how if something came to this planet, if it was trying to create a knowledge database and community connection, it would plug into the nervous system that runs beneath the surface, the synaptic wilderness beneath our feet. And watch. And wait.

She taps her nails against the Diet Coke can. "You're the one who found her. You could feel her down there. You have a connection. So what's that green antennae of yours telling you?"

"I believe," he says, "it has peaceful intentions."

"A human is locked inside there like a prisoner, and your assumption is that this thing is peaceful?"

Right then the girl stirs. First an arm unfolds damply. Then a leg.

The scientists back up, one of them so suddenly he knocks over a tray of tools.

"Your little plant lady is waking up," she says. "Should I be worried?"

"Fungus is not a plant," he says.

"And tomatoes are a fruit, not a vegetable. Who cares? They're plant enough."

"Fungus actually has more in common with humans than plants." He gestures to the girl, who begins to hack up something gray and bilious. "Case in point."

The girl takes one ragged breath, allows it to sit in her lungs for what seems like a minute, and then exhales. Her eyes are barely open, slivers of exhausted irises peering out from beneath her lids. Her skin is ashen and moist, like the inside of a mealy apple.

Director Ricketts sets down her can of Diet Coke so suddenly that it tips over and sizzles a puddle across the desk. She leans toward the intercom and says, with some urgency, "Vacate the lab."

The scientists don't waste any time hurrying through the exit and sealing the air lock behind them. They'll be blasted with UV light in the first room, sprayed with decontamination foam in the second, stripped in the third, showered in the fourth.

The girl is trying to sit up, but every movement is clumsy and labored. She doesn't look starved, but she looks soft. Without definition. Her body atrophied. She presses her arms against the table, rises a few inches, and flops back down. She shouldn't be able to move at all, given how long she's probably been trapped inside this thing — Isaac has a feeling it's been a long, long time — so that seems to imply stimulation of some sort, like a baby kicking in the womb, readying for the day it will be released.

Eventually she gives up. She lies there panting for several minutes. Damp curls of hair helmet her head. Peaches can see her try to open her eyes more fully and then squeeze them shut in the painful light of the room.

"Dim the lights," Isaac says. "Now."

Director Ricketts says, "Excuse me?"

"Will you please dim the lights, Director Ricketts?"

She hoists her painted-on eyebrows like crowbars and gives him an assessing gaze. Then she walks over to a wall panel and adjusts a series of knobs, and a twilight haze softens within the lab.

Another minute passes, and Isaac can see the girl's eyes blinking with the same steady rhythm as her lungs cause her chest to rise and fall. They are a good fifteen feet apart, but he can tell her vision is unfocused, as degenerate as her muscles.

For the rest of the day and through the night, little changes, but when they return to the lab in the morning, they find the window dirtied with spores. At first Ricketts orders the glass wiped clean, but Isaac stops the staff from following the directive, stepping closer, eyeing it from different angles. "Just wait," he says.

"Wait for what?"

"I think she's trying to tell us something."

"With spores?"

"They're not spores. Can't you see? They're letters."

17

◎

Nora reaches for her pistol, but it turns out there's no need.
The hand of the professor goes limp soon after it closes
around Jack's throat. She might hear a word—"Help"—
clotted with phlegm, but if not, she can certainly see the plea in the
man's eyes.

Jack rips away the fungal coat, tossing the meaty layers aside until the body is moistly unpeeled. Gordon is unresponsive when they
shake him. Jack yells, "Robert! Robert, can you hear me?" and then
asks her if they should call 911 and risk exposing others or do chest
compressions and try to resuscitate him themselves.

"Hold on." She leans her face close to Professor Gordon's, and the
plastic fogs with a faint breath. "He's still alive."

He needs a doctor, but first they need to destroy whatever is
growing here before it spreads.

She can see the panic in Jack's eyes—the professional calculations he's making, the cost of the lab, the cost of his career—and she
worries he'll choose his own future over the future of others. But
then Professor Gordon lets out a bubbling gasp, and life wins. Jack
nods and says, "Get Gordon out of here."

"What are you going to do?"

"There's a bottle of whiskey in the far cupboard."

"Hardly seems like a good time for a toast."

"I'm going to burn this shit down."

She grabs Professor Gordon beneath the arms and tries to drag
him to the hall, but he's limp and heavy and hard to move.

Jack rushes to a cabinet half covered with fungus, scrapes the lip of it away, yanks open the door, and reaches to the back of the shelf. He pulls out a handle of Jim Beam and yells, "Bottoms up!" He takes one small hit, then shakes it out through the room. Some of the fungi noticeably shrink against the splatter. A few of the cauliflowers explode their storms of black spores.

There is a Bunsen burner sitting on a counter like a candlestick waiting for its flame. He splashes a stream toward it, tosses the bottle aside, cranks the gas, and sparks the ignition. Tongues of flame spread greedily. He doesn't linger. He hurries toward Nora to help with Professor Gordon.

They leave the room, and as they close the door behind them, amid the fire's spitting sizzle, Nora thinks she hears a wail of pain.

The fire alarm goes off as they leave the building, and the fire trucks pass them in a blaze of whirling light on their way to the hospital. They drop Professor Gordon off outside the emergency room, where Nora flashes her badge and tells the nurse the man was exposed to a toxic contaminant in a lab and needs to be treated in isolation with antifungals.

In her backyard, on the stone patio, they set down the specimen jars. "Whatever's inside them can wait," she says. They have a dozen altogether, but only one matters: the one his grad student brought back to the lab. The label is discolored and peeling, but the tidy penmanship is still legible. These are the coordinates of what could very well be their source. She swipes the pine needles off a glass-topped table and they unfold a map of western Washington. Jack takes a red pen to it, marking down a location on the Sound. McNeil Island. "That's right," he says as if to himself. "She had mentioned this place. She'd take the ferry out. She liked to bird-watch there and thought the conditions were perfect for a fungal survey." He bites down on the cap of the pen. "But why here? Is this a true parent site or an ancillary location?"

"It's the parent site," Nora says.

He tips his head to look at her. "How do you know?"

She stabs her finger down on the island, indicating a black dot.

She explains that the map is outdated, that this wildlife area runs right up against the former site of McNeil Prison, which was abandoned and left to rot for several years before the state decided to rebuild.

"What did they rebuild?" he asks.

"The Black Creek Correctional Facility." She lets this sit for a moment before finishing: "Home to Albus Crotter."

"Oh, shit," he says.

"Oh, shit, indeed."

Her phone rings. She lets it go for several seconds before pulling it from her pocket. The number is unlisted, so she sends the call straight to voice mail.

"You said he's comatose."

"Not comatose. But the fall broke him. Shattered his spine. Severe brain damage."

"And yet . . ."

"I think it's safe to say he's found a way to escape."

"He's the parent. The point of origin. The axis of growth for morphogenesis."

"But why is this happening now?" she says. "It's been five years since the meteor storm. It's been a year since he was caught. What's the convergence?"

"It's also been five years of drought. Nothing's been growing. My research has been shit because of it. Only in the past week or so did the rains start up again. Even bad things grow with water."

"But what about him?"

"He said he was communicating with God. Maybe this is it. Maybe this is God. God as death. The comet as some manifestation of God. A messenger from the infinite void."

"My mother would slap your face for sacrilege."

"I know she would. I'm just spitballing here. I don't know. Maybe Crotter was an early point of exposure? A beta model?"

"He was the key."

"The key," he says. "Sure. The key for the vehicle of transmission.

And once the rains started up again, the fungi had all the fuel they needed to take a road trip through Puget Sound. And beyond."

"There's no beyond. It's going to end here."

Her phone rings again, and again she silences it.

"So what do we do?" he says and walks out into the lawn, turns, and heads back toward her with his finger raised. "Call Black Creek, for starters." He goes still and his eyes brighten and for a moment she thinks he's had another breakthrough. Instead, he kneels down and fingers something from between the pavers of the patio. A quarter. He looks up at her with delight. "Hey! Minted the same year she was born."

Her phone rings again and before she can ignore the call, he's jogging toward the rear of the yard and into the needled shade of a ponderosa pine. The one Mia had called her wishing tree. Quarters and dimes and pennies barnacle its trunk, tucked between the plates of terra-cotta bark. One found in an oil-rainbowed puddle in the parking lot of a hardware store. Another found in the grass beneath a bench overlooking the Sound. This one was shaken out of Jack's jeans; this other was excavated from the couch cushions. Mia never told them what she wished for because she believed that sharing forfeited the wish. The coins reach no higher than four feet yet skirt the entire trunk.

Nora follows him there, and he says, "I'm kind of surprised they're still here."

"Of course they're still here. Why wouldn't they still be here?"

"I don't know. I guess it seems like all the wishes should have disappeared with her."

As he slots the quarter into the tree, Nora's phone rings again.

"Somebody really wants to talk to you," he says. "Better get it."

She accepts the call with a sigh and brings the phone to her ear. "What?"

A female voice offers the bright, sunny welcome of what is certainly a telemarketer. "Mrs. Abernathy?"

Nora is ready to hang up; the phone is already falling from her ear as the voice continues chattering at her with a honeyed Southern drawl. "I know how this is going to sound—and it's going to sound extraordinary—but I believe we've found your daughter."

Her thumb hovers over the End button. She must have heard incorrectly. Her mind isn't in the right place. She should hang up and she should call Black Creek, because the two of them are close—they're so close—to getting to the bottom of this.

"Mrs. Abernathy?" the voice calls out again, and she slowly lifts the phone and mashes it against her ear so that there can be no mistake this time. "Mrs. Abernathy?"

Her voice is a whisper when she finally speaks. "What did you say?"

"I believe we've found your daughter."

"Her body?"

"No, ma'am. Her living, breathing person."

She transfers the phone from one ear to the other. Jack is staring at her with his eyebrows pinched together. "What is it?"

"You're saying"—Nora clears her throat—"you're saying she's alive?"

"Yes, ma'am. That's exactly what I'm saying."

She can barely figure out how to make words. "Who is this?"

"Do you happen to know where McChord Field is?"

"The air force base?"

"We'll have a helicopter waiting for you there in a half hour."

18

◎

Jack doesn't want to believe because it hurts so bad when that belief gets torn away. It's happened over and over again. He will see a reflection in a window, hear a voice in the cereal aisle, spot a messy tangle of hair in a car rushing past him, and feel certain: It's her. She's still out there.

Every now and then, somebody would bring up the possibility of a memorial service—his parents or mother-in-law. But neither he nor Nora would accept that kind of finality. There was no body, so there would be no grave.

This impossible moment is why. He tries to imagine what she will look like now—at thirteen—stretched out, bonier, with the knobby knees and sharp elbows of early adolescence. If she had never left, she would probably be a pain in the ass—like all thirteen-year-olds —and spend too much time on her phone and yell about the unfairness of chores and homework and everything else, slamming doors, testing the limits of teenage attitude. But he wouldn't mind. He'd welcome and love every minute of her eye-rolling disdain for him, and he would comfort her when friendships collapsed, relationships disappointed, and tryouts didn't go as well as they could have. He would briefly stop applauding to wipe away tears when she eventually walked across the stage to collect her diploma. He would wave at her from the other side of security when she headed off to board a plane for college, probably Pomona, maybe Carleton or Dartmouth. She would become an architect or a director or a lawyer. Maybe a professor like her dad or a cop like her mom. She would find a spouse, and they would have children, maybe two, possibly three, but not just one, because she had been lonely as an only child. And then Jack's hair would silver, his back would hunch, and his bones would break easily like stems of glass, and eventually he would fall on an icy sidewalk and die, so Mia would be the one missing and imagining the ghost of him everywhere.

There are different stages of grieving. Immediate denial gives way to a brain-blackening choke hold that lasts for years . . . which gives way to occasional bouts of teary paralysis . . . which gives way to the next phase and the next phase and the next phase. It never ends. You never get past it. A lost child is a bottomless hole.

He hates this hope. He absolutely hates it. Because when the girl in the window or down the cereal aisle turned out to be someone else, a phantom, Mia was taken from him again and again and again.

So he doesn't want to believe. He can't believe. He won't believe.

On the helicopter, he and Nora don't talk. Words feel unattainable right now, as do the many questions prickling their minds. They are buckled onto a bench seat, side by side, and before they had even taken off, Nora grabbed his hand. Her grip is so tight that his skin whitens and his tendons ache. The roar of the engine might as well be the blood in his ears. The rhythmic shiver of the rotor might as well be the breath in his lungs. Have they been flying now for three minutes or three days? He's lost track.

The clouds hang low and the chopper skims across the pulpy gray top of them. The rotor wash churns their surface, forming a gray whirlpool when they suddenly descend. Jack has lost his sense of direction and is surprised to see the ocean open up beneath them. Whitecaps froth. Rain spits. The wind knocks the chopper around, and the pilot corrects their course. An island looms. Spires of black rock surround the tree-studded hump. There seems to be nowhere to land, so when the chopper lowers further, he wonders for a panicked moment if they're going to crash, if this is an emergency landing. He isn't worried for himself. Instead, he fears, after all this time, that he will never see her, that the wish of his quarter will never come true.

Then the chopper tilts forward in a steep decline, and he sees through the cockpit window the arrangement of concrete buildings below. Their squares and rectangles are half sunk into the black rock and green grass, tucked among the island's natural features.

The helicopter pad is on a roof, and as soon as the landing skids touch down, a door to the building opens and a man steps out into the rain. He wears a black rain jacket and rain-spotted khakis and looks the definition of *ordinary*. Like someone who should be fertilizing his lawn in the suburbs or selling data plans at Verizon. It takes Jack a moment to recognize him as the man from the other day. The man who apologetically blocked his way on the logging road in the Olympics.

Isaac holds up an arm, maybe in greeting or maybe to shield himself from the heavy block of wind thrown by the rotor blades. He opens the cargo door and waves them forward, so they unbuckle and climb out and shout their greetings as the engine winds down. He says, "I have something rather extraordinary to show you."

Twenty minutes later, after they sign forms they're too rushed to read, after they're escorted through a labyrinth of windowless corridors broken up by security locks, they arrive in a room that functions like an observation deck. A bank of computers, a stack of surveillance screens, an intercom, a picture window that offers a view of a dimly lit laboratory.

Two guards wait for them here. They wear fatigues under Kevlar. Assault rifles are strapped across their shoulders but held before them at a downward angle; their fingers are straightened off the triggers yet ready to fire at a moment's notice. A woman with a rigid spray of hair rises from a roller chair and says, "Oh, wonderful. I'm so glad you decided to come." Her bright red smile is split by some of the whitest, squarest teeth Jack has ever seen.

He barely hears her introduce herself. He barely notices her manicured hand, held out to shake. Because his eyes are on the window, where *Mia Abernathy* is spelled out in black, messy, mold-spotted letters.

"Where is she?" he says, pushing forward. "Let us see her. Please."

Nora is beside him, studying the name of her daughter, tracing the lines of it with her finger. Then they both peer through the glass, squinting into the dusky space and trying to understand what they see.

Then Isaac lifts the dimmer switch and the lab is flooded with light.

There is a tree that grows in the far north. A Norway spruce called Old Tjikko. The tree above the ground might be a hundred years old, while the roots below are nearly ten thousand years old. It lives. It rots. It falls. A new trunk grows again from the same well. That's all Jack can think of right now. Old Tjikko and its cycle of death and rebirth. Not simply with regard to his daughter, but with regard to them. As a family. They fell, and now — somehow, impossibly — they have twined together and risen once more.

She is there. Wearing a surgical smock. Standing in the middle of the lab. Staring directly at them. She is older, taller, broader in face and shoulder, but unmistakably their daughter.

"Mia," he says.

19

saac watches their eyes. Jack and Nora both wear masks, but he doesn't need to see the whole of their faces to understand how they feel. Tears spangle their lashes and dribble down their cheeks. They clearly aren't listening to Director Ricketts when she tells them no, they are not allowed to enter the lab. Not yet. Not until she knows more about what exactly they're dealing with. They not only signed an NDA upon entering the facility, they terminated their parental rights. They are now here as consultants in what will be considered a biological trial, aiding in all communication efforts with the specimen.

"Can we call her Mia? Instead of a specimen?" Isaac says in a low voice. "Let's try to be sensitive to how they must be feeling right now."

Director Ricketts blinks at him several times as if to restore her focus. "Please don't tell me how to do my job."

The parents lean against the glass, their hands starfished against it, as if they might push through. Nora is tense and quiet, but Jack whimpers and pounds at the window and yells out, "Mia, Mia, Mia," each time louder than the last.

The girl does not respond at first except to cock her head one way, then the other.

"What's wrong with her? Why isn't she saying anything? Where did you find her? How long has she been here? Where has she been all this time? Was she kidnapped? Was she injured? Does she understand what's happening? Has she been psychologically evaluated? Has she had a physical?" Nora asks the questions so quickly that she can't possibly expect answers. She sees and hears nothing but her daughter.

Isaac has only so many answers—he hasn't been able to examine the girl himself except from a distance—but he tries to talk to them. In as soothing a tone as he can manage, he explains where the girl was found, how she was unearthed. But you can't give parents back their child—presumed dead for five years—and expect them to engage in any sort of logical conversation, let alone one that defies all reason. He might as well be saying, *Here are bones, the bones can dance.*

"Mia!" Jack screams one more time and that's when the girl starts toward them. Slowly. Her feet seem heavy, as if unrooting with each step. Her joints move as if stiffened with rust. More than a minute passes before she makes it to the window.

"Why is she moving like that?" Nora says.

"Because she's not used to moving at all," Peaches says.

The parents breathe heavily, their lungs shuddering. They slide their hands across the glass until their palms are in the center, their fingers overlapping. When the girl reaches her own hand up and stations it on the other side of the glass, her parents cry out and lower their heads as if in prayer.

The door to the hall opens and a guard enters. "Director Ricketts?"

"Can't it wait?" she says, her eyes sharp on the parents and their child.

"I'm afraid not," the guard says. "Something is happening."

"Something is happening here as well. A lovely reunion."

"Our surveillance is picking up on a biological anomaly in the Sea-Tac metro." Another beat before he continues. "A fungal event."

This finally gets her attention. "Do you mean like what we encountered in the Olympics? Is there more growth?"

"More growth of a different kind. Several hospitals are reporting patients having psychotic episodes that appear to be tied to fungal infections. And the police scanner —"

"Show me."

She always smiles. But Isaac has learned to read the curve of her mouth, the flex of her cheeks. When she is angry, she shows all her teeth and widens her eyes until they seemed peeled entirely of their lids. When she's disappointed, her face droops even as her smile curls upward. When she's intrigued, as she is now, one side of her mouth rises higher than the other, a crescent cutting her cheek. "Back in a jiff," she says and nods at Isaac, indicating he will continue to monitor the parents until she returns.

The father seems oblivious to anything except the girl. But the mother — Nora — turns toward the sound of the door clicking shut. She notes that Ricketts has left and focuses her attention on Isaac. "You can't keep us from her."

"There are risks."

"Fuck the risks." There is a hard finality to her voice, but it is offset by the tears flooding her eyes. "Put us in suits, if you have to, but let us in. Please let us in."

Ten minutes later, the air lock hisses open. Through the doorway comes a flood of UV light the blue-silver of a star. In the chamber, Nora and Jack lumber forward, their shapes as slow and bulky as astronauts in their hazmat suits.

Isaac expected them to rush forward, but once inside the lab, they pause. The next few steps must feel impossible. Their daughter is waiting for them. Standing ten yards away. Jack holds out his arms, as if to welcome her into a hug, and the girl shadows the gesture, mimicking the movement.

There isn't time to stop what happens next. First Jack and then Nora unzip their suits and flop back their hoods. They rush toward her.

The guard in the control room says, "Should I go in?" and Isaac says, "No. There's no point now. They've made their choice."

He drops his hand to the intercom button — and then slides it over and hits the lock button instead, sealing them in the lab.

"What about *her?*" the guard says, and Isaac knows from his tone that he means Director Ricketts.

"I'll take the blame."

He watches through the window as Jack and Nora pull their daughter into an embrace. She remains still, but they won't stop moving, kissing her, touching her, tangling their arms around her, combing their fingers through her hair. It must be a curious thing, parenthood. You create something that is and is not you. Like growing a new limb, a second brain. Whatever joy or pain the child experiences belongs to you as well. He remembers his mother then — her constant meddling, her desperate need of him — and forgives her.

Nora — who had been wearing a mask even before she entered the facility — smothers her daughter in kisses. There is no fear of contagion because not being able to breathe the same air as her daughter would be worse than death. Isaac wonders if he will ever experience such a profound feeling of love. To be willing to risk death for one kiss.

It is then that Director Ricketts enters the room. Her smile is at its most dangerous when she approaches. "What in the F-word is going on here?" she says. She reaches into her jacket pocket, removes her keys, and tosses them up with a rattle. When they land in her palm, her grip tightens, and they spike from her knuckles.

"I know you're —" he says, but he never gets to finish the sentence. Her fist swings upward, striking him.

Blood trickles from the corner of his eye. He wipes it away and studies the red tipping his fingers.

20

◎

Mia doesn't talk. Her eyes track them. Her movements are fumbling but responsive. But no matter how many questions they ask, she remains silent, as if her voice atrophied along with the rest of her. "Do you remember the wishing tree? Do you remember Tigey? Do you remember the night you disappeared? Do you remember us?"

Nothing. Maybe a slight tic of her mouth, a flare of her nose, a widening of her eyes. Jack's reaching. For anything. He's going to keep knocking until someone answers.

He can cry only so much. He can say her name only so many times. After the initial shock and wonder wears off, he truly takes in his surroundings and notes the equipment available to him. And he does the one thing he's been unable to do these past five years. He gets to work.

He kneels beside the shed macrofungal husk. The exterior has the hard-shell plating of a polypore, like a conk or an alder bracket, while the interior is fibrous and damp, the yarn-like hyphae clumping together into a sloppy mycelium. He runs his hand along it, and his palm comes away with a damp sheen.

Nora says, "Why did it wait?"

"What?"

Earlier, Nora found a small pair of surgical scissors on a tray. She's using them now to cut Mia's toenails. Their daughter sits on the operating table, her legs dangling, while Nora crouches before her, snipping at what look like thick curled talons. The clippings dirty the floor like wood shavings. "Why did this thing wait so long? Before giving her back to us? Why did we have to hurt for five years?"

"Five years," he says and shakes his head, because it feels more like a century. His hair is graying. His liver hurts. He can't come up with a reason to get out of bed most mornings. He lost his daughter, divorced his wife, and committed slow professional suicide. Time slows down when delivering its best poison.

"Jack?"

He realizes then she wasn't asking a rhetorical question and venting her pain; she actually wants to know. He should have guessed. Nora irons her bedsheets and organizes her magazines alphabetically because she believes in order and precision. Everything needs to line up in her life and in a case. Cause and effect. Why her? Why five years? "Is it the rain again? Rain falls and people die? Rain falls and our baby lives? Rain falls and everything's suddenly unfamiliar? Is that it? Because if that's it, you'd think my tears would have done the job already."

"Well, five years is nothing, really. There are plants older than the Bible. Stone is older than mankind."

"It's something to me."

"I know. I'm just—"

"Explain the timeline, Jack. How did we get from that night to this day?"

He's shaking his head as if he doesn't quite believe it himself. "Something fell from the sky. Buried itself in the ground. And took her with it."

"Why?"

"Well, I can only hypothesize. The rules of this world, after all, aren't the rules of other worlds. On Titan, for instance—that's one of Saturn's moons—on Titan, there are rivers and lakes made of methane. It's not a gas there. It's a liquid. Instead of water, methane is the apparent source of life."

"Stick with the rules of Earth," she says. "Earth I understand."

"There are two stages to most mushroom growth: The underground and the fruiting. The underground can take days or months or even years."

"Years," she says. "Five goddamn years."

"Usually a spongelike layer forms beneath the surface. The fungus grows hidden in the substrate until it's ready."

"Ready for what?" she says.

"Could be rainfall, like we've been having. Could be warm temps. Could be nutrients. Or some combination of factors. That's what signals the fruiting stage, where the buttons pop." He walks the length of the fungal pod and knocks on it with his knuckles. "But again, I can't say the same rules apply here. There are new rules every day, feels like. I don't even know what to call this."

"It's not fungus?"

"It is," he says. "And it isn't. There's no scientific name for what we're talking about. It's like learning a new language."

"But you're going to do your best? Not for your tenure portfolio or whatever. But for us?"

"I'm going to do my best." Jack begins his tour of the lab, yanking open drawers and cupboards, withdrawing tools, shaking solutions, hoisting a microscope onto the counter. The overhead speakers project the voice of Ricketts. The tinny quality takes away the music of her accent. "Might I ask what you think you're doing, Mr. Abernathy?"

"Dr. Abernathy," he says.

"What are you doing?"

"Oh, you know." The only thing you can do when faced with the unknown. "Science. Just a little science experiment."

"We have people here, very capable people, some of the best in their field, who can take care of that for us," Director Ricketts says. "If you could—"

"He's not just her father." He is surprised to hear Nora shout. "He's a professor of biology. He specializes in fungus. Let him do his fucking job."

"Yeah," he says quietly, just for Nora. "Let him."

He locates a tissue collector, a grafter that shaves and sucks biomaterial into a tube. "Can I have your hand?" he says to Mia and she stares at him a long moment.

Nora nods encouragingly and takes her hand and lifts it into the air. "It's okay."

Jack places the tip of her index finger on the nose of the grafter and thumbs the button. It snaps a bite out of her. Instead of blood, a gray-white fluid oozes out of the wound. He and Nora share a look that communicates what they are too terrified to say. Have they lost her after all? Is she still theirs?

Whether it's day or night, he doesn't know. How many hours pass, he isn't sure. Every once in a while, he glances at the window to the control room. The faces on the other side of it are constantly shifting. Sometimes it is Isaac Peaches, sometimes Ricketts, sometimes both, and sometimes neither. A guard eyes them now. A square-faced man with a square-shaped body. Maybe the night watchman.

"You know how I said I wasn't sure what we were dealing with? I could only make secondary comparisons?"

"Yes," Nora says, coming to join him at the microscope.

"Maybe I'm a little closer now."

"Tell me."

"It sure looks like fungus from a distance."

"From a distance." She lays her hand on the head of the microscope. "What are you seeing up close?"

"Take a peek."

She brings her eyes to the lenses and adjusts the diopter a touch. "I'm not sure what I'm supposed to see, but . . . it looks like a landscape."

"That's actually a perfect description. When you're at a vista, right? You're looking at mountains or a canyon, you can see strata. Different layers of time stacked up. In the same way here." He taps the stage for the slide. "There are different zones in this. Both flesh and fungus."

She lifts her gaze to meet his. "What are you saying?"

"We're dealing with something more like lichen."

"Lichen? But isn't that furry and leafy?"

"I'm not saying it's lichen. I'm saying it has similar properties in that it's a symbiote. A combination of algae and fungi. They work together."

"Why?"

"Because they each get something out of the relationship."

"Explain."

He explains how a common characteristic of fungus is that it forms beneficial and mutualistic relationships with other organisms. "So think of algae as the spoon and fungus as the hammer. Fungus gets food from the algae and algae gets structure from the fungus."

"What's the spoon and hammer of it all in this case?" Nora says. "What's this thing getting out of our daughter?"

"Intelligence for one. Human intelligence. Hypothetically, of course. But if it's accessing her, it's also accessing an understanding of this alien world."

"Hold on. *We're* the alien world?"

"To this stuff we are. Yeah."

"What else?"

"Mobility," he says and paces in a quick circle as an illustration. "She can run the same way that the wind can carry a spore."

"I don't even know what to say."

He's trying not to be heartbroken. He's trying to find hope and possibility in this discovery. His daughter is still here. His daughter is still alive. She's just changed. She's just *more*. Is that any more frightening than a teenager who vapes and drinks, who texts and drives? Yes. Okay. Maybe it's a lot more frightening. But he needs not to feel despair anymore.

He can see that he's losing Nora, so he puts his hands gently on her shoulders and says, "Stay with me here, okay? Let's focus on the good. She's here. She's not gone. She's different, but we can work with different."

Nora nods her head with some difficulty, fighting back tears.

"Think about how versatile mushrooms are for a minute," he says. "I just read this research study in the National Library of Medicine about fungal computers. Basidiomycetes. It's fungi they think has the electrical and thermal and chemical capability of computing and networking data. That's not science fiction. It's science. And I recently did a consult with Boeing, another with an architectural firm — they're thinking about trying to make things out of fungus. Everything from biomes on Mars to houses here in Seattle. Because some fungus is like wood. And some is foamy. And some is more pliant, like a polymer. It would be ecofriendly, obviously, but you could also repair elements of a structure by simply regrowing them. Is a fungus city any crazier than what we're seeing right now?"

"But," she says with a hard swallow, "are you saying this isn't her? It's just a Mia-shaped house? A piece of architecture?"

"No. I'm trying to say it's her, but it's not just her. It's *more* than her."

Nora returns to their daughter and Jack follows. Mia is staring at them. Maybe her mouth trembles slightly, the beginning of a smile. Whether she understands any of what they're talking about, he doesn't know. They touch her, squeezing her shoulder, rubbing her back, as if to remind themselves she's real.

Nora says, "You said they each get something out of the relationship."

"I did."

"So what is Mia getting out of it?"

"What are *we* getting out of it, you mean. Because this isn't just about her. It's about humankind. She's just one sample. One case study of what could be many."

"Don't call our daughter a case study. You sound like them," she says, nodding toward the observation window.

"Sorry."

"What is she — what are *we* — getting out of this relationship?"

His shoulders rise and fall in a shrug. "Maybe," he says, "the chance to survive."

"Survive what?"

"What's happening in Seattle . . . I was thinking of it as a contagion before. But maybe there's a better word." Nora and Mia are both staring at him intently when he finally says the word: "Invasion."

21

nnabelle had a brother. A twin. Named Adam. They looked so much alike — blond-haired, blue-eyed, always a pink flush high in their cheeks — that throughout their early childhood, people had trouble telling them apart. One of them might have a distinguishing freckle and one of them might have a scar on one elbow, but nobody could ever remember which feature equaled which kid. The twins enjoyed the confusion they caused so much that they styled their hair the same and wore each other's clothes and sometimes swapped classrooms at their elementary school. This was in the Houston suburbs, where the roads ran straight, the lawns were an unspoiled green, and the houses all shared a similar design. People delighted in sameness.

Then middle school came, and with it, all the strange, awkward transformations of that age. Hair where there wasn't any before. Lengthening bones, thickening muscles. Adam's voice dropped three octaves in a month, and just like that, he no longer wanted to be mistaken for his sister. Adam no longer wanted even to spend time with her. They went from cozy inseparability to pained severance. He shaved his head. Everything he wore had holes in it. He pierced his nose with a pin heated over the stovetop burner. He wanted his birthday celebrated a day later than hers. He wanted his bedroom relocated from the main floor to the basement. He had gone from a reflection of her to a broken mirror, all jagged edges and distorted familiarity.

Their father was a state senator and the owner of a construction firm that specialized in sports arenas and shopping malls. He saw his family as an extension of his career, so he favored and spoiled Annabelle because she remained the *good girl,* and he came down hard on Adam, who was an *embarrassment* and a *disgrace.* Her brother had broken her heart, so Annabelle delighted in seeing him punished. She leaned into her parents' love by playing flute in the orchestra and signing up for student council and volunteering to usher at the Cornerstone megachurch and maintaining a 4.0 GPA. Adam's extracurriculars were limited to weed, oxy, light beer, and a failed garage band called Monstyr Attax!

Annabelle sported a lipsticked smile, and he a performative sneer. He dented the walls with his fists. He shattered the taillight of their father's Mercedes with a swing of his skateboard. He graduated with a 2.0 average, emptied his college savings account, and took off for Austin and then Boulder and then LA. They heard from him intermittently over the years, but in general her parents preferred not to speak of him, as if he could be dug out and burned off like a wart.

Even Annabelle grew so accustomed to his absence that when people asked if she had any siblings, she said no, she was an only child. She continued to listen to her daddy by enrolling at Baylor, his alma mater, and later on at Texas A&M, where she pursued graduate work in international studies. Her family's stance was firmly nationalist. Business and politics were two sides of the same coin, her father said, and God and the American military were two sides of the same bullet. Globalism was Commie talk, a pansy denial and dilution of America's power. When Daddy died of a coronary, she inherited his construction firm and decided the best way to carry forward his legacy was to focus on border security. The Department of Homeland Security invested hundreds of millions in the construction of the Texas portion of the border wall — until the comet changed everything. People suddenly wanted to be protected from what was in the sky, not what was in the south, so she pivoted her focus to a new division within the DOD devoted to extraterrestrial resistance.

Whenever people whined about conservatism or nationalism or whatever ism they were shamefully machine-gunning on social media or MSNBC, she wanted to point out a very simple fact: Strength wins. America is the strongest institution in the history of the world. Keep it that way. Period. The comet had upended their geopolitical certainty, making it the greatest threat to American dominance since the nuclear standoff of the Cold War. And that's because Americans didn't know what weapons and resources were out there. It was an arms race. And the threats were now without as well as within their borders.

She learned about Adam's involvement with the Roofless Church through her office. The sect — or cult, as most called them — was being investigated as a possible terror group. Adam was flagged as a member of a compound in northern Minnesota. "I thought you were an only child," one of her colleagues said, and she knew then how her father had felt. The pride and the embarrassment that came with blood.

She flew up and they met at a lumberjack-themed diner for lunch. He arrived fifteen minutes late. A car with three other men waited for him in the parking lot. She rose from the booth to greet him. He wore all black. His hair had fallen out, and his eyes gave off a starry glow. He gave her a close-lipped smile that felt pitying. She wasn't sure whether to offer a handshake or a hug, but in the end instinct took over and she wrapped her arms around him. He felt as cold and sharp and fragile as an icicle. They took their seats opposite each other and she said, "We've got to get something in you" — pushing a menu over to him — "before you waste away to nothing."

He said he was getting all the sustenance he needed.

"You've been smoking that stuff, haven't you? You're a metal-eater now?"

"Metal is," he said and assumed a position of prayer, lifting his head toward the ceiling and opening his palms as if to catch something.

"I don't even know what that means."

He didn't respond except to smile at her serenely.

"Well," she said. "You seem happy. I'm glad for that, at least."

"I know why you're here," he said.

"I'm here to see my long-lost brother," she said.

"You're here to use me."

"That's not true at all."

"I know who you work for, Annabelle."

"Let's figure out what we're going to eat, how about?" She unrolled her napkin and spread it across her lap, then neatened her silverware. "I bet a place like this serves a nice slice of pie."

"I want you to have something," he said. He reached into his jacket and withdrew what she at first believed was a weapon. But instead of jamming it into her breast, he set it softly on the table between them. It was a long metal wand, thinly branched at the top like a tuning fork. Its silver-blue sheen identified it unmistakably as omnimetal. The gentle tap of it against the wood let off a hum that shivered the ice water in her glass.

"What is it?" she said.

"Growing up, we spent all that time at the church, right? Holding up our hands, praising Jesus, and singing Christian soft rock? All those people who emptied their wallets and gave up their Sundays, they desperately wanted something this world wasn't giving them."

"Was it the same thing you were looking for at the bottom of a bottle or coke vial?"

"It was, yes." She'd meant it as an insult, but he didn't take it as one. "It was exactly that." He widened his eyes with excitement. "We're all searching for something else. And this is it. This is something else." He nudged the wand toward her, but she leaned back until the booth stopped her.

"You're making me nervous, Adam."

"You know why every church has a spire? It's because we know — instinctually — that you've got to look to the sky if you want to communicate with a world other than this one. Put up a big antenna."

"I just want to talk to you, Adam. You and me. Brother and sister. Without all of this nonsense in the way. I'll forget my government if you forget your church. Just for a few minutes. Let's talk. Let's just talk."

He told her that if she really wanted to talk to him, she first needed to listen. He touched the omnimetal rod and then he touched his ear.

A gum-chewing waitress swung by with a pot of coffee and asked if they had any questions.

"I've got loads of questions," Annabelle said, her eyes on her brother as he rose from his seat and gave a small bow. He left her then, this time for good.

At first Annabelle kept the rod in a drawer, ignoring it, an unwelcome reminder of something that felt pained and unfinished. But one day she felt the air humming as if a train were passing by in the distance, and the sensation poured through her entire body like a tickle. She checked the hallway. She looked out the window. She wondered if a test was being conducted on the grounds. Then she returned to her chair and realized what the source of the sound was.

She opened the drawer. She took the rod in her hand. Every hair on her body prickled, and gooseflesh tightened her skin. Rather than bring the rod toward her ear, she leaned her head toward it, because in addition to feeling the tremoring sensation, she heard something. Whispering. The voices were legion, overlapping, but at least some of them seemed to belong to Adam.

She couldn't make out what was being said. Not with any clarity. Snippets of words here and there. It was like trying to read code without knowing Java or listening to twenty radio stations at once. Was this — to borrow her brother's phrase — some kind of antenna? Or something else? What were the implications if the metal could absorb *more* than energy on a quantum scale?

A part of her brother was still here, having merged with the metal. And a part of the girl was still here, having joined with the fungus. If that kind of absorption and convergence was possible, what did death even mean anymore?

The answers to these questions inspired her for their scientific challenge, yes. The curiosity and adventure of her work. But there was also an angry ambition that drove her. Thaddeus Gunn — the principal director and supervising authority for their shadow agency — did not seem to think much of anybody, including herself. He dismissed her suggestions. He hung up on her midconversation. He referred to her as a grunt, a roughneck who got the job done without really understanding it.

She might not be a scientist but that didn't mean she wasn't hungry for knowledge. She wanted to discover something of consequence as a rebellion against him but also because she had grown up the favored child, and, as much as she hated herself for it, she couldn't help but crave that same feeling of approval and recognition that came when her father hugged her close and called her his perfect girl.

Ten miles from Seattle, Annabelle can already see the fires. Several blocks blaze throughout the metro area. Cords of black smoke tie the ground to the clouds. The F5 Tower is missing what looks like an entire floor of windows, the glass replaced by an orange gash of flame.

She sits in the hold of the helicopter as they shuttle across the water of Puget Sound. The steady thrum of the rotor can be heard even through the headsets. She wears an unzipped hazmat suit with the hood puddled around her shoulders. "What you did back there," she says to Isaac, "was beyond unacceptable."

"I'm sorry," he says — but is he really?

"By allowing the parents inside, you not only defied me, you compromised the integrity of the lab. You introduced unknown pathogens and bacteria to an isolated space. The specimen has been exposed. Jack and Nora have also been exposed. All three could be ruined as a result."

"Were you ever going to let them go anyway?" he says. "After what they'd seen?"

She pulls aside his headset gently. Now she hears her words twice, spoken from her lips and projected from the headphones around his neck. "If they die, their deaths are on you." She brushes his hair away from his ear. "And I don't appreciate your tone. Not one bit."

"It's just," he says, "if you've lost a child, aren't you already dead?"

She traces the cartilage of his ear with her finger, and his breath flutters. Then her fingernails turn inward, pinching, twisting. He closes his eyes and grits his teeth against the painful heat of her grip.

"Well?" she finally says. "Are you ready to apologize?"

"I'm sorry. You're right." His tone is shrilly honest. She has a way of making him believe, and she can tell he means it when he says, "It won't happen again, Mother." It isn't the first time he's called her that, and he quickly corrects himself. "Director Ricketts, I mean. It won't happen again."

Only then does she release him. He presses both hands against his ear as if it might fall off. The throb of his pulse remains in her fingers. She understands how to create the most exquisite pain out of the smallest gestures.

She clears her throat, consults her tablet, and in a cheery voice that will hopefully get them back on track she begins to debrief him on what they should expect when they arrive at Virginia Mason. The hospital has cordoned off an ICU for all patients exhibiting the same curious and violent symptoms. There has been an exponential rise in cases the past few days, and the police have been taking their arrests to the hospital instead of the station.

Director Ricketts opens up an app that broadcasts the police scanner, and in a short burst of noise, they hear the same kind of complaint in the scramble of voices: "There's something seriously wrong with this guy" and "Not sure if it's PCP or LSD or bath salts or what, but she's out of her mind on something" and "His own family. How could he do that to his own family?"

They swing north of downtown, buzzing the Space Needle, and bend south again to approach the Virginia Mason campus. There are several news trucks parked outside the hospital, along with squad cars flashing their rack lights. The helicopter lands on a roof, and Isaac opens the cargo door and climbs out, then offers his hand to Director Ricketts. She zips herself snugly into her hazmat suit before stepping into the punishing downdraft of the rotor wash.

The hospital's chief of medicine, a physician named Camille Johnson, meets them at the entry to what is now the contamination ward. Her hair is cut short, a tight web of curls dyed orange. She wears a mask, a PPE shield, and an apron over a long-sleeved green surgical smock tucked into gloves.

They flash their badges and make their introductions.

"Not every day the Department of Defense shows up at my hospital," she says. "Then again, not every day I see something like this."

"We believe we can help."

"Good. Because after COVID, I think the people in this city would rather drown themselves in the Sound than go through another quarantine." She gives Peaches a head-to-toe look, taking in his checkered button-down and pleated khakis. "Something wrong with your ear?"

"Oh," he says and touches the tender swell of it. "No. I'm fine. Thank you."

"Well, if you're coming inside, we'll be happy to suit you up."

"That won't be necessary," he says.

Her forehead wrinkles with a question, but before she can ask it, Annabelle says, "Don't you worry about him."

Dr. Johnson takes on a lecturing tone: "I'm saying the obvious here, right? It's not just the risk to him. It's the risk he poses to others if he walks out of here with—"

She goes silent at the sight of his hand. He holds it in the air between them, as if to shake, but he just wants to show her. Moss furs his knuckles. Vines creep out from beneath his fingernails, curling around and around his fingers, gloving him green before blooming in a burst of white-petaled flowers.

"What are you?" Dr. Johnson says, clinical more than fearful.

The vines retract and he shakes out his hand, shedding petals to the floor. "I'm someone uniquely gifted with the ability to solve your problem."

"As I said," Annabelle says. "Don't you worry about him."

Dr. Johnson nods warily before waving them forward. They pass two police officers wearing masks, and she pushes open the door to the ICU. The rooms are arranged in a circle, at the center of which is a nurses' station. From here, you can spin around and take in a 360-degree view of every glass-walled room. Twenty of them altogether. The privacy curtains are pulled back. The lights are on. There is the feel of an aquarium, because inside each room stands a patient.

They are different ages, genders, ethnicities, but there are commonalities among them: They all wear the same hospital smock. They all have a hand cuffed to the safety bar of the bed. And they all waver in place, as if fighting an invisible wind, and stare blankly out at Annabelle and Isaac. Every few seconds, one of them will bark out a cough, a phlegm-thickened rattle. Many have thick gray trails of mucus running out of their eyes, their noses, their mouths, and even their ears.

Dr. Johnson says, "They all came in screaming. Gnashing their teeth. Thrashing against their restraints. But as soon as we get them in here, they calm down."

"So there's some sort of stabilization as a result of proximity?" Isaac says. "They're among familiars."

They watch as one patient, and then another, then another and another and another — all of them — lift a hand. They extend their index fingers and bring them to their mouths as if to say, *Shh.*

Then the fingers sneak between their lips. Their teeth snap down, biting as hard as they would on a stalk of celery. Skin breaks; blood blooms. And with the blood they begin to draw on the glass walls of their rooms. They all crouch together, beginning at the floor, working their way up, and curling down again, creating a slow series of circles that spiral inward and take up the entirety of each window. It is a monstrous choreography, a strange ballet.

"Go on," Annabelle says and nudges Isaac forward. "Do your work."

Isaac takes a short walk around the ward, listening to them cough, studying the ciphers on the glass more carefully. When he returns to the nurses' station, Dr. Johnson asks, "It's got something to do with that damn comet, doesn't it?"

Isaac says, "The sky laid the seeds five years ago. Now the rains have awakened them. In Puget Sound and the Olympic Peninsula, we're dealing with a sudden proliferation of new plant and fungal life."

"Including yourself."

"Including myself."

"But you're not one of them."

"No, I am most certainly not."

"Then what are you?"

"You don't have to answer that," Annabelle says.

"It's okay," Isaac says, though he takes his time responding. "There are examples of lichens that seem to grow with the specific expectation that birds will harvest them and make them into a nest."

"Okay?"

"They've learned how to work with others to make a new home. I think that's what we're seeing right now with a lot of the alien flora. It's been waiting, learning, adapting. It's testing out this new environment and trying to find the best way to grow in it."

"Are we even talking about science right now?" Dr. Johnson says. "Because this sounds like the stuff of myths. Green men and gray men and the like."

"Can't it be both? A lot of myths and legends began as a way to make sense of a truth people couldn't quite grasp."

"The bloodwork reveals they're all experiencing a fungal infection."

"The bloodwork isn't wrong," he says.

Annabelle says, "We'd be very curious to see the blood and tissue samples you've harvested."

"Harvested?" Dr. Johnson says.

"Yes?"

"That's a word that makes this sound like a farm."

"In a way, it is."

She gives Annabelle a sidelong look before waving to a nurse with rhinestone-studded glasses and asking her to bring over one of the files.

"Which one, Dr. Johnson?" the nurse says.

"Doesn't matter. They're all the same."

A few manila folders are slapped on the counter. *Noble, Darla. Gordon, Robert.* Isaac takes one and flips it open. He reviews the chart on *Chives, Augustino,* licking his fingers as he flips from page to page. Dr. Johnson shakes her head at him. "Here we all are, taking every precaution, and here you are, no mask, no gloves, licking your bare fingers like you just finished a plate of ribs."

"He's not the same as you or me," Annabelle says. "In case you haven't noticed."

He finishes the final page and says, "Would you please introduce me to Mr. Chives?"

Dr. Johnson leads them to a man with a squat build and a graying crew cut. His paunch pushes against the hospital gown. His eyes are pouchy, and he looks as though he hasn't slept or shaved in a few days. He seems not to see them as they approach. He is too busy painting his blood along the glass. His mouth hangs open, revealing coffee-stained teeth.

"Are you seeing what I'm seeing?" Annabelle says, tracing her finger along the glass, following the shape of what he's drawn there.

"It's a code," Isaac says. That's why she originally hired him away from Big Ag—because he could see and manipulate genetic sequences to build better seeds. Drought- and blight- and fungus-resistant.

"And?" she says.

Isaac leans into the glass, studying the crosshatched glyphs. "We'll crack it, of course. Code is language. It's meant to communicate and instruct. We'll need to photograph each of the etchings separately for comparative study."

Annabelle says, "I'd say this is rather promising, don't you think?"

He tips his head. "Promising?"

She motions a hand around the room, indicating the collective. "The way in which they appear to be locked into a kind of hive mind." This is her job. She encounters the kill power of a brain-hijacking spore, and she immediately thinks about how she can use it. Control the uncontrollable. Science as a military-industrial tool. She's generating a wish list of organic mind-control serums, dreaming about how the nation might one day put this threat to use and control a political or business leader or even entire populations.

"Excuse me?" Dr. Johnson says, and they both look at her. "I've got a phalanx of reporters outside. A new patient every hour. And the mayor, governor, and police chief on the phone. You all don't seem to be in a rush, but I am. You all don't seem to be nervous, but I am."

Most people live in a bubble. If they didn't read the news, it wouldn't matter who was president or whether a peace treaty had been signed or which corporate leader had stepped down in a scandal. They are unaffected by the theater of the world, even though their phones may incorrectly magnify their connection. How must it feel, then, to be one of them? To know that something mythological rained from the sky? That everything has changed and nothing has changed? You're still paying your car insurance and worrying over a discolored mole and ordering a soy caramel latte with sprinkles from the barista even as the news tells you that something in the Louisiana bayou is killing children, and a village in France was discovered encased in ice. It's all so far away, a source of entertainment or vague unease until it's in your backyard.

That's when Annabelle realizes that not just Dr. Johnson but every nurse and doctor in the unit is staring at her. There is a mixture of fear and neediness on their faces. They aren't reading the news anymore — they are the news. The comet is here. In their backyard. And they want it gone.

Dr. Johnson pokes a finger at her. Even muffled by the mask, her voice comes as a clear shout. "You're standing there, acting all amazed, saying how promising all this is, while I'm left to wonder whether we're ground zero for the next pandemic. Talk to me. Do we need to shut down the interstate? Do we need to quarantine the city? What's happening?"

"Oh," Annabelle says, "I'm sorry if we've inconvenienced you," and Isaac visibly cringes, because he has been trained to know that tone of voice. Annabelle always pours extra syrup over her anger. "I was under the mistaken impression that expert advice and government resources might be of use about now. How about we cut out the middleman and hurry things along by just going straight to the source." She knocks at the glass, chiming it with one of her rings. "Augustino?" she says and his eyes wobble before focusing on her. "Augustino Chives? Will you just come out and tell us? Tell us what you want?"

The man looks at her, his lips trembling.

"What's that?" she says. "I can't quite hear you."

His mouth opens. And a geyser of gray-black bile splashes across the window.

22

J ack checks on the guard sleeping in the control room—sees the slow rise and fall of his breathing, his head lolling to the side—and notes the pistol holstered at his hip. Then he goes to the air lock. It is a steel pocket door with a recessed handle. He tries it, but it doesn't move. A control pad is situated chest-high on the wall. He presses that as well—a few combinations of buttons—and each time it lights up red.

"Don't keep pushing that thing," Nora says.

"Why?"

"Because an alarm will go off."

He pushes one final combo, because that's the kind of person he is, and then sizes up the number of cameras in the lab. Four that he can see, one stationed in every corner.

"What are you thinking?" Nora says. She has finished with Mia's toenails and fingernails and now she stands behind her daughter, trying to untangle the clumps from her hair. Grooming her.

For the ten years he and Nora were married, Jack never visited a barber. Once a month, Nora would tell him she was sick of looking at his untidy mop of hair, and she'd take him out on the porch, seat him in a chair, spritz his head with a water bottle, and scissor away his curls. She didn't talk much when she cut it, but then again, she never talked much. This was her way of talking without talking, expressing her love.

"Nobody knows we're here," he says, and their eyes lock with understanding. They're in a government facility secreted away on an island off the coast, and their daughter appears to be some sort of synthesis of kingdoms, the next rung on the evolutionary ladder. Not the kind of thing you want on the evening news if you're on the geopolitical front lines looking to harness a biological weapon.

"They're not going to let us out of here," Nora says.

"Even if they do, they won't let her come with us."

"What's next?"

His hand sweeps the room. "This was never meant as a holding cell. I'm guessing they separate us in the morning. Isolate and observe. Controlled exams follow. And then—"

"No. I mean, what's *our* next move?"

In the past he always thought long term: This many years of research equals a dissertation. This many years of service equals tenure. This many years of investment equals retirement. But that's all irrelevant now. There is only this moment and the next. They need to get out of here, and to hell with everything else.

"Do you remember the family tower?"

Her smile is fleeting, but it's enough to encourage him to keep talking. When Mia was a toddler, Jack would wrestle with her in the living room. He would invent moves constantly, saying, "This is what I call . . . the spider monster," and crawl his fingers up and down her tummy in a tickle. And "This is what I call . . . the backbreaker!" and pick her up quickly and bring her down slowly upon his knee, making a bone-crunching sound. She invented her own moves—the panda bop, the bitey thing—but Nora is the one who invented the family tower. She normally watched them from the kitchen while reading the newspaper or filling out a report, but one day she leaped up from her chair and smooshed herself on top of Jack and said, "This is what I call . . . the family tower!" She invited Mia to join in and the girl flopped onto them both with a roar and a giggle.

Later that night, when Jack and Nora were tangled up in bed, the door opened. A wedge of light from the hall fell over them, and Nora paused, panting over him. "Is it her? Tell me it's not her," she said. And he said, "It's her." The little footsteps padded across the floor, moving toward them, and her chirpy voice asked, "Whatcha guys doing?"

Jack pulled Nora down on top of him and yelled, "Family tower!"

Mia didn't know any better, so she climbed up on the bed and jumped on top of them with a laugh that was soon followed by "I had a bad dream. Can you tuck me in again? And sing to me?"

"Sure, sweet pea," Jack said, "let's go."

In the lab, Nora asks him why he brought it up as he goes to the window again to check on the sleeping guard. "Because," he says, "we've used misdirection before. I say we use it again. And I say we do it now."

"Now?"

"It's night, right? I mean, I think it's night. The brass is gone. The JV squad is working the late shift. Let's make a move before they think we're capable of it."

"What's the move?"

"This is what I call . . . the seizure!" With that he falls to the floor and begins to kick his legs and shudder his arms.

Nora rushes to the window and bangs on it, startling the guard awake. He looks around, bewildered, before settling his gaze on her. "Please," she says. "My husband is having some sort of episode."

Her *husband*? He continues to spasm his body even as he fights a smile, wondering if she even realized she said it.

The guard's voice crackles through the overhead speakers. "I'm sorry, ma'am, but there's nothing I can do."

"He needs a doctor. Please."

"I'm under orders. I'm not supposed to let anyone in or out."

"You have to. You have to get him out of here."

Jack arches his back and rolls his eyes and bends his limbs in unnatural directions, doing his best while also wondering how much longer he can put on a show. Having a seizure is exhausting. He should have tried a coronary instead.

"He's dying!" Nora says. "You're just going to let him die?"

The guard's voice is slurred with sleep but certain when he says, "You made the choice to go in there. I don't have a choice when it comes to letting you out."

It isn't working. They're not going anywhere.

Jack flops his body over so that his back faces the observation window and goes still. He tries to slow his breathing. Hopefully he looks like he's dying. His eyes settle on his daughter. She stares at him blankly. He mouths the word *Sorry.* He tried.

It is then that she hops off her seat at the edge of the table. She pads her way barefoot across the floor with more surety than he has seen in her so far. A straight spine. Level steps. A determined path. When she moves past him, he can't help but sit up, forgetting for a moment that he's supposed to be suffering a medical emergency. Nora too has gone silent, distracted by Mia's approach.

Their daughter stands centered before the observation window. The guard on the other side of the glass blinks expectantly, as if waiting for her to ask something of him. He has mussed brown hair, bloodshot eyes, and a sloped chin.

Mia raises her arm as if to throw a punch. Something has happened to it. The color and texture have shifted. It appears now like something plated, armored. Chitinous. She swings her fist forward and the glass fissures in a sudden web of silvery lines. She swings again and it shatters altogether. After several hours of stasis, this happens with a speed Jack can barely process.

The guard is so surprised that he barely remembers where his firearm is located. As he fumbles for his belt holster, Mia leans through the ragged hole in the window. Her back arches. Her throat surges. There is a damp rush and she vomits — or maybe *spits* is the right word — a splatter of gray right in the guard's face. It slimes across his mouth, nose, and one of his eyes. The substance has a glue-like consistency. He tries and fails to wipe it away. He falls to the floor, clawing at himself, and Mia wastes no time climbing through the shard-edged hole after him.

• • •

Fifteen minutes later, they are in the locker room — the changing station where they originally donned their hazmat suits. Their wallets and keys remain in the cubbies here, and they collect them. Their phones are gone, but Nora's service pistol is still there.

The guard is with them. They've learned his name is Kenny. He keeps trying to negotiate, and Nora keeps telling him to shut up. He would have suffocated had they not helped clear the muck off his face. He coughed and wheezed for a good minute, desperate for air, before he finally realized his own M9 was trained at his head.

This facility is a concrete maze. Kenny led them to the locker room, and he will lead them out of here and into the open air, but first he needs to be cuffed. Nora has a pair in her purse. "This is stupid," he says as the bracelets tighten around his wrists. "You're being stupid. We gave you back your kid. We're trying to help understand what's happening to her. And this is what you do? Attack me? Pull a gun?"

"Kenny," Jack says, "I realize you have to put in some effort here, since your job is on the line, but shut the fuck up."

Kenny stops talking after that, but he sighs a lot, walks as slowly as he can, and stares meaningfully at every security camera they pass, hoping someone might pop out of a doorway and catch them. But the halls are mostly empty at two a.m. At one point, they hear voices up ahead, but Nora presses the muzzle into Kenny's cheek and puts a finger to her lips. Jack creeps toward the corner and is ready to peer around it when he feels a hand on his arm. Mia. He pulls back and she steps forward. He hears her snort softly, as if to dislodge something from her sinuses, and out of her mouth comes what looks like a gray-green ball. She plops it into her palm and rolls it around the corner. There is a muffled thump, like a gunshot heard through a pillow, and a voice cries out, "What the hell?" The exclamation is cut short by a choking cough, and a few seconds later they hear bodies drop with meaty thuds.

Mia looks at Jack, and one side of her mouth hikes up in a smile. A familiar dimple hollows her left cheek, and only then does he feel like he's truly found his daughter.

They continue on. Jack is so worried about what's waiting for them as they turn corners and tromp up staircases that he doesn't realize they've lost Mia. He calls to Nora, and she looks at him with a mixture of panic and anger as if to say, *Again?* "I know," he says and he holds up his hands, which tremble with the familiar panic surging through him. "I know."

But Mia is only one hallway back. She stands before a door. A door that turns out, upon closer inspection, to be welded shut. "We need to go, sweet pea," he says and places a hand on her shoulder. "We need to go now. Please." She resists him one more moment before following.

"What's behind that door?" Jack asks and Kenny says, "I've asked, but nobody's been able to tell me. It's just a place nobody goes no more."

23

Nora leaves Kenny at the docks, handcuffed to the railing. The patrol boat they steal is painted black with a small cabin topped by a gun turret. A light rain falls as they motor out of the inlet and into the dark chop of open water. She hates boats and she hates the ocean, but what choice do they have? Jack grew up in a family that water-skied in the summers, so he finds his way around the controls without too much trouble.

Navigation is more of a problem. He steers them due east and snaps on the fog lights, encasing them in a hazy glowing globe. The gray bellies of waves roll constantly before them and he keeps the throttle low in case any rocks should rise like fangs from the water.

Nora closes the cabin door and muffles the noise of the briny, seething ocean. Bile bothers her throat. Her arms are out to help her keep her wobbly balance. It's not motion sickness so much as dread. The ocean is chaos. The ocean is a vast unknowing mystery. The ocean is just another version of the black nothing of space and the blazing seed of the comet that ruined everything.

The cabin lights are dimmed to keep the reflection off the windows. The LED strips on the floor and the faint green light of the control panel are all she has to work with when she rips open a cupboard and fumbles past a flashlight, a coil of rope, a box of flares, a flask of whiskey.

"I'll take that!" Jack says, and she says, "Now's not the time for you to lose control."

"Come on. Just a taste. I promise." He reaches a hand back. "Unless you want me to stroke out on you. Because after all we've been through, my blood pressure is through the ceiling."

"One taste, Jack."

He snatches the flask from her and unscrews the top and knocks back a drink. "Hallelujah, Jesus," he says and tucks it into his jacket.

She hoists up the seat of a bench and locates what she's looking for: the life vests. She pulls hers on and snaps the buckles into place, then yanks the straps until she feels a tight, reassuring hug. Only then can she breathe. She slams one into Jack's chest and he takes it with a "Thanks," not really looking, too focused on steering them through the night.

Then Nora holds out the third life vest to Mia — and hesitates. Their girl somehow seems to stand perfectly still, despite the roll of the boat. In the middle of her pallid face, her eyes are black and watchful. She is familiar and she is a stranger. She is their daughter and she is something else. "Mia?" she says. "Just in case something happens . . ."

But she never finishes the sentence, because Mia holds out her hand. The fingers are curled into her palm, gripping something.

"What is it, Mia?" Nora says. "Do you want to show me something?"

When the fingers open, mushrooms spring from her palm.

So many years ago, after Nora's water broke and Jack drove her to the hospital and tried to guide her breathing, when the contractions made her ribs feel like they were going to break, Nora asked for an epidural. It wasn't part of her pregnancy plan; she had hoped for a natural birth. But the pain owned her more fully than she could have imagined. The anesthesiologist rolled her onto her side, inserted the needle between two vertebrae, and said everything would be fine soon, soon — but he was wrong. The warm numbness he promised never came. The treatment failed. When they realized this, she was already dilated eight centimeters, so there was no point in attempting a second epidural. She reached a threshold then. A threshold of pain and endurance. There was no way out except to push, so that's where she focused all her mental and physical energy. Something like that is happening now. It began when her phone rang with the news her daughter had been found — and it continued through the moment when Mia hardened her arm into a kind of bludgeon. Nora has passed a threshold of uncertainty and belief. There is nothing she doesn't believe in anymore. Anything is possible. Everything could happen.

She reaches out — hesitantly — and plucks one of the pink, hatted mushrooms from her daughter's hand. It is cold and damp and spongy in her grip.

"Okay," she says. "Now what?"

Mia opens her mouth. Wide enough that Nora can see the shadow inside it.

"No." Nora is someone who always carries hand sanitizer in her purse and uses a paper towel to open bathroom doors. "Absolutely not. That's not safe. That's —" But she stops herself. What feels like a lifetime ago, she stripped off her mask. At this point, what does it really matter?

She brings her palm to her mouth and licks the mushroom from it. Her teeth grind it down and she swallows the sour paste. She fans a hand at her face, fighting off a gag, then says, "I did it. Now what?"

The answer soon becomes clear, not with words but with images that blink to life in her mind. Her vision of this world is overlaid with another. There is an electrical whine in her ears. Her skin tingles and her tongue feels like it's growing fatter. "What's happening?" Nora says and puts her hands to the side of her head as if to hold it in place. She is rocking or the boat is rocking or the sea is rocking or the Earth is rocking. "What's happening?" she says again, but she already knows the answer.

In the way of mother and child, they are two even as they are one. Life cradling life. Sharing. Talking to each other.

Why is it that you can forget a thousand smiles and sunlit days, but you can never forget a cruel word or a slammed door? That's the sticky trap of memory. It rarely gives you what you want. Over the past five years, all boundaries have collapsed between her personal and professional life. As a detective, you focus on the bad things, so her life is focused on the bad things. When she looks at others, she sees addiction, unpaid debts, and love affairs gone wrong. When she looks at herself, she sees an abandoned marriage and a lost child.

But memories are surfacing. Mia is helping her see what was once eclipsed. The three of them seated at a window table at Macleod's as Mia dipped her French fries into her hot cocoa. The three of them walking along the pier and tossing bread crumbs and naming the greediest, fattest seagull Fred. The three of them walking the entirety of the Safeway parking lot to collect all the spare change people dropped. The three of them adding a chewed-up wad of grape gum to the Market Theater wall. The three of them trying to count the cobblestones along Pike Place even though Mia couldn't make it past thirty. The three of them stopping to listen to a pink-haired man strumming a guitar with a sticker on it that read THIS MACHINE KILLS FASCISTS and applauding when he finished. The three of them hiking through the Hall of Moss in the Hoh Rain Forest and Mia blowing out her diaper in the child carrier backpack. The three of them sledding at Crystal Mountain, and Mia licking a snowball before tossing it to give it slime power. All of this came together in her mind like a steadily twisting knot of roots upon which her notion of family grew.

But there was more, much of it unfamiliar. Scarves of cosmic colors. Moons that looked like the skulls of dead gods. Flowers with babies curled up in their blooms. A mouth that yawned open and spilled out tentacles. Or was it an eye opening? Or was it a door opening? A door. A door. A door. Someone was knocking at the door.

And here was Mia, tromping through the nighttime woods with her father, hunting for mushrooms. Mist oozed through the bracken, moss-furred boulders and thick-waisted firs. Meteors strobed the sky. She told him about finding a hole — a big hole — but he didn't listen. When she grew tired and whiny, Jack loaned her his phone. She perched on a stump and watched cat videos and played games. Until she heard something. A damp sound. Like tongues moving in mouths or worms twisting out of their tunnels. She set down the phone, hopped off the stump, and took a few steps. And then her foot wouldn't move. She wondered if her shoe was caught by a root, but she couldn't see through the mist swirling around her ankle. Then the earth opened up and swallowed her down.

There is a lurch and at first Nora thinks it's in her mind before realizing she is lying on the floor of the boat's cabin. Mia is kneeling beside her, and Jack is asking if she's all right while reversing the throttle and saying he's sorry but they hit something, they hit something big.

Out on the deck it is difficult to tell the difference between rain drizzle and salt spray. Dawn is coming, and the clouds pulping the horizon are a sick green. Her shoes slip in the damp and she returns to the cabin door and clutches its frame. She isn't sure where they are, but with the black walls of forest all around them, she can tell they're inland. She guesses the Salish Sea, if not past Port Townsend.

Jack usually saunters more than walks, but on the boat he moves with a steadier sense of confidence than she. He rushes over to the starboard and then the port side, leaning out over the water and saying, "Shit. Oh, shit, shit, shit." The boat—its engine idling—begins to drift in the current. The yellow haze of the fog lights sparkle on the water.

A metal ladder leads to the gun turret. His feet ring out as he climbs up it, not answering her when she asks, "What? What is it? Did we hit a shoal?"

The boat rocks. The waves slap. A frond of salt water hisses across the deck. Finally his voice calls down from above. "Climb up and see."

"I don't want to climb up and see!"

Mom!

It's not something Nora hears—it's something she feels. She is being called with some urgency. Inside the cabin she finds Mia standing on her tiptoes, staring out the rain-speckled window at something visible over the bow. Nora joins her there.

"What is it?"

At first it is difficult to understand what she is looking at — maybe a black slab of rock jeweled with barnacles — and then it bobs and rolls over and she sees the white underbelly and understands. It is a whale. An orca.

The view suddenly brightens and she understands that Jack has found a spotlight above. Its beam cuts the dark and homes in on the whale. There is a gash near its fin where the boat struck it. A wave rolls over and buries the whale from view for a few seconds, and when it bobs up again, the foam frothing off it, she sees something that stops her breath.

She initially mistook the white clumping its skin as barnacles. But she was wrong. It's fungus. Mushrooms bulge out of its eyes and blowhole and coat the tongue of its gaping mouth.

24

Dr. Johnson gets on the phone with the mayor, and Director Ricketts gets on the phone with DC. The Pentagon approves the National Guard deployment of one thousand troops. More immediately, Sea-Tac airport has been shut down, all incoming flights diverted, and the police are working to barricade the interstate corridors. But borders are porous. A true quarantine won't be possible, but they can at least slow the spread.

While they talk, Isaac busies himself with his own work, scanning the bloody glyphs with his phone, uploading them onto his laptop. He asks for a quiet space to study, and Dr. Johnson puts him in the hospital chapel.

He sits in the front pew, bent over his computer. The windows are dark when they're not lit up with the red flash of an ambulance. A backlit cross hangs over the pulpit.

When he worked as a genome engineer, he spent his days reading and modifying the sequence and expression of genes. He developed programs and systems, one of them called SPLICER, that calculated possible cleavages and unions between biology and synthetics. Trying to make a stronger seed. To bully evolution. Any nucleus was programmable. DNA was up for negotiation.

He boots up SPLICER now. He doesn't have all the information he needs on proteins and transcriptional activators and catalytic domains of this fungus, but he has a rudimentary pattern. If the rings of a tree can tell you about the history of a forest, then the swirl of these ciphers can point toward a larger narrative. A genetic sequence that will tie back to a source. An origin. A kind of motive for the crimes currently being committed.

While the computer hums in his lap, running analytics, his eyes wander the sanctuary. He can't remember the last time he was in a church, but there is a hush to it he appreciates — the same calming stillness he used to experience in a laboratory and now finds in the forest. This is where you come to think hard and figure things out. He studies the alcoves set into the walls of the chapel. Here is Mary in one, Jesus in another. Saints are tucked into the others. Some he cannot name, but here is Julian. His mother's favorite. Saint Julian, who listened to the stag's prophecy, who tried to run but still ended up killing his parents. The other day Isaac read a magazine article about how religion is dying, and he wonders what new saints and gods will rise up instead.

A half an hour passes before the SPLICER program completes. The air pressure in the chapel shifts as the door opens and heel-driven footsteps click along the aisle, approaching him. "Well?" Director Ricketts says.

"Most mushrooms decompose other things. And contribute to and feed off the decomposition. They're called saprophytes. Or necrotrophs."

"And that's obviously what we're seeing here."

"Yes. That's the very definition of it. These people are rotting alive." He pauses at the memory of Augustino Chives coughing violently and something blackish muddying his chin and splattering the window. "There is a fungus in northern Oregon, in the Malheur National Forest. Genus *Armillaria*. It's perhaps the largest organism on Earth, spread out over several hundred miles. And it's a killer of fir trees. It moves from host to host, and they die off."

"Host to host, body to body."

"Our immediate reaction is to feel fear, of course. But there are other perspectives. Dead trees are good habitat for beetles and grubs, for instance. There's one. More larches can grow when fir trees die. There's another. The presence of the fungus is bad — to use a rather simple word — only if you're a fir tree."

"Or a human, in this case."

"Or a human, in this case," he says, nodding.

"But what about the girl?"

"Some say there are over five million species of fungus. Who knows how many times over that number has expanded since the meteor strike."

"What are you saying?"

"I'm saying there's a garden growing. A rich, abundant, unfamiliar garden. I'm one thing that's grown out of it. The girl is another. Augustino Chives is another."

"Keep talking."

"Some fungi are necrotic. Some. But not all. Morels, for instance. Morels harvest nutrients off a tree, but they don't aid in decomposition. They're called mycorrhizal. In general you can think of mycorrhizae as givers, not takers. Or cooperators — maybe that's a better word. To put it in the most oversimplified of terms: Necrotics are the baddies, cooperators are the goodies. The cooperators help with soil chemistry and plant nutrition and basically act as the internet connection of the underlying forest."

"So just like people, you've got takers and you've got cooperators."

Isaac says, "And our girl back at the lab, Mia — I'm guessing she's a cooperator. If we're dealing with a sudden crop of new growth, she's our best-case scenario. For communication, negotiation, allyship."

"Or indoctrination."

He almost says *Yes* but can manage only a sigh. Because he knows she is referring to him. He is the indoctrinated.

Director Ricketts approaches the pulpit and stares at the cross as if ready to pull it down and wield it like a sword. "Whereas what's happening here in the ward . . ."

"What's happening here is something different. Malignant. And scary. This is our worst-case scenario. This necrotic spread is here to gobble us up."

"So how do we contain the spread?"

"Right now we're dealing with the equivalent of a wildfire. There are infant fires spreading. Sparks carried by the wind, shall we say. And they could flare up dangerously on their own. But it's the source that matters most right now. It's the source — the parent site — we need to extinguish."

"You mean contain," she says.

"I guess."

Her eyes flash at him. "You guess?"

He tries to keep her gaze but finds himself ducking his head. "It's the source we need to contain."

"And how do we find the source?"

"I think I already did." He hates himself for enjoying the pleased smile that splits her face when he shifts the screen toward her. "Look."

‖‖‖‖‖‖‖‖‖‖‖‖‖‖‖‖‖‖‖‖‖‖‖‖

Jack is reminded of his mother's death. COVID was spiking, protesters had taken over downtown Seattle, the White House was caught up in a cycle of scandals too numerous to keep track of, and she was felled by a heart attack. He had spent weeks swallowing everyone else's pain and frustration, and suddenly none of it mattered. All the trouble in the world was eclipsed by his own personal tragedy. Once addicted to the news, he didn't read the paper or look at his phone for weeks because he had only so much empathy.

That's what's happened to them now. Though it seems impossible, Nora and Jack had willfully put what was happening in Seattle out of their minds, because they just didn't have the bandwidth for anything other than Mia.

But the whale has brought them back. The fungus is spreading. There is death in the air and in the water. The farther they travel, the more they discover. Not just orcas, but sharks and sturgeons and halibut and salmon floating in the inlet. As Jack motors the boat forward, the carcasses thump softly against the hull, their bellies rolling over white in the wake. The smell of rot rides the air.

"I don't even want to think about what's already in my lungs," he says. "I don't want to go through this again."

Mia tugs at his sleeve and offers him a hand blistering with mushrooms.

"It's okay, Jack," Nora tells him.

"What is that?"

"She's trying to protect us."

His eyes flit between Nora and the hand and the sea. "Aren't we supposed to be the ones protecting her?"

"Just take it."

"But what is it?" he says. "Like medicine?"

"It's more than that."

He dutifully pops them in his mouth and grinds them down and gags at the earthy flavor and mucusy texture. Then his eyes widen, his pupils dilate, and he says, in a dreamy voice, that he has to sit down. He doesn't bother with the bench. He drops to the floor and holds his head in his hands. Nora takes the wheel while he struggles to come to terms with the fact that he's no longer himself. *Himself* has become *themselves*—the three of them are joined in a kind of mental marriage, a collective point of view. Nora's hand is Jack's, and Mia's ear is Nora's, and Jack's heart is Nora's. Separate but together. A *they*, a *we*.

A pole net is bracketed to the wall of the cabin, and Jack watches Mia remove it and exit the cabin. He remains on the floor, but his mind travels with her to the deck. He is here and he is there, leaning over the railing and dipping the net into the water to scoop up a steelhead still slapping its tail weakly. She brings it back into the cabin, dribbling water, and his vision of her catches up with the reality of her as she's beside him. She takes the fish firmly in her hands and runs her thumbs along the gummed-up gills and the milky eyes. They all examine the residue scraped away by her fingernails.

"Do you know what this is?" Nora says.

The girl's face is clenched like a fist when she looks at her mother and father. They don't hear a voice, but they feel it, like the bass of a car radio speeding past.

The door is unlocked. When the door is unlocked, things come inside. Some of those things are bad.

"The door to where?"

The door to the other side of the comet.

"That doesn't make sense."

There are other worlds than this one.

"What are we supposed to do?" Nora says. "Close the door?"

It's too late to close the door.

"Then what do we do?"

We do what you do.

"What do I do?"

When bad things happen, you stop them. You're a hunter. Let's hunt.

"Okay," Nora says. "Let's hunt."

They know where they need to go. Nora and Jack had figured this out before they heard the news of Mia, and they reach McNeil Island in the gloom of dawn. The clouds are so low that a gray wispy ceiling presses down on them, tighter and tighter with every mile they travel, as if the world has run out of room.

At first they cannot distinguish the island from what they initially believe is fog. But the fog has a shape. A border. Miles wide. If they refocus their perspective, they can see the island as it rounds out of the water and domes into the sky, connected to the cloud cover by trembling vaporous threads.

Jack powers down the engine. "It's not an island," he says. "It's a biome."

The border isn't a perfect delineation, like a wall, but it's close. They sink into the haze. The engine idles and he allows them to drift, not knowing how far they are from land. They first see the basalt cluttering the shore. Then the bony manzanita thickets. Then the black jawline of evergreens. The air is so thick with spores that a greasy film instantly clings to their skin.

"Who knows what we're breathing in," Nora says.

Mia takes her hand. *It's okay. I'll protect you.*

Jack knows there are several docks, including one for the ferry at the Black Creek Correctional Facility, but it seems better in a case like this to take an indirect approach. A rock jetty curves like a tongue off the shore, and Jack steers toward it and reverses the throttle. Their momentum slows and they putter close enough to drop anchor, tie the boat up, and clamber over the railing onto the algae-slick rock.

With every step they travel, the air grows murkier, and sound warps as it does underwater. A twig might snap twenty yards away, but it sounds close enough to snatch. A bird cries out a warning, and there might as well be a flock of them all around. The trees crowd around them. Their trunks are slick and their branches weighed down by a fungal coating. The ferns don't swish so much as slap at their legs. Mia wears nothing but a hospital gown. Jack offers her his jacket but she shakes her head no. She's not cold. And her feet pad along quickly, not at all tender to the forest floor.

Here is a family of owls on a tree, but whether they're still alive or not, it's hard to tell. They are mucked over, glued to the branch, and might as well be a burl on bark or a gall on a leaf.

Farther along they encounter a deer. Its grayed antlers branch upward. It doesn't startle, remaining rooted in place. When they walk right up to it and examine it further, they discover porous holes running through it and gray cracks along its ribs that ooze black. There is nothing left. The deer has been consumed entirely by the necrotroph that stole its shape.

Is this what awaits Seattle? As the spores spread, will the biome gradually expand and shroud the city? Will the houses and sky-scrapers be plastered gray? Will the forms of people root to side-walks and park benches like molten sculptures? Everything they're seeing right now is only days old. The biomass of fungus can grow exponentially, doubling in unit time. It is the ultimate colonizer. What will the Sound look like in two weeks? What will the Pacific Northwest look like in two months?

Jack's foot catches in the undergrowth and he nearly trips. When he looks down, he sees something grinning up at him. What looks like a gray round face. A slimy hand manacles his calf. He kicks at it and it opens its mouth, revealing gray-black gums, and hisses. His foot is yanked suddenly downward and he's lost up to his knee. Another yank and he's down mid-thigh. He cries out for help and Nora and Mia take his arms and pull and pull and pull — and finally he falls forward as the thing withdraws with a sucking sound back into its burrow.

As soon as the thing is out of sight, Jack doubts what he witnessed. Because what grabbed him was recognizably human. He's reminded of his own laboratory when they discovered the Tapir locked inside that thick fungal casing. Would he have eventually become a black-gummed creature that hissed from the shadows? How many different subspecies were they dealing with? Fungus was typically simple, but the diversity of growth and behavior seemed to hint at something more like a colony.

The wall of the forest gives way to a meadow, its grass glopped over and matted. In the near distance they can see the correctional facility, big stone structures drifting in and out of view. There is no fence, because the sea serves as a moat and because the low-security prison houses the geriatric and incapacitated.

As they march forward, they can see the guards and nurses and patients alike waiting for them outside, as gray and still as statues.

||||||||||||||||||||||||||||||

Corn is vulnerable to blight by an airborne fungus called *Ustilago maydis,* commonly referred to as corn smut. Hundreds of millions of dollars are lost every year because of it. When Isaac Peaches worked as a genome engineer, one of his directives was to find a way to stop its spread. He tried a thousand different modifications that might create stronger, more resistant strains before finally getting the idea of adding something to the mix: a killer protein. Instead of going on the defense, he would take the offense, an act so very unlike him that he surprised himself. This symbiotic strain of corn he designed had a built-in fungus, KP4, that ate other fungi. The idea was to infect the infection.

This is what he tells Dr. Johnson to try as he leaves the hospital.

"But KP4 is a toxin," she says, and he says, "So's chemo. Just try a low-dose version and see if you get any results." He's sure she will. But stopping the spread will also require contact tracing and isolation. Seattle is going to be in the news as a hot zone for the next few weeks at least. The good news is, the infection won't spread except sparingly, due to environmental factors. There are other areas of the world, after all, where omnimetal strikes have been discovered, so the spores must be there as well. But it's only here — so far, anyway — that they've flourished. It must be because of the funk. The mossy, earthworm-y funk of the Sound and the Olympics. In a normal year, it gets over one hundred inches of rain, the wettest geography in the country. It's its own special aquarium, the perfect incubator.

The doctor has more questions, but he can't linger because Director Ricketts is waiting for him on the helipad. The morning shift at the DOD facility discovered the lab compromised, a guard handcuffed to the docks, and the girl and her parents escaped. Teams are assembling to scour the coastline by boat and plane, but the fog stewing through the Sound isn't going to make it easy.

Director Ricketts blames Isaac. And he will be punished accordingly. But first they have work to do. When he was in the chapel, his SPLICER program translated the fungal pattern as a circular key chain, the necrotic zone of which is growing more rapidly and expansively with each new infection. Every patient had a slightly different code, but they all linked back to a parent generation from which the mycelium network began. It wasn't that different from DNA testing, and the original source, the master infection, was a man named Albus Crotter, a serial killer who liked to leave his mark on his victims. The same holds true now.

He is listed as an inmate at the Black Creek Correctional Facility, located on an island on the Sound, and their chopper is whisking them there now. Beneath them the gridwork of the city is lit up red and blue with the rack lights of emergency vehicles. But the chaos seems far away, and Director Ricketts is rigid and silent in the seat beside him as they leave Seattle behind, cutting through the gray nowhere of the clouds over the water.

IIIIIIIIIIIIIIIIIIIIIIIIIIII

The Black Creek Correctional Facility appears more flesh than stone, as if mortared with fungus. The hallways are so thickly pasted they appear rounded instead of squared, like the passage of a digestive system. Pulsing cauliflower formations bulge from the floors, walls, and ceilings. Jack says, "I think these are the spore catapults. A kind of bursting cell. And I'd need to do an autopsy to know for sure, but I bet if we checked the respiratory system of an affected person, we'd find smaller versions of the same. Imagine this hallway as a throat."

"I don't want to," Nora says.

Spores snow the air. Jack trails behind Nora and Mia, studying a coral-like formation with black hairs spinning out of them. "Hmm," he says, and she says, "Jack. Enough."

"Okay." He jogs to catch up and nearly slips more than once. "Sorry."

They find the occasional face or arm sculptured out of the gray. Some of them blink or reach, their fingers trembling like anemones in a tide pool. Along one section of wall there are five mouths with gray tongues lolling out from between teeth. A black syrup dribbles and oozes from them.

Down one corridor comes what sounds like the mewling of a thousand voices. Something bangs against a metal door so hard, it bulges outward. They startle and look around worriedly, but for a time they believe they might travel through this necrotic womb un-molested.

Then the light dims and the end of the hallway seems suddenly to retreat. They realize then that a kind of sphincter is tightening before them, closing off their passage. They hurry forward—too late. The way is blocked. A puckered gray swirl prevents them from traveling any farther.

Jack and Nora kick and claw at it, and then they stand aside and let Mia have a turn. Her fist hardens into what looks like a conch. "Go ahead," they say. "Just like the window in the lab. You've got this."

She pulls her arm back — and slams it forward, hammering the blocked exit. She doesn't crack through. She doesn't so much as dent it. But there is a response. It comes in the form of a squelching sound. The floor shifts beneath their feet. The ceiling surges and then flops down nearly to their heads. The walls tighten. This is not a slow and steady change. It's a sloppy, baggy compression, like they're trapped in an irritated intestine that is committed to digesting them. Fluids ooze. Spores darken the air. They're choking and they're blinded and they're fighting the damp weight of the hallway closing around them.

Jack gets shoved one way, then another. He calls out for Mia and Nora, but they're separated from him, and he feels like he's tangled up in a thousand sopping blankets. The weight pushes him down and he feels something pressing against his chest — the hard corner of the flask. He manages to rip it out of his pocket. Unscrew it. Splash some whiskey out.

Maybe he's just imagining it, but after one dribble, the fungus seems to loosen its grip. When he shakes the flask out more fully, there is a kind of squeal and it pulls away entirely.

He finds himself on his knees, slathered in some sort of mucus. When he looks up, he sees Nora and Mia clutching each other in a ball and, beyond them, the open end of the hallway.

"Go," he says, and they scramble upright and stumble forward through the gap.

On the other side they rest for a moment, and he holds up the flask. "I remembered. In the lab. How it shrunk away when I emptied that bottle of Beam."

"Thank you," Nora says, and he says, "Don't you mean *Cheers*?"

"Your jokes are rarely funny, but especially not right now."

They continue on through the maze of corridors and finally find the source of the infection on a lower level — in a windowless medical ward. Here, Albus Crotter hangs from the wall. Puttied there. All the hyphae seem to spring out of his center, rippling outward fibrously. Like something waxen, his body melts in and out of the fungus, sunken in places and bulging in others. His jaw hangs open crookedly, his mouth overlong, a gaping cavity ridged with black and yellow teeth. Out of it pours a constant stream of spores, dirtying the air. His eyes dribble black oily tears that streak down the wall in rivulets.

The remains of dozens of bodies fill the room, all lying or crouched on the floor in postures of pained worship. Crotter worked as a cell tower technician, and he found another way to transmit his message in this afterlife. In his diaries he had written about the voices he heard at the tops of the towers, the humming dialogue with what he thought was God. God was speaking through him. God had found him, and this is His cathedral.

And maybe they hear it now. A whispering. It seems to come from all around them, warning them away or urging them forward. The air feels thick enough to swim through. Mia leads the way cautiously, stepping around the molten, rotted bodies. Then the three of them stand before him, only inches away. Maybe there is a ripple through the spongy floor, like the twitch of a muscle. Maybe one of the black eyes appears to widen with knowledge, their reflections captured in its inky globe.

And then, in a surge, the room comes to life. The coral formations discharge and the black wiry hairs whiz through the air and bite their skin, piercing them like thorns. The bodies come unstuck and muddily slop their way toward them with a sound like rutting pigs. Nora fires her pistol, making the dim air strobe with the muzzle flash, but the bullets have no effect beyond splashing their skin. When Jack punches one of them, his hand is swallowed up by its chest and won't come out, cemented into place. The things circle around Jack, Nora, and Mia in a steadily closing knot. Their goal seems less to strike than to grapple, to cling and smother, to bury, to make them stay, to make them theirs.

Only Mia has any effect on them. She hacks up a bile that melts the face off one supplicant. She hardens her arm into a plated bludgeon and knocks another onto its back; it splatters into a mess of porridge and bones.

Then she climbs up the wall, finding her grip in the ribbed strands of hyphae. There is a sound of guttural exhalation as Crotter's mouth expels a chimney-black cloud of spores, hazing the air of the room. She slams her hand directly into the source of it and pushes, pushes, all the way up to her shoulder. The teeth clamp down and she lets out a tiny scream that Jack and Nora can hear through their whole bodies.

Then she yanks back and rips out what looks like a squirming black squid. Its tentacles lash at her, tangling the air. She grits her teeth and squeezes her fist, strangling the brain of the thing until the pulp of it oozes between her fingers.

The arm of Crotter comes unstuck from the wall and strikes her heavily. She is knocked from her perch to the floor. Her hand opens and the black-tendriled thing wriggles away from her grip. It flops and squiggles, at first trying to escape, then circling back toward Mia. Scurrying toward her face — her mouth.

Nora has emptied her pistol. She pops out the clip. She finds another in the pocket of her holster. She slams it into place. She aims down the line of the barrel. And fires.

At first she thinks the gun is jammed, because there is only a metallic click. No gunshot. And then she realizes, as the black squid explodes from the impact, that these bullets came from the sarge. And they were made of omnimetal.

With that, Crotter goes still, and all the bodies in the room collapse.

||||||||||||||||||||||||||||

When the helicopter descends on McNeil Island, the rotor wash churns the fog away so that they touch down in their own spinning sphere. The grounds are slathered with fungi, and the Black Creek

Correctional Facility rises up — glopped and warted over — like the nightmare factory that it is.

Isaac says they should wait for backup, but Director Ricketts isn't speaking to him, so her only response is to charge a round into the chamber of her M9, yank open the bay door, and step outside without him.

Because she can see the three of them. Limping out of the entrance to the building, their arms around each other. The father, the mother, and the girl. Especially the girl. She wants the girl — and what then? Mia becomes, at best, another pet, like Isaac. And at worst? A lab rat in a cage. What was it she called him earlier? Indoctrinated.

"What should I do?" the pilot asks, and right before Isaac rips off his headset and follows her, he says, "Tell all units to swarm. We've got our target."

He curses himself as he climbs out into the murky daylight because he said what she wanted him to. She's trained him as a mimic, a microphone for her desires. Even now he's chasing after her, following her path. He belongs to her. He is her. That's what his mother used to say when cuddling with him in bed: "You're me. I made you."

And now she has her arm extended, her pistol ready to fire. He can't hear her words over the sputtering whine of the helicopter powering down, but he knows she's yelling for them to raise their hands and drop to their knees.

The three of them hesitate. They are grimed over with what looks like mud and blood. The girl still wears her hospital gown and one side of it is a shredded red. The father is putting himself in front of her. The mother is reaching for something inside her jacket.

Peaches knows he doesn't have much time. He can sense Director Ricketts's finger tightening around the trigger as if it were his own.

He closes the distance between them with seven long-legged steps, and that's all the time it takes for him to finally let go, to reveal himself for what he truly is. He can feel the fungus splashing up around his feet and the grass bristling up as if electrocuted. He can feel the clothes tearing off him as his skin spikes into roots and unspools into vines. The pistol discharges wildly when the green twines around her neck and waist and legs, whipping around and around her, sewing her arms against her sides, tearing through her hazmat suit and cutting into her cheeks to cinch shut her mouth until she is mummied, and he is unrecognizable.

Gone is the meek and slender man. In his place stands something mossy, branched, and seething with blooms.

The fungus withers and blackens around him in a steadily spreading circle. A moth lands on him and tastes one of his flowers. A centipede falls off him and scurries away. A beetle scuttles across his foot and up his leg. Worms and salamanders rise from the soil all around him and test the air to see if it's safe again. He has given himself over to the symbiont. He is the green man.

Jack, Nora, and Mia stare at him uncertainly.

He never learned the story of how Julian became a saint after killing his parents but he now understands it must have had something to do with atonement. "Go," he tells them.

They start off a few steps and then hesitate. "Where?" Jack says. "Where are we supposed to go?"

If they run, they can only go so far, because the girl likely can't survive outside of a damp environment. If they hide, they devote their lives to campsites and cash-only motels, to peering out between window blinds and hoping a red laser sight never tracks its way across their foreheads. Nothing awaits them but a future as long and rotten as a hollow log.

"Maybe there's another way," Nora says.

"I'm listening," Isaac says.

"When I met you before, you said something that stuck with me," Jack says. "You said you work for the government, but you don't work for the government."

"What are you suggesting?"

"You're one of them," Jack says, and Nora says, "But you're not one of them. You're just pretending to be one of them." They begin and end each other's sentences as if reading from the same script. Isaac hardly knows whom to look at, his attention bouncing between them. "You're one of us."

"As of a few minutes ago," Isaac says, "I suppose that's true."

"What if it continues to be true? What if you continue to work for the government while not working for the government?" Jack says, and Nora says, "And what if we join you?"

"We?" Isaac says.

"The three of us become the four of us," Jack says. "We work together."

"Work together how?"

"The wrong people are in charge," Jack says. "Instead of running, what if we stay? What if we work — from inside the system — for change?"

"The four of us," Isaac says.

"Or maybe even the five of us," Nora says and nods at Director Ricketts.

"No," Isaac says and the vines tighten around Director Ricketts on reflex. "No, that's not a good idea. She's dangerous."

"She doesn't have to be," Jack and Nora say. They look at Mia, and she steps forward. "We can . . . change her mind?"

He understands then. It is as he said before: the girl is a cooperator.

"It's exactly what I told them at the hospital," Isaac says. "To save the patients, we need to infect the infection."

"Yes," they say.

He doesn't know if they're asking him or telling him, but the invitation feels right, and he gives them a nod.

The girl approaches Director Ricketts, who struggles against her bindings and flinches away from her touch. "She doesn't want to hurt you," they say, their voices harmonizing.

The girl gently pulls the vines away from her face, unzips the hood of the hazmat suit, ungags her mouth. Her lipstick has smeared. Her hair is wild with dirt and leaves. She spits out a white petal and then unleashes a torrent of words, trying to threaten, then bribe, then beg. This goes on for a minute, and no one responds, and her words bluster away into a choking sob.

The parents join Mia. They put their hands on Director Ricketts's shoulders, holding her firmly in place. It is only when Mia opens up her palm and displays a fresh eruption of mushrooms that Director Ricketts begins to scream for help, help, help. But no one can hear her. The helicopter, fifty yards away, continues to idle its engine, ready for a quick takeoff.

Her words are muffled by Mia's hand clapped over her mouth. Jack pinches her nose. Nora holds her still. Eventually Director Ricketts has no choice but to swallow. They release her — and she coughs and pants and hangs her head. Minutes pass. They wait patiently. Maybe they can hear the sound of helicopters and boat engines buzzing in the near distance.

When Director Ricketts finally lifts her face, her expression has calmed and her gaze locks on them each in turn and she says, "Let's begin again."

ACKNOWLEDGMENTS

Thanks to Katherine Fausset and Holly Frederick at Curtis Brown and to Noah Rosen and Britton Rizzio at Writ Large for closing deals and coaching along the business end of the Comet Cycle.

Helen Atsma is now at Ecco, but her fingerprints remain over all these books, and I'm eternally grateful for that. At Houghton Mifflin Harcourt, thanks so damn much to Jaime Levine, Fariza Hawke, Marissa Page, and Michael Dudding for all the heart and muscle you've put into both sharpening these books up and getting them out into the world. A brilliant copyeditor is an amazing gift, so a huge round of applause to Tracy Roe, MD, the best in the biz.

Thanks to Dan Hernandez at Carleton College for answering all of my weird and annoying questions about academia, biology, and fungus in particular. And thanks to Michelle Martin at Prairie Creek Community School and to the naturalists at the Wolf Ridge Environmental Learning Center in northern Minnesota for serving as additional resources. You all helped bring my "out of this world" ideas down to Earth, authenticating the fantastical.

I pawed my way through many articles when researching *The Unfamiliar Garden,* but I'd like to especially highlight "The Social Network: Deciphering Fungal Language," by Abigail C. Leeder, Javier Palma-Guerrero, and N. Louise Glass, which appeared in *Nature Reviews Microbiology* in May 2011; and "How the Zombie Fungus Takes Over Ants' Bodies to Control Their Minds," by Ed Yong, published in the *Atlantic* in November 2017. I also took many notes when watching the fantastic documentary *Fantastic Fungi.*

My parents are both naturalist nerds—and my mother in particular is trained as a botanist—so if she hadn't constantly quizzed me on trees and mosses and seeds and flowers as a kid, I don't know that I would have written this book as an adult. And of course I need to thank Lisa, my wife, for her love and support and patience over all these years. And you know what? I've never thanked my kids before in the Acknowledgments, but Connor and Madeline, if not for my deep and total love for you, I could never have imagined the terrifying possibility of loss that informs this novel. So you better stay safe—and keep out of the woods during apocalyptic meteor showers.